I0666114

THE
ABSENT
MEMORY

JEREMY THOMAS FULLER

BOOKS BY JEREMY THOMAS FULLER

THE METALWOOD SAGA

SEASON ONE

The Metal Wood

The Stone Flame

The Death Edge

The Fatal Cure

The Prime Trees

SEASON TWO

The Absent Memory

The Crystal Curse

The Silent Binds

The Twin Fury

The Splinter Soul

STANDALONE

Attention Deficit

THE ABSENT MEMORY

THE METALWOOD SAGA
BOOK 6

JEREMY THOMAS FULLER

STARMIST
ENTERTAINMENT

STARMIST ENTERTAINMENT

166 Geary Str STE 1500 #1259
San Francisco, CA 94108
United States

jeremythomasfuller.com
instagram.com/jeremythomasfuller
facebook.com/jeremythomasfuller
bsky.app/profile/jeremythomasfuller.com

Cover designed by Maria Spada
Author photo by Zack Griset
Set in Stix Two

Fourteen Trees in a barren land
Fourteen Souls where the weary stand
Fourteen Gifts from the wise one's hand
And two great woes for the Fall of man

—Valaraldan nursery rhyme

PART ONE

ONE

KYTHAELA SAT on her storyteller's log, looking around the fire. Elven children stared back at her, their gazes calm and respectful. Kids were still raised well, here in the great city of Ilyrion. The elves hadn't lost that, at least, after all this time.

She raised her eyes above the fire, looking at the city that was visible in the distance. At night, Ilyrion shone with thousands of glittering lights, its own firmament below the sky. Kythaela took a deep breath, letting it out slowly. The silence around the campfire was palpable.

Her memories were returning.

"The Twins," she began. "Long worshipped by elves, these mysterious deities have been part of life on Valaralda for tens of thousands of years.

"But who are they, really? Are they gods, or are they men? Where did they came from? What do they want? Where do they live? Fruitless questions, some might say.

"But sometimes that is the best kind of question."

She paused, giving her words a moment to sink in. Story-telling was an art—pacing was important. The children remained silent, listening to her vigilantly. She smiled at them.

"Some say the Twins are gods who created the seven Prime Planets: Valar, Mar, Eryn, Sya, Y'abel, Ayel, and Ashi. They made the planets and set them loose to drift in the universe, each a part of its own solar system. The Twins hid a part of their power on each planet, the legend says, waiting for elvenkind to find it and harness it.

"But some profess this tale to be a lie. They claim the Twins are simply elves, not gods—regular men who lived on ancient Valar before the Great Awakening. They were charismatic leaders, benevolent masters, loved by all. The Twins, in this story, were the greatest kings the world had ever known. Many swear that this is true.

"Still others say the Twins are moons, not men. The twin moons that forever orbit Valaralda, gazing down at us at night, guiding us, watching our paths. But watch as they might, the moons are powerless: just heaps of rock, swinging in great arcs through the sky. Silent, passive beacons in the dark.

"But many reject that story, too. So what truth remains? What *are* the Twins? Why do we worship them, curse them, use their signs? Why have we built great churches to them, written books about them, studied their origins? Surely there must be a nugget of *something* true, underneath it all.

"Which brings us to our final legend.

"In this story, the Twins are Trees: Tevelarel and Laravon. The Trees grew from seeds at the moment of the Awakening, bringing forth light and power and magic to the worlds. No one knows where the seeds came from—they just arrived.

"Now the Trees stretch forth their branches, embracing elves and men, sending forth waves of power from the high mountain where they stand. People and beasts and the very plants themselves embrace the Twins, feeding in the luxury of their magical wellspring.

"One Tree is black, and one is gold. The legend says they keep each other forever in balance, forever in check. For if one Tree were to destroy the other, it would throw the worlds into darkness such as none can imagine. And so the Trees are paired, a yin and yang, forever frustrating each other, forever keeping each other at bay.

"And their great power, such as it is, pulses in magnificent strands, flooding the planets with magic. Magic that the intrepid can harness, using for purposes good or ill. It is the very source of Prime magic: light and dark to rule all. This magic Awakened the minds of men, bringing about the Second Age.

"But the Trees, magnificent as they are, cannot be found. No one knows where they are. And if something cannot be found, can it be said to exist?

"These are all good stories. Powerful stories."

Kythaela stopped, letting her last words ring into the silence that followed. The fire crackled happily, smoke rising to the Valaraldan heavens. The children were silent, awed.

"Unfortunately," Kythaela said into the night, "none of these stories are true."

TWO

"WHAT DO YOU THINK?" Trey asked, and the artificer glared up at him. Trey realized he was hovering again. Oops.

He backed away a few feet, giving the man some space. Artificer Ramul had already turned back to his work, a loupe on one eye and that strange tool he used in his left hand, some kind of cross between a screwdriver and a pair of pliers.

"I think it's done," Ramul said.

"Really?" Trey asked, a rush of excitement filling him as he leaned forward again, intent on the sword Ramul was working on. Twenty thousand years old and it almost felt like this was the first sword he'd ever seen. Well, it wasn't.

But it was the first *shocksword* he'd seen.

"Trey," Ramul said, "this thing could get you into a lot of trouble."

"I'll be careful."

"I'm not talking about that. You could get thrown in jail if the wrong person catches you with this. You understand that, right?"

"Yes, yes," Trey said. "Darkprime magic is illegal on Valar-alda. I get it."

"It's the *wood* that's illegal," Ramul said, standing.

"I know. But I didn't make the wood—I just brought it with me from Earth."

"That *might* hold up in a court of law—and it might not. We can't just go around murdering people to create dark-prime Trees, you understand. We're *civilized* here."

"I know."

It was illegal to create darkprime wood anywhere on the continent of Esara, where the city of Ilyrion was situated. The elves there weren't *nearly* as murderous as the Cothellon had been. They actually had *morals*. So there was no Civil Service here, no killing of innocents to power magic. And as a result, there was no darkprime magic. Not legally, at least.

But there might be a loophole.

If you had darkprime wood created by the Cothellon—before the planet gated to another solar system entirely, joining Valaralda in the sky—then you *might* be okay.

Unless you were gatesending.

That particular magic wreaked havoc on the mind, so it had been completely outlawed.

The Department of Magical Research had its fingers in everything.

So many rules. So much to consider. Valaralda really was a different place. A place of elves, of a high-minded, ancient people, where they were pretty sure they knew everything and were extremely skeptical of anyone from off-planet.

Luckily, Trey was originally from this place.

He just couldn't really remember it.

The shocksword was just lying there on the workbench, gleaming. Trey could almost feel the latent power it held, just waiting to be unleashed. His hands itched with anticipation, and he found himself hopping from one foot to the other. Legal or not, he wanted to try it out.

"Do you think it works?" he asked.

"I'm sure it does. When you brought me the Tree Ring Staff, I finally figured it out. It was what I had suspected all along."

"What was the secret?"

Ramul brushed off the question. "It's technical," he said, his face guarded.

When Trey had first met Ramul a few weeks ago, the man had been studying magical artifacts. Nobody knew how they were made, but Ramul thought he had almost figured it out. When he had heard about the Tree Ring Staff, the magical artifact that provided limitless power to the wielder, he had salivated. This could be the secret, he had said. So Trey had let him study it.

It hadn't taken long for the artificer to unlock the secrets buried in the wood. Then Trey had had the idea of making a sword, and there they were.

And it was beautiful.

"So what now?"

Ramul gave Trey a crooked smile. Trey tried to ignore the man's terrible teeth. "Now, you fight," he said.

Finally.

Trey reached for the shocksword. It was long and almost rapier-thin, with a wooden handle made of dark elm. Ramul had done something to the wood, something that Trey hadn't understood. Supposedly he had recreated the Tree Ring Staff, but just for one wood. Now it was an inexhaustible supply of power, much like the Staff itself was. Trey wondered what "technical" thing Ramul had discovered to make it all possible. Maybe if he had his old research papers, he'd be able to figure it out.

There was an icon on the handle, some kind of glyph. It

looked like a T, with a little circle on the bottom. "What is this?" Trey asked, pointing at the symbol. It looked strangely familiar, like he'd seen it somewhere before.

"Just a decoration," Ramul said. Trey watched him for a moment, trying to detect a lie. Ramul returned the gaze, his expression flat.

Trey turned back to the sword and picked it up, marveling at how light it was. It was a good thing, too—Trey wasn't exactly a muscle-bound fighter. A light sword would be much easier to swing one-handed.

"Do you know how to fight with that?" Ramul asked as Trey hefted the sword.

Did he? "I'm not sure."

Ramul frowned. "Shouldn't you know whether you can fight or not?"

"It's the gatesickness," Trey said. "My memory is spotty. I can remember the past few hundred years pretty well, but when I go back further, it comes and goes."

Which was why gatesending was illegal on Valaralda—going through a gate messed with your head. It could either take memories away, or give them back. There didn't seem to be much rhyme or reason to it, or at least no one had ever figured it out. Trey and Arra had found out about the side effects on accident. Trey had gone his whole life thinking he was human, thinking he was in his thirties.

But none of that was true.

He was an elf, and he was at least twenty thousand years old. He'd pieced that much together by comparing memories with Orym and Arra. Both of them were around his age. The three of them had lived on Valaralda before traveling to Earth —or Mar, as the locals called it.

He still had trouble wrapping his head around it all. It

didn't help that the memories were inconsistent. Vast stretches of time—thousands of years—were dark, as if the memories had been snuffed out, or as if they'd never existed to begin with. He'd once tried *really* hard to remember something—anything—from one of the dark periods. All he'd gotten for his trouble was a flash of purple and a splitting headache.

He'd given up trying after that.

"You okay?" Ramul asked. Trey realized he was just standing there, staring off into space. He'd been doing that more and more lately, as memories returned to him. He'd have to be more careful, lest he call undue attention to himself. The elves on Valaralda were a picky bunch, even if he technically was one of them.

"I'm fine," Trey said, looking once more at the shocksword in his hand. "Mind if I take this out into the yard?"

"Be my guest," Ramul said. "Just don't hurt yourself."

Trey grunted. After twenty thousand years, it would certainly be a funny way to go: killed by your own sword.

He walked out of the workshop, hoping that at some point in his long, convoluted past, he'd learned how to use a sword.

TREY STEPPED out into dazzling sunlight.

Valaralda was beautiful, he had to admit, and the similarities to Earth were striking. What were the odds of that, anyway? Orym would probably know. Nothing about the planet seemed *truly* alien. Sure, the plants and animals were a little bit different. All the names were elven, of course, but Trey found himself unconsciously translating things into English. It made things easier for his poor brain.

He squinted, brandishing the shocksword. He could feel the pulsing warmth of the darkprime elm in his hand, ready to be used. Trey stood there for a moment, hoping memories of sword fighting would surface.

But nothing happened.

Perhaps he should start with the magic. He saw Ramul coming out of the workshop, crossing his arms and leaning against the wall, watching him. Great. Supervision was just what he needed. He felt his palms getting sweaty.

He took a deep breath and activated the magic.

It was as easy as a thought. Blue lightning flared up all around the sword, traveling in squiggly lines up and down the metal. Trey felt shockstriking magic surging through him; he could actually hear the electricity as it coursed along the sword.

It was *far* cooler than he'd expected.

He felt a silly grin coming to his face. He put one foot in front of the other, mimicking a sword fighting stance he'd seen in an old movie. He held the sword forward, pointing up, as if brandishing it before an enemy.

"En garde!"

It seemed like the right thing to say. He'd probably read that phrase somewhere. He had no idea what it meant.

"Nice," a woman's voice said from right behind him.

Trey jumped, almost dropping the sword. The electricity dissipated as he lost concentration, but he turned as quickly as he could, pointing the sword at the assailant who had snuck up on him.

It was Arra.

"Hey, you," Trey said, still pointing the sword at her.

"Looks like you really want to stick me with something," Arra said.

Trey felt his cheeks getting hot. "Well now that you mention it..."

Arra walked up to him confidently, brushing her hair back as she approached. Trey found himself admiring the sway of her hips as she moved.

"So *this* is what you've been up to," she said, a slight smirk on her face. She reached out to the sword, feeling its edge, touching the dark elm in the hilt. Her hand brushed Trey's, surprising him. He jumped.

"Sorry," she said. "What is it?"

"It's a shocksword."

"Your idea?"

Trey nodded.

"Tired of the Tree Ring Staff already?"

"I don't know. It just seemed kind of silly to fight with a staff. I wanted something a little...sharper."

"Do you even know how to use a sword?"

"I don't know. I was hoping if I just held it, maybe tried a few moves, I'd remember."

"You fought well with that Staff, you know."

Coming from her, that was a big compliment. She was more of a fighter than he'd ever be. "Thank you," he said. "You weren't so bad yourself."

She smiled, stepping forward and wrapping her arms around his neck. "We made a good team," she said, leaning up and kissing him firmly. He closed his eyes, enjoying the kiss, tasting strawberries on her tongue. The shocksword slipped out of his hand, clattering loudly on the ground.

They both jumped, startled. Then they burst out laughing.

"Some warriors we are," Arra said, still tangled up in his arms.

"Hey! We saved the world."

"We did, didn't we?"

The sun shone in her dazzling blue eyes as she looked up at him. Trey felt something like a shiver go through him. She was just so *perfect*. He smiled back at her, his heart swelling with joy.

"So," Arra said, stepping back, "do you need any help with that sword? I can teach you."

Trey had seen her fight with a sword, during the battle in the Prime Forest. He knew she preferred to use a bow, but she was equally skilled with the sword. Something felt wrong about accepting help from her, though. He felt like he should *know* this already—like he'd learned it before. Sword fighting was something he could do, long ago in a life long past. He knew it.

But it wasn't coming to him now.

"Yes," he said. "Help me." It sounded silly when he said it that way, but there it was. He needed her.

Arra leaned in again for one more kiss. "En garde," she whispered, and he heard the rasping sound of metal being drawn.

Suddenly she had a sword pointed at his chest.

"Um," Trey said. "Can I—"

"Pick up your sword?"

"Yes." Trey knew he was blushing. Off to a good start already.

"Very well, sir," Arra said, her tone lofty. She backed off a pace and bowed to him, a smile still on her face.

Trey picked up the shocksword and hefted it. This wouldn't end well. Arra would probably tear him up before he even got a chance. But maybe—just maybe—it would unlock his memories.

Plus, she looked damn good holding that sword of hers.

He lifted the shocksword, activating the magic again. But something was wrong. He felt something *else* in his head, something pulling at him from the sword. It felt euphoric and dangerous. It felt dark. He staggered as the feeling washed over him, trying hard to keep his balance as waves of power flowed through his body.

In his mind he thought he heard an evil voice screaming his name.

THREE

"ARE YOU OKAY?" Arra asked, looking at him with concern. Trey shook his head, trying to clear it. It didn't work.

"That was strange," he said. "The magic's never done that before."

Or had it? Darkprime magic always felt *good*—almost like a drug, if used too much. But this was much stronger than he'd ever experienced before. He'd been told that some dark-mages burnt out on the magic, succumbing to its siren song. Was he going down that path? It was a chilling thought.

"Nelenor," Ramul said, walking up to him.

"What?"

"The dark Twin. He calls to you through the wood. Beware of Nelenor: he is a cruel master. I *knew* I shouldn't have made that sword."

"A Twin?" Trey asked. He looked at Arra to see if she knew anything, but she just shrugged. "I thought the Twins were a myth. A religion."

"They're certainly a religion," Ramul said. "But not a myth. Not to those of us that believe."

So that was it—Ramul was a Believer. Trey had encountered many of them on Valaralda, some more devout than others. Invariably, Believers would insist that the Twins were their "master." Trey thought it was just an excuse for bad behavior. He'd never call anyone his master.

Except for Quynn.

Still, there had definitely been *something* in the sword. Something had called to him. Something wanted him. Maybe he'd better take it easy.

"You want to stop?" Arra asked.

"No," Trey said, "I need to figure this out. Stand back—I'm going to try again."

"Are you sure that's wise?" Arra asked, but it was too late.

He activated the magic.

Blue lightning flared up along the sword, and Trey once again felt the familiar surge of power flowing through his body. It felt good, as darkprime magic always did, but this time there was no voice, no call. No Twin.

Whew.

"It's fine," he said, swinging the sword experimentally. It left glowing arcs of light in the air as it moved. *Super* cool.

Arra frowned. "Are you sure?"

"All good," he said, stepping backward into the center of the yard. "Let's give it a go." Arra lifted her sword and followed him, the frown still creasing her face.

What happened next was kind of a blur.

Arra moved faster than he had thought possible, slapping his sword aside, ignoring the electricity surging around it. Trey tried vainly to slice at her, but she blocked him quicker than a blink, moving smoothly from position to position. It was as if she'd been training her whole life for this.

Which, of course, she had been.

Within moments, Trey found himself on the ground, his

sword flying through the air to land halfway across the yard. Arra stood over him, sword pointed at his neck. She smiled a beautiful smile, wisps of hair escaping from her pony tail. She was breathtaking.

And she was deadly.

"Best two out of three?" Trey asked weakly. Ramul clapped from his position against the workshop.

Arra lowered her sword and extended her hand, helping him up. She was strong—probably stronger than he was. She'd lived her life in the woods, learning to fight and survive. Of *course* she'd be better at this stuff than he was. Still, it did bother him a bit. He'd thought for sure some kind of memory would have returned to him. How had he lived twenty *millennia* without learning sword fighting? It was ridiculous.

He walked over to retrieve his sword. "Can you teach me that?" he asked.

"Sure," she said, "but it will take a while."

"No time like the present."

"I thought you had an appointment at the University?"

Oh. Trey had nearly forgotten about that. His appointment was extremely important—it was his way back into the Anthropological Society, the way he would return to his old research, his old life. He'd *discovered* something, way back twenty thousand years ago. Something terrible. And he needed—desperately needed—to remember precisely what it was.

He glanced at the sun, checking the time. Persephone was tilted about a third of the way past its zenith. Good. He hadn't missed the appointment—he still had plenty of time to get to the University.

Wait a second—what had he just done? He'd reflexively checked the time using the sun. And not just any sun—Persephone, the alien sun that lit this solar system. How had he done that? Were his old memories finally coming back?

He waved the sword around. Still nothing. It just felt awkward and strange, like a dead piece of metal. His head felt no different from before. No memories flooded in, no sudden realizations or groundbreaking discoveries. He was just Trey, the bookseller from New San Francisco.

"I have a few more minutes before I have to leave," he said. "Maybe you can teach me something easy."

"I can try."

But then something else happened.

Arra dropped her sword, clutching at her heart. She stepped forward, her mouth open. She fell.

Trey darted forward, just barely catching her before she hit the ground. He lowered her carefully to the grass, long hair streaming out beneath her on the ground. Her eyes were rolled up into her head and she was breathing unevenly. Trey was at a loss. What should he do? He patted around his pockets, hoping for some prime birch. He could heal her with that.

Then her eyes opened, and she took a deep, ragged breath. "What happened?" she asked, looking up at Trey with beautiful blue eyes.

Trey hovered over her. "I don't know," he said. "How do you feel?"

"Kind of...drained, I guess. It's passing." Her breathing seemed better.

Trey laid a hand on her forehead. It felt cool to the touch, but sweat was beading on her brow. He frowned. "Have you eaten anything today?"

Arra sat up weakly, allowing Trey to help her. "I don't think so," she said. "Maybe that's all this is."

"Arra, you have to take better care of yourself."

"I don't need a lecture," she said, eyes flashing. She pulled away from Trey and got to her feet. "Shouldn't you be getting to your meeting?"

Trey looked at her, standing there defiantly. She was a strong, beautiful woman. She didn't like being coddled. Fine —he could live with that. He stood, returning her stare. His head told him they'd been madly in love. His heart had a place for her, like a puzzle looking for its missing piece. He *knew* they'd been in love, but that had been thousands of years ago, and the memories were dim. It was like reading about yourself in a book: you knew who you were supposed to be, but it didn't feel like you. It didn't connect. He knew she felt it too, the confusion, the doubt. He longed to gather her in his arms, to whisper into her hair.

But instead, he crossed his arms.

"You sure you're okay?" he asked.

"I'm fine," she said. "Come on, I'll walk with you."

"Okay," Trey said. "But there's something I need to grab, first."

He'd brought the Book of Amplification with him, and it was still in Ramul's workshop. It was the other priceless magical artifact he had: the Staff and the Book. He'd left the Staff at home, considering it too dangerous to bring with him everywhere. The Book was another matter—it didn't have any direct use. It simply amplified any magic the wielder was already performing. It didn't do anything on its own.

"I'll be right back," he said. Arra nodded.

He walked into the workshop, pausing a moment to let his eyes adjust to the dim light. The workshop was small, and it was packed to the brim with oddities. Books, tools, parts and pieces were strewn everywhere. A half-assembled machine of some kind was lying on one desk. Another desk held an open manuscript, with Ramul's neat handwriting flowing across the pages.

Something about the scene felt familiar to Trey. It was almost like he'd been in a place much like this, long ago. A place that was very near and dear to his heart.

Memories came flooding back to him, suddenly, unexpectedly. He clutched the edge of a desk as he remembered.

FOUR

TARATHIEL.

Yes, that was the name Trey had in those days. It sounded strange, a foreign word in a memory that didn't feel like his. But it was him, in some millennia now far gone.

Tarathiel blinked his eyes, looking around the room. Where was he? Oh, yes. His home in Errenmel. *Their* home.

He was sitting at his desk, his latest research arrayed in front of him. Papers and books were strewn everywhere, and more books lined the walls of his office. He was holding a quill pen—he'd always been old-fashioned like that—and he'd clearly just been writing something. He peered down at the page.

It was covered in hieroglyphics. The symbols were pictures, taken from the ancient language spoken by the priests of Akhenaten, the Moon God. The people of Nekhrumet didn't worship the Twins—they had their own religion, and their own language to go along with it. But that language was dead and gone now, lost to the desert sands. It had taken Tarathiel years to learn as much as he had.

He looked down at the page again, seeing translations

written in below the hieroglyphics. He peered at the first one, rubbing bleary eyes.

Guruthos, the page said in his neat handwriting. And next to it, the translation: *shadow of death.*

Tarathiel felt icy fear wash over him as he read the words again. He'd been hoping the word would translate into something pleasant, something nice. That perhaps he'd been wrong about this whole thing. But no.

The language of the hieroglyphics was still kept alive, if barely, by the last remaining priests of Akhenaten. Tarathiel had found one of them, and the man had told him all he knew. There was some debate as to the meaning of a few of the words, though. Tarathiel had labored a long time, translating reams of text from the various books he'd unearthed. This was one of the last, the key word that kept appearing over and over. *Guruthos*. It signified something terrible, something powerful. Something he'd started calling "the Fall."

Whatever it was, Guruthos was gone now. If it were ever to return, it would mean the fall of civilization. The texts were very clear on that point. And so the name had stuck.

The Fall. The shadow of death.

He read the whole sentence quietly to himself.

SAN NA I GURUTHOS, *belaith ah graug, onna Ambarhal ah û mellon im.*

"AND SO THE shadow of death, mighty and powerful, in Ambarhal and everything within."

The sentence was a fragment—it didn't quite make sense.

And he'd seen that word crop up before—Ambarhal—but he still didn't know what it was. This was getting him nowhere.

He rubbed his eyes. Perhaps he wasn't cut out for this work with languages. He'd always thought he'd had a good head for it, but maybe he'd been wrong. Maybe he should be outside, farming or fishing, not inside with books and pens.

Perhaps he just needed more sleep.

"Don't be so hard on yourself," Alleria said as she padded softly into the room. Tarathiel turned in his chair, smiling at her. She was carrying a tray with a bowl of something steaming. His stomach rumbled as he smelled it, and he realized he hadn't eaten anything in a long time.

His wife set the tray down and kissed him on the neck. He reached for her, and she sat in his lap, looking down at the writing he'd been working on.

"The shadow of death," Alleria said, frowning. "That doesn't sound good. Are you sure that's right?"

Tarathiel sighed. "I'm never sure," he said, "but yes, I think it's right. Whatever the Fall is, it means death. Death on a large scale."

Alleria leaned against him. "Eat your soup," she said. "Death can wait."

"We have to do something!"

"We *are* doing something."

"But all the Senate does is *talk!* The Fall is coming back for us. We may not have much time. We need to *act*, not sit around debating things for months or years!"

Alleria smiled at him. "Dear, haven't you learned by now that Senators *love* talking? It's what they're good at."

Tarathiel ground his teeth. "Politics are so annoying."

"I know. That's why you have me around!" She squirmed on his leg.

"To be annoying?"

"To be a Senator, silly." She squirmed again.

Tarathiel felt his face flush. He reached his arm around her waist, pulling her closer. "That's not the only reason," he whispered, nuzzling at her neck.

"Is it for my cooking?" Alleria asked, grinning wryly.

"Yes," Tarathiel said, his research forgotten, "it's your cooking."

"Your soup will get cold," Alleria scolded, turning to straddle him.

He grabbed her and kissed her.

Death could wait.

FIVE

TREY BLINKED, coming back to himself. The memory had been so *real*. He could still picture his office, his books, his writings. He could still smell that soup. He could still taste Alleria. He could still remember the feel of her body against his.

He ached for her.

He licked his lips, feeling how dry they'd become. They'd been so in love back then. So happy. So free. As the memory began to fade, Trey wondered if their relationship would ever return to how it once was. Arra still felt almost like a stranger to him, sometimes. He didn't know what to do.

Then he remembered why he had come back into Ramul's workshop—he was there for the Book of Amplification. And there it was, sitting right where he'd left it, atop one of Ramul's cluttered tables. He took it and they left, waving goodbye to the grim-faced Ramul.

Ramul's workshop was on one end of Ilyrion University, and Trey's meeting was on the other, at the Anthropological Society. They had a long walk ahead of them, and Trey worried about what was to come. Would the Society help him? Would they grant him his old position? Would they at least give him the research he'd so painstakingly done before the Sending twenty thousand years ago?

Something *bad* was coming to Valaralda. Something that would destroy not just this planet, but Earth, too—and everything else in the vicinity. He *knew* it, somehow. He just knew it. It had been the discovery of a lifetime, but now he couldn't remember the specifics.

He needed the Anthropological Society's help.

They were walking through the beautiful quad that formed the center of campus. Trees and flowers and grass grew everywhere, with bench-lined walkways curving throughout. A tall clock tower stood in the very center of everything, itself wrought into curves and branches, made to resemble a tree. Students walked to and fro across the lawn, strolling hand in hand or looking at electronic devices. A few of them flicked their eyes back and forth, staring at unseen things projected by their implants. One was even using magic: he saw a girl fly through the air, boosted by leafrunning. Other students were shouting at her, urging her on.

There was a Prime Tree on campus—one of four that graced the city of Ilyrion. It was right there in the middle of the quad, huge and lifelike, beautiful and strange. Trey still hadn't gotten used to seeing the massive Trees. They were big, yes, but that wasn't all of it. There was something about them that gave Trey the chills, but he couldn't quite put his finger on *why*.

As he got closer to the Tree, he saw that there were students there. Hundreds of them, surrounding the Tree. Many were on the ground, picnicking or kicking balls around or just lying there, reading. But then Trey raised his eyes, and he was shocked to see hundreds more students, floating in the air on little platforms ostensibly made of wood. They were everywhere in the sky, a constellation of them, doing home-work, or napping, or kissing.

He kept walking, passing by a ring of people, circled around a woman. She had two knives out, one in each hand, each long-bladed and sinuously curved. There was a big chunk of wood in front of her, and the woman was flicking at it with her knives, twirling and spinning in a kind of dance. Little chunks of wood flew away as she moved, spinning into the air and glinting in the setting sun. A shape emerged grad-ually from the wood, and Trey suddenly realized that this woman was Sculpting it, using the carving as a kind of performance.

He stood there, transfixed, watching the woman move. She was incredibly skilled, mixing Movement and Sculpture perfectly, cutting feature after feature into the wood before her.

But then the *real* magic happened.

The sky opened up above them, and rainbows cascaded down. Not one or two of them—*five* rainbows curved down-wards from the sky, playing along the grass, the multicolored light dazzling and dancing. Trey felt his heart grow light as he watched them play.

Then the rainbows disappeared and the sky grew dark, and stars were there, shining up above them in a patch of night sky. The sky was strange, detached from the daylight everywhere else. It was like looking into a hole, as if they had their own personal telescope. And then a shape appeared in the sky, flying between the stars. It was long and spiky, that shape, silver and jagged and somehow *evil*. And it was loom-ing, getting larger and larger as the crowd watched. It was traveling at an *incredible* speed, zooming through space faster and faster. The crowd started growing nervous, and Trey had to fight his instincts to duck, to run, to get away from this terrible thing that was approaching.

And then everything disappeared, and the world was back the way it had been. No rainbows. No stars. No terrible instrument of destruction hurtling through space.

Three inches of the wooden sculpture disintegrated into dust.

The crowd broke into applause, cheering and whistling. The mistweaver sheathed her knives and bowed, beaming.

It had been quite a performance.

"You okay?" Arra asked.

Trey nodded. "The magic here," he said. "It seems so effortless, so...integrated."

"They haven't had to hide from humans," Arra said. "They can do whatever they want."

"What would Earth have been like if the elves had existed openly? If magic was known?"

"I don't know," Arra said. "It wouldn't have been the same."

"It would have been better."

"Have you had any more memories of our life before?"

"A few."

"Are they good or bad?"

He looked at her. "Good." She blushed, reading something in his eyes.

"You remember...us?"

"Sometimes," he said. "We were really in love."

She didn't respond to that.

They continued walking arm in arm, passing elven students who paid them no attention. The sun was beginning to dip below the horizon, lending a somewhat gloomy feel to the campus.

"Sometimes," Arra said, "I still feel like we just met. And

sometimes I feel like I've loved you my whole life." She looked up at him then, blue eyes gray in the twilight. "Thank you for taking it slow with me."

"I'll wait as long as you need."

"Thanks."

"You sure you don't have somewhere else you need to be?"

"I don't think so. Why?"

"Well, you *are* a Senator now. I figured you had important meetings and...stuff."

Unlike Trey, Arra had immediately been thrown back into her old life. People had fawned over her, pledging their loyalty, giving her dresses and trinkets and things. And they'd even given her her old job back: Senator. It seemed awfully quick to Trey. They hadn't even *recognized* him.

Arra pulled her arm away. "You're jealous?"

"No," Trey said, although he was. Nobody even *believed* he was the Tarathiel of old. Maybe it was his ears. He looked like a human, not an elf. People here had trouble taking him seriously as a result.

"You *are* jealous," Arra said, but she looped her arm back through his. "They didn't actually make me a Senator, you know."

"They didn't?"

"It's just the title—they didn't give me a vote. It's for PR purposes. Speaker Imala wanted to look good in front of everyone, I guess. Alleria, from ages long past, resplendent in her gown, regales the audience with tales from afar." She sighed. "It's all just show."

Trey hadn't known that. "I'm sorry. I had no idea."

She leaned into him as they walked. "It's okay. Maybe if I work at it, they'll eventually give me some actual power in the Senate."

"Do you want that?"

Arra was silent for a moment. "I'm not sure."

"Hey, you two," a familiar voice said from somewhere to the right. Trey looked around and saw Orym standing there, waving at them.

"Orym!" Trey said. "Where've you been?"

"Mostly hanging out with the Space Agency. They've got some really impressive gear they're working with. They never let me touch any of it, though." He pouted.

Trey chuckled. "Always the scientist."

Orym beamed. "Yes, indeed." He turned to Arra. "You're looking beautiful tonight." He bowed slightly to her, giving her the formal greeting, the sign of the Twins on his hand.

Arra bowed back, equally formal.

"Orym," Trey said, "were we ever friends? Before everything. Before we left Valaralda."

Orym narrowed his eyes. "Were you that kid who failed all my science courses?"

"I don't remember."

"That was a joke," Orym said. "*Everyone* failed my science courses."

They laughed.

"Besides, I'm pretty sure you and I didn't meet until the Sending."

"Who chose you for it?" Trey asked. "Or did you volunteer? I'm having trouble remembering much of anything from back then."

"Well, there were twenty-eight of us," Orym said, "and I was a volunteer. Fourteen to become Prime Trees, and fourteen to find the Defense Mechanism. I guess things didn't quite work out how we planned. I wonder...do they even know how to make Prime Trees here on Valaralda?"

"I assumed they did," Trey said, "but I've never asked."

"I don't think they do," Arra said.

Orym stroked his chin. "I'll have to find out. There's so much we don't know yet." Then he brightened. "Where are you two off to?"

"Trey has an important meeting," Arra said.

"Oh?"

"It's not *that* important," Trey said. "I'm just meeting with the president of the Anthropological Society. President Myrddin."

"Just the president," Orym said. "Not that important."

"Maybe it is."

"You want your old job back."

"Yes," Trey said.

"I really don't think they can do that."

"Why?"

"Money," Orym said. "I heard about a bill that was passed a long time ago, right after the Sending—after we left this planet for Earth. The Anthropological Society was nearly entirely defunded."

"What? Where'd the money go?"

"The Department of Magical Research. I guess the Senate figured archaeology was a wasted effort."

"But they were wrong," Trey said. "So wrong. I really *believe* the Fall is coming, and the Defense Mechanism is the only way to stop it. We have to find my old research. We have to find the Mechanism and activate it. And we may not have much time."

"Myrddin will probably see it your way."

"I hope so."

"I saw it, you know," Orym said. "The Fall."

"You did?"

"I was there when they discovered it, just a few weeks ago. Everyone at the Space Agency went nuts."

"What does it look like?"

"Like a cloud of exotic particles. I didn't get a good look at it. They made me leave."

"Do you think it's true?" Arra asked. "That the Fall could kill us all?"

Orym paused a moment before answering. "It could be," he said. "But I think there may be more here than meets the eye. We need more data."

"I'm *sure* it's that dangerous," Trey said, "but you're right. I need to get my old research, maybe do some more digging. If the Defense Mechanism really is spread out across seven planets..."

"We have a lot of work to do. I'll let you two get back to it."

"What are you up to?" Arra asked.

"I'm heading back to the ISA building—the Space Agency, sorry. The Director called me in for a meeting. I have no idea what he wants—they don't seem to think I'm capable of helping with their research."

"You, too?" Trey asked.

"It's hard getting back to life here, isn't it?"

Trey nodded. "Too much time has passed." He brushed a hand back through his hair. It was getting kind of long. Maybe he should get it cut.

"Oh, that reminds me," Orym said, rummaging about in a small bag he was carrying. "I have something for you." He brought out a tiny black box and a little thing that looked like an earpiece. "It's a communicator. Nothing like they have here, of course. Just something I cobbled together. I fashioned it after the old Cothellon technology, but with a few of my own twists."

"Such as?" Trey took the communicator, looking at it quizzically.

"Such as interplanetary transmission," Orym replied. "It beams signals off of satellites orbiting Earth and Valaralda. We can talk to each other, even if we're on different planets. The transmission isn't instant—it can take anywhere from two to fifteen minutes to get the signal across—but it's a lot better than nothing." He pulled another set out and gave it to Arra.

"Who else has these?" Trey asked.

"Only Dillon, so far. And you two. I thought my son and the Prime Mages should have them, at least. Who knows what might happen next? I wanted to be prepared."

"Why is it," Trey said, "that you're always handing out radios?"

Orym stepped closer, placing a hand on Trey's shoulder. "I'm sorry about what happened," he said quietly.

He was talking about Callan. Trey's best friend—his *only* friend, really. Orym had given Callan a radio, back before they'd fallen from New San Francisco. Back before he'd met Arra and the elves. Before all of this had started.

And Callan had betrayed him. He'd sold them out to Quynn, who was pretending to be Trey's father. Callan had just wanted to see his sister again, but it had been a fruitless hope. His sister was dead, killed for Civil Service. Killed to make a darkprime Tree. Killed to feed the Cothellon plan. And Callan had been killed as well—Quynn had murdered him in cold blood, right there in front of Trey. A pointless kill for a pointless man.

"I'm sure it will come in handy," Trey said.

Orym squeezed his shoulder. "Oh, I almost forgot about these." He pulled out two white cards, handing one to each of them. "Guidecards. Maps of the world. It autodetects your position, feeds you information about where you are.

Contains history, tourist destinations, things like that. You'll figure it out."

"Thanks," Trey said. "You really think of everything."

Orym clapped him on the back. "Well, I'm off to the races."

"Good luck," Arra said.

"Are your apartments okay?" Orym asked. "It was the best I could get, given the circumstances."

"They're more than adequate," Arra said. "Thank you again for your help."

Orym nodded. "Of course. Anything for the Prime Duo." He laughed. "I think I'll start calling you that. The Prime Duo." He laughed again, heading off down the path.

"He'd better not call us that," Arra muttered.

"I don't know," Trey said, "it has a certain ring to it."

SIX

IT WAS GETTING close to dinner time when Trey and Arra arrived at the Esara Anthropological Society headquarters at the east end of campus. Trey wasn't sure why Myrddin had set the meeting this late—maybe he didn't want to be seen with Trey.

A young woman was sitting at the front desk when they entered, and she looked up at them with a bored expression. "Yes?" she asked. Trey could already tell that she was going to be very helpful.

"Trey, to see President Myrddin."

"Do you have an appointment?"

"Of course."

"And who is this?" The woman looked at Arra.

"This is—" Trey started, but Arra interrupted him.

"Alleria," she said, her tone slightly imperious. "Senator."

So she was already adopting her old name? Trey wondered if he should do the same. He didn't really like the name Tarathiel, though. It sounded pompous.

The woman at the desk didn't seem fazed. "I'll tell him you're here," she said, hitting a button on her desk.

"The Society must have fallen on hard times," Trey said quietly, looking around. The front office wasn't much to speak of. It was very small, with nothing but a receptionist desk and two little chairs in it. A picture adorned one wall—it depicted a pyramid in a desert, with what looked like a few Prime Trees around the edges. Hieroglyphics decorated the frame.

"He'll see you now," the receptionist said, pointing to the hallway on the left. She didn't even bother looking up.

"Should I stay out here?" Arra asked.

"Come with me," Trey said. "Maybe 'Alleria' can help persuade him."

She didn't catch his sarcasm. She followed without a word.

There was a door at the end of the hall, marked with Myrddin's name. Trey pushed through it and found a portly gentleman with a gray beard and gray hair.

"You must be Trey," the man said, standing and giving a short bow. "I'm Myrddin."

"Nice to meet you," Trey said, resisting the urge to stick his hand out. It was an old human tradition that the elves had never quite latched on to.

"Please, come in," Myrddin said, ushering them into his office. "And this must be the lovely Alleria I've been hearing so much about."

Trey glanced at Arra and saw that her posture had changed; she was standing very straight, her expression even. "Greetings," she said to Myrddin, inclining her head slightly and giving the sign of the Twins. Her imperious tone was back.

He offered them chairs, and they took them. The office was sparse, with few shelves and even fewer books. There was a small window, but it looked out on another building just inches away—not much of a view. Hard times, indeed. It must have been the defunding Orym had mentioned. The Society had no money for nice offices with nice views.

"It has been a long time since a Senator has visited these offices," Myrddin said. "The Senate has not been as...support-ive...of our ventures in recent years."

"You receive your funding from the university, do you not?" Arra asked.

Myrddin nodded. "Indeed we do, and the university is funded partly by the Ilyrion government. Lately our prospects have not been good. The Department of Magical Research is the university's biggest draw, the main reason it receives funding. But the Department has not had a new magical breakthrough in quite some time. As a result, support has all but dried up. Our position in the Senate continues to erode."

"Surely the Council of Mages continues to help?"

"They, too, are waning. Perhaps magic has had its day on Valaralda. Society demands progress—technological progress. Magitech is no longer the way forward, it seems. Citizens long for the future."

"That puts the Anthropological Society in quite a bind."

"Indeed. We are the worst of the lot. Forget technological breakthroughs—what new discoveries are there to be found in our planet's history? None. But I am getting ahead of myself." He turned to Trey. "What can I do for you, sir?"

Trey cleared his throat. "You know of the Fall, I assume?"

Myrddin frowned. "We've heard the rumors, along with everyone else."

"And you don't believe them?"

"Do you have new information?"

Trey leaned forward in his chair. "I'm Tarathiel," he said. "I discovered it."

"Ah, yes," Myrddin said. "I had heard you two claimed to

be alive twenty thousand years ago, but I wasn't sure if I believed it."

"Do you now?"

"I believe in facts. Facts and proof. Elves do not live for twenty thousand years. I believe gatesickness has overtaken you both."

"I led the original excavation near Nekhrumet," Trey said. "My team discovered the writings of Akhenaten, the Moon God of Nekhrumet. Surely you've read my accounts of those discoveries."

"I've read Tarathiel's accounts," Myrddin said. "Tell me: who was on that team? Which archaeologists did you bring with you to share in your findings?"

Trey racked his brain. Who *had* been with him? He had vague memories of the expedition, of digging under the sands, but he couldn't remember who was there. He couldn't remember any specifics, really. It was agonizing, knowing you did something, but being unable to really *remember* it.

"I don't know," he admitted.

"Here's the thing," Myrddin said. "Tarathiel was a renegade, even in his day. His great project, the Sending, deprived the world of many of its greatest leaders, scholars, and magicians. It *crippled* society, setting us back a generation of progress. Nearly two hundred good elves were lost to that foolhardy plan, and for what? Nothing was ever heard from them again. It didn't take long after that for gatesending to be banned. It wasn't just the side effects, you know. We couldn't risk another Sending. We couldn't risk losing more elves."

Trey was taken aback. He knew it had been a struggle back then, that no one had wanted to go along with his plan to reunite the seven planets. But he'd won that battle, had he not? He had convinced them all. He'd won the vote. Hadn't he? His memories were murky.

But now to hear that he'd caused such harm, that the Sending was reviled—it was too much to bear. He opened his mouth, but Myrddin wasn't done.

"You see," he said, "I've studied Tarathiel. I wrote my dissertation on him when I was a student. Do you know what they call his little project now?"

Trey shook his head.

"They call it the Folly."

The room whirled. Surely it hadn't been that bad. He'd been trying to save the *galaxy!* How was that folly?

"What is it that you want from me, Trey?" Myrddin asked.

Trey cleared his throat. He was finding it hard to think. This was not going the way he'd planned.

"Speak up, son," Myrddin prompted.

Anger flashed. He was *not* this man's son. "I want my old job back," he said, his voice shaking. "I want access to my original work. I want to continue that research, to find the Defense Mechanism, to save us from the Fall. I want to...to... to..."

He trailed off. He couldn't do this. He was terrible at confrontations. He felt a headache coming on. Next to him, Arra was silent in her chair. Was she not going to come to his rescue?

Myrddin stood, looking at Trey sadly.

"I studied Tarathiel," he said. "He was misguided, yes. But he was also a man of action, a strong man who did what needed to be done. He was as intelligent as he was charismatic. He was a leader. And you, I'm afraid, are not him."

"But I *am*—"

"We do not have the funding to take on another researcher at this time. And even if we did, I'm afraid we don't know where your records are."

"You *lost* my research?" Trey was flabbergasted.

"I do apologize for not being of greater help to you," Myrddin said. "Good night."

Trey was stunned. He couldn't even think. The thoughts just kept bouncing around in his head, unwritten. He felt anger suffusing him, paralyzing him. His headache was growing worse. Should he say something? Should he leave? He stood slowly, letting the moment grow. Only one thought was left in his mind.

"You may have just doomed the world," he said, his voice cracking. Then he spun and stalked out of the office. Behind him, he heard Arra following.

SEVEN

TREY RUSHED DOWN the hallway and out of the Society offices, Arra struggling to keep up with him. When he got outside, he stopped, looking around at nothing in particular. His head was a frenzy of emotion.

Arra laid a hand on his arm. "That didn't go very well."

Trey glared at her. "You weren't much help."

Arra removed her hand. "Don't blame this on me. You need to stand up for yourself."

Trey tried to bite down his anger, with little success. "The *Folly*? What the hell is that about? We were trying to *save the world*. I thought I'd convinced them of that."

"Remember," Arra said, "I was there too. I went with you on the journey. We did this together."

Trey sighed. "I remember," he said. "I just wish we could fix it together. How am I going to get the Defense Mechanism working if I can't get any support here?"

Arra shook her head. "Maybe there's someone else we can ask. I'll see what I can do in the Senate, but don't hold your breath."

"You certainly acted the part in there," Trey observed. His tone was more snide than he'd meant it to be.

"What's that supposed to mean?" Arra asked, her eyes narrowing.

"Nothing. Never mind."

Dark was gathering. Lights were coming on all over campus, illuminating the trees with a pleasant orange glow. But Trey's mind was too flustered to notice the beauty. What should he do now? His one avenue of support, the Society, had proved a dead end. He needed to get to the other planets. He needed to search for more writings. He needed—

"Tarathiel?" an unfamiliar voice said. Startled, Trey turned to see an older man approaching. The elf was skinny, his skin a little shriveled. But he had a friendly air about him, as if he were the least dangerous person on the planet. Trey found himself instantly taking a liking to him.

"Do you know me?" Trey asked.

The elf stopped in front of him, looking at him with something like awe in his eyes. He was wearing a chocolate brown suit that was more than a little shabby.

"It *is* you," he said. "You look just like him."

"I'm sorry," Trey said, "I don't believe we've had the pleasure yet. I'm Trey."

The man's head bobbed. "I'm Lashel. I work for the Society."

Trey nodded at him. "Pleased to meet you. How did you know I'm Tarathiel?"

Lashel beamed at him. "I've got your picture. Dozens of them, actually." He squinted at Trey. "The hair is different, and you've gained a little weight, but it's definitely you."

Was he really that out of shape?

"Did you...study me?" Trey asked.

Lashel nodded vigorously. "I actually wrote a book about

you," he said. "I can give you a copy, if you want. It's called *Tarathiel: Age of Discovery*. It didn't sell very well."

"Why not?"

Lashel shrugged. "I guess people no longer believe in the Fall."

"I heard they call it the Folly."

Lashel winced. "True. People are people, I guess. Always on to the next big thing. They forget what's come before. Listen"—he stepped closer to Trey, his voice lowering—"I've been working on some stuff of my own. I'd love it if you could take a look at it sometime."

"I've got a lot on my—"

"I think it may be important," Lashel interrupted. "You see, I was looking through your old translations, and I—"

"I really don't have the time."

"But if you would just *look* at what I've been doing—"

"Really," Trey said, "now's not a good time." The man was getting annoying. Trey was flattered to finally be recognized, but he didn't have time to review someone else's work. Not right now when he had the fate of the world resting on his shoulders. "Maybe later."

Lashel looked crestfallen. "So what were you doing in there?" he asked, motioning toward the Society office.

Trey sighed. "I was trying to get reinstated. The Fall is coming, and we're way behind schedule. We need to get the other planets online so we can activate the Mechanism."

"Ah," Lashel said. "That's what I wanted to talk to you about. Your research—"

"Not now, Lashel," Trey said.

"Of course," Lashel said, his face falling again. "You're a busy man. I'll let you get back to it." He made as if to leave.

"Hey," Trey said, and Lashel turned back to him eagerly.

"Yes?"

"Do you think you could put in a good word for me? You know, at the Society?"

"Sure I will," he said, grinning. "I still can't believe it. The great Tarathiel, back from his big adventure! My kids will be so excited when I tell them."

Trey wasn't sure that was true, but he didn't want to dissuade the man. "Thanks," he said.

"Don't mention it." There was almost a skip in his step as he left.

Arra laughed. "I don't think he even knew I was here."

"If *he* can recognize me," Trey said, "why doesn't anyone else?"

Arra shrugged. "Who knows? The people here are kind of strange." She almost sounded like she missed Earth.

Trey turned away. What should he do now? He'd blown his opportunity to rejoin the Society. Now he was on his own, the only person who believed in the looming threat. He had no resources, no friends. He didn't even have his old research.

"Hey," Arra said, nudging him. "It'll be okay. Let's go home. We can have dinner and think it over."

Trey looked at her. He was still frustrated from the meeting, still worried about what was coming. But Arra was with him, supporting him. She was looking at him in that way she had, as if nothing else in the whole world mattered. He felt his heart melting. He put his arms around her waist, kissing her on the nose.

"That sounds great," he said. "Thanks."

"For what?" she asked, blue eyes unblinking.

"For being you."

They strolled away as the last light left the sky.

PART
TWO

EIGHT

"DO WE HAVE *TIME* FOR A STORY?" Rylan asked.

Dillon shrugged. "We have somewhere else to be?"

Maybe. Rylan *had* wanted to visit the renown city of Nekhrumet, after all. The desert city was apparently famous for its beauty, its art, and its...other things. Things of the female persuasion. He'd seen a picture of one of them: dark-skinned and dark-haired, she was one hell of a beauty. She had one hell of an ass, too, from the looks of it.

He realized Dillon was still looking at him expectantly.

"Guess a story would be fine," Rylan said, turning back to the old woman. Mirra was short and wrinkled, with braided white hair that had little wisps sticking out everywhere. Her skin was deeply tanned, no doubt from years living out here in the Thesserin Desert. She was ugly as sin, but she seemed nice enough.

He looked around the room. Fourteen strange-looking miniature trees lined the windows. Everything else in the ramshackle room was covered with junk—plants, beads, papers, old food—stuff just strewn haphazardly around. The smell in there was a bit pungent. Not rank, exactly—just earthy, like plants. Rylan wrinkled his nose. He'd never get used to the smell of plants.

"Be ya seated, little ones," Mirra said in that odd accent of hers. "Old Mirra be tellin' ya a story for da ages."

Rylan found a short little stool with a bit of dirt on it. Brushing off the dirt, he sat, swinging his legs. He hoped the story would be interesting. And not too long.

"Da story begins," Mirra said, "in a great an' terrible jungle."

CARIEL WAS AN ELF.

She could remember that, if not much else. Vague visions swam in her head, waving around like palm leaves reflecting the sun. She didn't know why she knew it, or how it could be —she just knew she was different. She didn't have the claws of the rylak, the thick upper body and long limbs. She didn't have hair all over her body—it was mostly just on her head, where it belonged.

The Wilds were beautiful, in their own way. Beautiful and deadly. And hot. She took one last look at the thick jungle before turning back to the village. She could feel sweat making its way down her back, dripping from her armpits. She swatted at a bekal as it flew past, intent on drawing blood. The bekal were just beginning their mating season; soon there would be hordes of them, millions upon millions of the insects flying everywhere and getting into everything.

But she'd tarried out here too long already. Bending down, she picked up her heavy water bucket and began trudging back to the village of Skallgr. Hloldr would not be happy if she took too long.

Memories popped into her head as she walked. They came

at the most unexpected times, appearing without any context. Mostly they were more confusing than helpful.

She knew she was not on her home world. She knew she was on a planet called Eryn. A planet filled with hot jungles and violent creatures. *How* she got here, she could not remember. Nor why she was here. Or even how long ago it had been.

Whatever had happened, Eryn was her home now. The Kalmansa Wilds were her home.

And she was its slave.

"WAIT," Rylan said, interrupting the story. "I don't understand half of what you're saying. What's a bekal? Who's Hloldr? Where is Skallgr?"

"Ah, little ones," Mirra said, "don't ya be frettin' da names. You be from Mar, be it so?"

Rylan nodded slowly. He was still having trouble thinking of Earth as Mar.

Mirra smiled, showing broken teeth. "I use words you be understandin'," she said. "Bekal be like a mosquito. Bites you here." She slapped at her forearm. "Listen now. Mirra translate what she can."

"How do you know what a mosquito is?" Rylan asked. Surely they didn't have them here on Valaralda. Had Mirra been on Earth, somehow?

"Never be minding," Mirra said, smiling patiently.

Dillon elbowed him. "Let her continue," he whispered. "I want to know where this is going."

"Fine," Rylan said, eying Mirra. There was something not quite right about her.

"Now, where be I?" Mirra said.

SKALLGR WAS BLESSEDLY quiet when Cariel returned. The rows of wooden houses were silent, standing like sentinels in the harsh jungle sun. A few rylak were walking down the street, but they weren't looking her way. She watched their hairy, muscular forms ambling along the dirt road, growling at each other in conversation.

Careful not to spill any water from her bucket, she made her way to Hloldr's house. It was a rickety wooden thing made out of mangrove—not the most stable substance to build things out of. But Hloldr, her master, was proud of it, in his own strange way. He was always prowling around, convinced the other rylak were trying to steal it from him.

Which they probably were.

He wasn't home when she got there. She quietly poured the water into his big stone cistern, careful not to splash any on the dirt floor. She was thankful for this moment of quiet. They were so rare.

Suddenly the door slammed open, rocking the walls of the house. Cariel stood swiftly, bowing her head and putting her hands behind her back, trying to appear as submissive as possible. Inside, she was trembling.

She smelled Hloldr before she saw him. The rylak gave off a peculiar stench, hard to describe: like sweat mixed with garlic. Sometimes she could also smell blood. She was grateful that now wasn't one of those times.

Hloldr stalked inside, long toeclaws scraping the earth. "Where have you been?" he snarled, his voice low and raspy. She had worked long and hard to understand the rylak's strange language of guttural growls and barks. Yet she had never quite gotten used to it.

"I was getting water," Cariel replied, doing her best to

approximate the sounds. She knew she sounded dreadful to her master's ears, but it was the best she could do. She kept her head facing the floor, cringing inwardly. She should not have stopped to stare at the jungle again.

When the slap came, it was far worse than she had expected. They always were. She fell to the floor, reeling from the blow. Hloldr had kept his fingerclaws retracted, thank the Twins—otherwise she might not have survived the hit. Still, the strength of it brought tears to her eyes. She struggled to hold them back.

"Bring me food," Hloldr commanded. When she didn't get up immediately, he hit her again. "Now!" he barked, and she could hear his fingerclaws coming forward, making that subtle rasping sound all slaves learned to listen for.

"Right away," she growled, her voice coming out closer to a mewl. She stumbled up, trying to regain her balance without vomiting. Her vision still swung from that last blow —the rylak never knew their own strength. Frail little elves were too weak to withstand their abuse for long.

Hloldr watched her, golden eyes glowing as she left the hut, trying to keep herself from crying. It was important to appear strong here in Skallgr. Strength was the most important quality for the rylak. Weak slaves were thrown out of the village, thrown out to fend for themselves in the Kalmansa Wilds.

It was a death sentence.

Not for the first time, Cariel wished she could run away.

NINE

THE SPACE AGENCY office building was huge. Sleekly modern, it towered above the rest of the university campus. Orym looked up at it before he stepped inside, marveling at the glass work on the building's exterior. It looked like a skyscraper wrought in miniature, all reflections and angles and lines.

He approved.

He hadn't been in this building before. He'd only seen the Space Agency's research facilities, and some of the monitoring stations. *This* building was where the corporate offices were, where the true wealth of the Space Agency was most evident. It wasn't the most-funded government division, but it was definitely near the top.

Once inside, he found himself facing a row of security gates. Someone walked through in front of him, and the gate silently admitted the person. It must have scanned the man's implants, Orym realized. Implants that he didn't have.

A concierge approached him, a genial smile on his face. "Good evening, sir," the man said. "Are you here for an appointment?"

"I'm here to see Director Arkiem."

"Your name?"

"Orym Duskmere."

"Let me check."

The man's eyes flicked away, focusing on something distant. Using his ocular implant, no doubt. It gave the man a kind of computer screen inside his brain, projecting information directly into the ocular nerve, controlled by eye movement and brain wave scans. Creepy stuff, if Orym were being honest.

But also *really cool.*

The concierge returned his attention to Orym. "Follow me, sir," he said, turning and leading the way through one of the security gates. They walked down a hall and into an elevator which had no controls at all, not even a screen or a number telling them what floor they were on. This, too, must be managed via implants, Orym realized.

"When the elevator stops, proceed to your left," the concierge said, bowing and stepping out of the elevator. Then the doors closed and Orym felt a surge as the elevator car sped upwards.

Three seconds later, he had arrived. He went left, passing through a glass door indicating that this was the Research and Exploration Department. A young man was sitting at a desk made of brightly polished metal. He looked up as Orym approached.

"Good evening," the man said, his eyes flicking just slightly as he accessed his implant. "Welcome to the ISA, Orym. Director Arkiem is ready for you."

The man led Orym to an office at the back, where the door proclaimed its occupant to be Doctor Arkiem Brightwing, Director of the ISA R&E Department. The young elf opened the door and waved Orym through.

The office he found himself in was all glass—smoky glass on the inside walls, clear glass on the outside. Even the *floor* was glass. A wide, glass desk took up one edge of the room, and it was completely empty: no papers, no computers, not even a beverage or a pen. There was a wide open area in the middle of the office, and two glass chairs sat against the other wall.

Orym felt like he'd stepped inside a very expensive fish tank.

"Welcome," Arkiem said, standing up from the desk. "You must be Orym."

"Yes," Orym said. "Director Arkiem?"

"The very same. Please, come in and have a seat."

Director Arkiem was younger than he'd expected. The man was thin, almost to the point of being frail, but his skin was smooth and his long, blond hair was lustrous.

Orym went over to one of the glass chairs and sat down hesitantly. It put him twenty feet away from the desk—an awkwardly large distance. Should he move the chair up?

"How are you finding Valaralda?" Arkiem asked, seemingly unaware of the awkward situation.

Orym shrugged. "Some things have changed," he said, "and some have not. The planet is as beautiful as I remember."

"It has been twenty lifetimes since you were here, correct?"

"Yes, although I don't remember much of it."

Director Arkiem crossed his arms. "Tell me," he said, "how is it that you've been alive that long?"

Getting right to it. "Honestly?" Orym said. "I have no idea."

"Come now. You have a reputation. I know that somewhere in that head of yours, you must have a theory or two."

"Nothing I can prove."

"How much do you remember from your time on Earth?"

"My first memories are right around 1700 A.D. I was born in Salem, Massachusetts. There was a high concentration of elves in the town at that time."

"You were born there? But I thought you were born *here*, on Valaralda."

Force of habit had led to that mistake. The thought was so ingrained into him, it was hard to shake. Hard to reconcile what he remembered with what he now knew to be the truth.

Gatesending could really screw with you.

"My apologies," Orym said. "My first Earth memories are there, in Salem. A nice elven family took me in. My memories were gone, so they raised me as their own."

"But you came to them as an adult."

"Yes, I believe so. My memories since then are clear, but everything before that is missing. I remember fighting in the Revolutionary War."

"How did you discover your true age?"

"It happened when we went through the planet gate, when Earth moved into this solar system. Some of my memories re-formed. Most things are still hazy, but I remember being here, living here on Valaralda. I was a scientist, even way back then."

"And you were Sent to Earth with the others."

"Just so."

"Yet somehow you—along with several others—managed to survive for many millennia. Far longer than any elf before you has."

"Yes."

"And you remember nothing prior to Earth year 1700?"

"Correct. Although—" He stopped.

"Yes?"

Orym wasn't sure if he should continue. It was an unformed thought, unproven. He hated half-baked theories.

"Please continue," Arkiem said, leaning forward in his chair.

"I have this strange vision that keeps coming back to me," Orym said. "It's almost as if I were on another world for a time."

Arkiem's expression flickered for an instant, as if he had been expecting this. "What was this...world...like?"

Orym frowned. The images were always so hazy, so indistinct. "I remember the color violet," he said. "And Trees." He instinctively thought of them as Trees, with the capital T. They'd been Prime Trees—he was sure of it.

"Anything else?"

"I remember a hill of some sort. Almost a mountain. And there were two Trees on it. They soared above everything else, almost as if they were the lords of the place. It was so..."

"Yes?"

"Disorienting. Confusing. I don't know." He lapsed, unsure how to continue. The vision had been coming to him more and more lately, but he didn't understand it at all. Perhaps his mind was overworked after being alive for so long. Perhaps traveling through the gate had changed it. Broken it.

"Is this why you called me here?" Orym asked.

Arkiem seemed lost in thought.

"Director?"

Arkiem blinked, coming back to himself. "Sorry," he said. "No. I brought you here for a different reason."

He tapped a blank spot on his glass desk and stood. Light suddenly erupted out of the desk, creating a three-dimensional image in the middle of the room. The images moved and swirled, interface elements sliding in and out as Arkiem manipulated them with his mind. Orym was astounded—this was far beyond any technology he'd seen on Earth. And now he knew why the office had so much empty space.

The images finally resolved into something Orym would recognize anywhere: Earth. The planet whirled lazily in the air, perfectly depicted in every way. The colors were amazing —Orym found himself wondering how the display technology worked, what other things they could do with it. He grinned at himself inwardly. No matter how long he lived, one thing would remain the same: his insatiable curiosity for all things technological. Perhaps it was because Orym had never been much of a mage.

Director Arkiem continued. "This, as you may have guessed, is Earth. We've been completing a survey of the planet, the first undertaken since the Sending twenty thousand years ago. Back then, we could only use long-range telescopes, since the planet was so distant. But now that it's here in the Persephone system, we thought we'd take the opportunity to examine the planet in detail."

It made sense.

"As you can see," Arkiem continued, "we've completed a three-dimensional map of the surface area. That was the easy part. Then we pointed everything else we had at it: radio telescopes, lidar, sonar, infrared imaging—the works. Plus a few things humans never developed, such as *dúathmain* telescopes."

He was talking about darkprime magic. Both darkprime and lightprime emitted an energetic field when used—not light, exactly, but something else. Orym's physics were a bit rusty; it had been hundreds of years since he'd studied the magic in earnest. But detecting it shouldn't be a problem with the right instruments, even at great distances.

"We discovered a number of interesting things," Arkiem

said. "For example, did you know that there are several pockets of lifeforms living deep underground in various parts of the world? Humans, from what we can tell."

Orym hadn't known that. "That's not particularly surprising," he said. "We don't police the humans anymore."

"After you Sundered them, you mean."

"Just so."

"It's funny," Arkiem said. "You say all the elves lost their memory when they got to Earth."

"We did," Orym said. "Most of it."

"But you knew enough about the magic to remember the Sundering. The ritual is fairly simple, I'll admit, but still— that seems awfully strange to me, that you would remember."

Orym shrugged. "Some of us must have remembered. There were writings, passed down to elves from generation to generation, written by the original group. They talked about magic, about the Prime Trees. There wasn't much detail—we didn't know how to make the Trees, or anything at all about darkprime magic."

"But you had enough information to wipe out nearly the entire human species."

"They were acting in the best interests of the planet," Orym said, shifting in his seat.

"They?"

"The High Council. They debated the Sundering for decades before they actually did it."

"You weren't part of that group?"

"No. I was working for the other side at the time. The Cothellon."

"Ah, yes. The renegade squad of elves bent on worldwide domination. Not unlike the High Council."

It amounted to the same thing. "The Cothellon got us here."

"But why? Why move the planet?"

"Lorelei never gave us the true reason, but I think it was Tarathiel's discovery—the Defense Mechanism. She believed Earth was part of it, that it needed to be moved nearer to Valaralda."

"How could she possibly have known that? She's not one of the original group, is she?"

"I don't think so, but who knows? None of us had any memory after the Sending. She could be anybody."

"And now that you're here...what? Does the Mechanism exist? Is there a switch to turn on?"

"I don't know," Orym said. "That wasn't my expertise."

"Maybe you should find out."

"Maybe I will."

Arkiem smiled at him. The expression was oddly cold. "Are you a mage?" he asked after a moment.

Orym felt his eyes narrow. "Only a very weak fallfoiler. Why?" He'd always wanted to be a mage. His whole life, he'd thought he was Mundane. The day he had discovered he could use darkprime magic...that had been a good day.

"So you're not one of those Prime Mages."

"No."

"But you're friends with some of them, correct?"

"Yes." Where was this going?

"Have you noticed anything strange about them?"

"Not particularly. They're like me. Trey and Arra are both from here, from Valaralda. We're all twenty millennia old, and we don't know why. None of us can remember most of our lives."

"Doesn't that strike you as odd? Your two friends are Prime Mages, yet you're not."

"Well, Trey is actually half of one."

"*Half* a Prime Mage?"

"Yes. He can only access three of the powers. Well, four, I guess. He can use gatesending quite well."

"And you don't know why this is the case?"

"We do not."

"Yet the fact remains that these two individuals are the only ones you're aware of who can use more than one type of magic."

"There may be one more, actually. Quynn. He was masquerading as Trey's father, but he was actually someone else. One of the Cothellon leaders."

"So that makes three known Prime Mages. But how are they made? Where did they come from?"

"I take it you don't have any here on Valaralda."

"We do not."

"Well, I don't know how Prime Mages are made. I don't know anything about them."

"Want to know what I think?"

Did Orym have a choice in the matter? "Sure."

"Prime Mages are a myth, a longstanding legend. Oh, we have stories of them. Stories of all-powerful mages with unimaginable powers. Mages who could call legions of beasts and men, who could split their essence, forming armies from just one man. Mages who could shake the ground with the flick of a finger. But they are just that: stories. Legends from a hundred thousand years ago, in the years following the Great Awakening. Nobody believes them now."

"So you don't know how to make them."

"I don't think they even exist."

Arra and Trey were proof that he was wrong, but Orym didn't want to argue the point. Why was he here, anyway? What did Arkiem want?

He looked again at the rotating model of Earth, floating there in the middle of the room. It was a beautiful planet. For a moment, Orym wished he could go back there. Go back and live in the forest. Go back to a simple life. An easy life. A life of hunting and farming and living.

But there were questions to be answered and discoveries to be made. There were more mysteries to uncover. Threats to counter. The Fall was coming—whatever *it* was. And when it came, Twins help them all.

There was a knock on the office door, startling him. The door opened slightly and a man's head poked through, looking back and forth between Arkiem and Orym. "Sorry to interrupt," the man said.

"Ah, Druindar," Arkiem said, "your timing is perfect. Come in, come in."

The elf named Druindar stepped into the office. He was tall and thin, with long, gray hair that hung limply down his back. He had an almost furtive presence, like he was constantly worried about something. Orym stood and gave him a small bow.

"Greetings," Druindar said, reaching his hand out in the human fashion. Without thinking, Orym took the proffered hand and shook it. The man's hand was limp and clammy.

"Orym," he said.

"Druindar." As he released Orym's hand, something small fell to the glass floor. It was a leaf. Was the man some kind of landscaper?

"Druindar is my Chief Magitech Officer," Arkiem explained. Not a landscaper, then.

"Magitech?" Orym asked, turning back to the Director. Something about Druindar was making him uneasy.

"You don't use that term on Earth?" Arkiem asked. "Interesting. It refers to the combination of magic and technology. We at the ISA often find that the best solutions involve both."

That made sense. "So you're a mage?" he asked Druindar.

"Indeed," Druindar said. He didn't seem inclined to elaborate.

"I asked Druindar to join us here tonight," Arkiem said. "He will continue the presentation."

"During our survey of Mar," Druindar said, taking over the holographic display controls, "we detected some unusual emanations."

"Emanations?" Orym asked. "What do you mean?"

"*Dúathmain.* We know darkprime magic is still legal on Earth, so we expected to see some. But the location is very strange."

"Oh?"

"The emissions are coming from somewhere under the Mediterranean Sea." As he spoke, a red dot started pulsating on the rotating model of the Earth.

"But why would that be?" Orym asked. "Are there people down there? Mages?" A thin red line began stretching out from the dot, racing upwards in a graceful curve until it shot off the planet and out into space somewhere.

"That is unlikely," Druindar said.

"But the Director said earlier that they had discovered humans living underground," Orym said. "Maybe some of them are underwater, too?"

"We detect no lifeforms in the vicinity," Druindar said. "And these particular *dúathmain* emissions are unlike anything we've seen before."

"How so?"

"Well, most darkprime magic occurs briefly, in fits and starts. The one exception we've encountered was your flying cities. When they were powered by magic, the emissions were very steady. But even then, they fluctuated here and there as individual mages entered and left the circle."

"You got rid of the fallfoiler mages," Orym said. They'd

replaced them with some kind of technology, allowing the cities to float without the aid of magic. Orym hadn't had a chance to investigate how exactly it worked. There was so much he didn't know.

"Indeed, we did," Druindar said. "We removed all magical requirements from the sky cities. We couldn't in good conscience leave those poor slave darkmages there." He smiled somewhat crookedly. The expression looked painted on, as if he were a kind of doll. It gave Orym the creeps. "Whatever magic is causing the emissions under the Mediterranean Sea," Druindar continued, "it's *completely* stable. A pure, flat waveform. Not only that, the intensity of the emissions indicates that the sheer power involved is immense—*far* bigger than anything we've ever seen before."

"Any theories as to what it is?"

"Not yet." He gestured to the red line that was still arcing out from the image of the planet. "This is a diagram of the emission. It follows a straight, very narrow path—almost like a laser, albeit a curved one."

"And where is this—laser—pointing?" Orym asked.

"Right at Valaralda," Druindar said. "At us."

TEN

"WHO IS HLOLDR?" Rylan asked. "*What* is he?"

"He be a rylak," Mirra said, not quite turning to look at him. "An evil race. Powerful race. De'r claws be somet'ing to behold."

"But where are they?"

"Eryn," Mirra said. "It be a planet far away. A planet no one ever visits. Tha elves be there, ya see. Dey be Sent there, tru da gates."

"But why?"

"Why did da elves be visitin' Earth? Why did magic be destroyin' *your* race? It be fate, little ones. It be *magic*. It be da Fall."

"Oh."

"Now listen. Listen to da tale."

Rylan tried to settle in, but something about this story was bothering him.

THE HUNT WAS ON.

Cariel was struggling to keep up. The rylak always ran quickly through the jungle, long limbs and strong muscles and cutting claws making it easy for them to traverse the thick undergrowth. They'd lived in the Wilds for millennia, evolving with the jungle, learning what it took to stay alive out here.

And Cariel had not.

It wasn't as easy for Cariel and the other elven slaves, but they were still expected to make the trip. They always carried the supplies: food, skondul liquor, spears and arrows. No medical supplies, of course—the rylak believed that only the weak died of injury or disease. And if you were weak, you were better off dead.

Rylak hunted pretty much every day. It took a *lot* of meat to keep them full and happy, after all. But it was usually smaller game: birds and fish and tapir and boar.

Today wasn't one of those hunts.

Today was the *big* Hunt. The Hunt for cavek. The Hunt that would feed them for a month. And the material rendered from that animal would last them for a *year*.

She swatted a bekal fly away. The spawning would likely begin tonight, and then there'd be millions of the tiny insects, getting into everything. She wondered if the red moon would be up tonight as well.

The elven slaves—there were just three of them today, all women—crested a hill and came out into a clearing. The rylak had stopped momentarily, staring out at something in the distance. Cariel stood, staying loyally quiet, grateful for the chance to catch her breath.

Hloldr, her master, was pointing and growling words she couldn't quite make out. She followed his claw, shading her eyes from the glaring sun. Up ahead, far in the distance, she could see a tree. It was massive, towering far above the rest of the jungle, shading everything around it from the intense sun. The tree itself was a strange color, somehow brighter than everything nearby. It was almost like the sun favored it, shining brighter everywhere it touched the massive tree.

It was very strange.

"You," someone growled at her, and Cariel flinched instinctively. But it was just Svalya, the pack chief. She wouldn't hurt her. Svalya always looked out for her.

"Yes?" Cariel growled.

Svalya bared her teeth at the poor pronunciation. "Why do you stare at the tree?" she asked. The female rylak towered over Cariel, and she could smell sweat and the peculiar odor of fur the rylak always had.

Had she been staring?

"The tree is strange," Cariel grunted.

"So are you," Svalya observed. "But I think you know what the tree *is*. Why will you not tell us?" She was flexing her fingers, claws unsheathed.

Cariel swallowed. "I do not"—she coughed as she growled the awkward word—"know."

"It is magic," Svalya said. This was a new word, only recently introduced into the rylak lexicon. For some reason the rylak always suspected the elves of magic, of doing things that should be impossible.

Cariel had no idea why.

"The tree is a mystery," Cariel managed, the words feeling like gravel in her throat. "I do not know what it is."

Svalya leaned even closer, her eyes menacing. Her wolf-like muzzle opened, revealing rows of razor sharp teeth. "I think you do," she growled. "Why are you afraid?"

Cariel was taken aback. "What?" The word came out as a whimper. Svalya pulled away. She must have seen something in Cariel's eyes.

"You think I will hurt you. You think you are in danger."

"The males," Cariel said. "They...look at me."

"As long as I am packleader," Svalya said, "we will not hurt you. Sex with elves is...unclean." She spit the words out as if they were distasteful. Cariel wasn't very good at reading rylak facial expressions—they didn't really *have* much in the way of facial expressions—but she was pretty sure Svalya meant what she was saying. Svalya wanted to protect her, for some reason. Her and all the elves. She didn't want Cariel to be afraid.

Maybe—just maybe—Svalya was one rylak she could trust.

"We run!" Svalya shouted, gesturing for the pack to continue. But she gave one final wink to Cariel before she turned, and Cariel felt something leap inside her.

Maybe life wasn't *entirely* hopeless.

The rylak set out at speed, and Cariel had to run to stay with them, clay pots and leather packs heavy against her back.

"They always ask about that stupid tree," Tilla said, running along beside her. Tilla was another slave, and she was speaking in the elven language. The language that had been outlawed.

"Shh," Cariel cautioned. "They will hear."

"Let them," Tilla said. "I long to be away from this place."

"You want so much to die?"

Tilla just looked at her, and Cariel saw that, in fact, she did.

Perhaps she had a point. There was nothing for them here, no way out of this terrible life they led. But wasn't being a slave better than being *nothing*? Wasn't life better than death? If Svalya was there to protect them, shouldn't they at least *try* to make something of themselves?

Cariel wasn't entirely sure.

"Don't do anything stupid," she whispered to Tilla. "If something happened to you..." She left the thought unfinished.

Tilla's eyes softened, and she reached out and squeezed Cariel's arm. "We'll make it," she said. "We'll keep each other strong."

Cariel smiled in return.

They left the clearing and entered back into the jungle. Here vines swept over her, leaves and spindly trees mixing with ferns and thicker trunks, a miasma of green and brown and green. Cariel followed as well she could; the rylak were cutting their way through indiscriminately, as usual. They made it look easy.

She thought she saw something, then, far up ahead. It was just a glimpse, a long way off through the trees. Maybe she was imagining it. Maybe it was nothing.

But if it was what she thought it was, they were all in grave danger.

"Wait!" Cariel growled, the sound coming out almost as a bark. She was proud of it—it almost sounded *right*.

Every rylak stopped and looked at her. She could almost feel their breath, feel their stares.

Shit.

"Sakul," she said, "up ahead."

Instantly the whole pack fanned out, threading through the surrounding trees, taking cover and taking stock. Sakul, Cariel knew, was a terrible thing. It was a bird, a very territorial bird which always flew alone. And if it struck you—if it managed to get its beak underneath your skin—you were dead, rylak or not.

Sakul killed *everything* it touched.

Hloldr was suddenly standing next to her, his thick hand

clutching her shoulder. "Where?" he growled, his deep voice impressively quiet.

Cariel pointed to where she'd seen the bird. Sakul were small but obvious, bright white with pitch black beaks. They were easy to see, if you were paying attention.

Hloldr followed her finger, trying to find the errant sakul. But there was nothing there, Cariel could see. No bird, no menace. No death looming on the horizon.

The sakul was gone.

"You lie," Hloldr said, and then he did the smallest possible flick of his finger across her face.

Pain flared out instantly along her cheek, burning in her skin. She felt blood flowing from the wound Hloldr had made.

"Our vision is better than yours," Hloldr said, his tongue wrapping indelicately around the guttural words. "We would see a sakul if it was there. Now *silence*."

He stood in front of her, chest heaving, and she could smell his arousal. He *wanted* her, the way all rylak wanted elves. He wanted to touch her, to make her his. He leaned forward, and for a devastating moment Cariel was sure that this was the time he'd finally do it. He'd take her.

But he just slapped her, this time without his claws.

It was enough to send Cariel reeling to the ground, sparks around her eyes.

But then she heard a grunt and Hloldr was reeling, too, staggering from a blow she hadn't seen. She looked upward, trying to clear her vision. Svalya was standing next to Cariel's master, hackles raised, a low rumble escaping her throat.

"Claws away," Svalya said.

For a very brief moment, Cariel saw anger flashing in Hloldr's eyes. He almost struck the packleader. He almost retaliated. But Svalya held her ground, daring him to strike.

The moment passed.

Hloldr slunk away, claws retracted. Defeated. Svalya looked at Cariel, her expression one of pity. "Do not lie to us again, pretty one," she said. And she turned and led the pack away.

Tilla reached down, helping Cariel to her feet. "Are you okay?"

Cariel nodded, wiping blood from her cheek, watching Svalya's back. "Come on," she said. "We have to go."

Tilla nodded.

They set out, following the pack. The sakul was nowhere to be seen.

WHEN IT FINALLY CAME, the cavek was just as terrible as Cariel had remembered.

She heard it before she saw it, of course. It thundered, even in the jungle, even though there were trees and vines and millions of plants everywhere. Still it came, heedless of the undergrowth.

She couldn't smell it. Cavek didn't smell like anything, interestingly enough. For such a massive creature, it was surprisingly clean. This, of course, made it much more difficult to detect.

And that, doubtlessly, was the entire point.

Rylak had been hunting this beast for generations, for millennia. It was a point of honor to take one of them down —if you planted the spear at the right place, if you were the one to kill the cavek, you were instantly honored above all else. You were placed high, given the choicest meats and the best women.

At least until the next Hunt, when the whole thing happened again.

Still, it was enough to motivate the rylak. They *wanted* this cavek dead. And they all wanted to do it *themselves*. This, Cariel knew, was folly.

And so it came.

When it finally crashed into view, Cariel shrieked. She couldn't help it. She clutched Tilla, cringing at the sight.

The cavek was *huge*. Easily a hundred feet tall and two hundred long, it was thick and bulky and gray like an elephant, yet strangely muscular and agile. Its four single-jointed legs were *strong*, incredibly long, tipped with claws the size of swords. It had a wide face with inset eyes, and its mouth was always open, baring scimitar teeth that could rip through trees and huts and rylak and *anything*.

Elephants. Swords. Scimitars. These were concepts from *before*, from the life Cariel had led before she'd been Sent to this savage planet. Why did she remember these things but nothing else? Why did she see swords when she looked at the cavek's paws? Why did she think of an elephant when she looked at its bulbous body, at its thick, dry skin, at its ears? What had *happened* to her?

She didn't know. And now the rylak pack was surging forward, spear tips at the ready, poison already dipped and gleaming and prepared to strike into the cavek's three hearts.

Maybe they could kill it.

If the rylak had the nerve. If they had the skill.

But first, it was the *cavek's* turn to strike.

And so it did, swiping its front left paw at the group of rylak in a devastating arc. Cariel winced as three rylak—*three* of them!—flew backwards in the air, guts spurting outward from vast rents in their stomachs. They landed somewhere three hundred feet away, slammed against a tree or fallen a hundred feet to the ground.

Dead. Bloody. Mincemeat.

Just another meal for the cavek.

But the cavek wasn't done. It snarled, the sound ricocheting off the trees and leaves, its spit thick and warm as it rained down on elves and rylak alike. It lunged forward, mouth wide open, intent on its prey.

Rylak, Cariel knew, were just a snack to it. There were other animals out there, other beasts inside the jungle, which were larger than rylak. Other things that would give a *real* meal to one such as the cavek. These were what the cavek normally hunted. It didn't need to kill the rylak. It didn't even need to notice them.

Except now. Now it was provoked. Now it would fight. The cavek continued its lunge, scimitar teeth bared. And the six remaining rylak, Hloldr and Svalya among them, brandished poison-tipped spears.

And charged.

ELEVEN

THE PIG and Whistle was bustling—far busier than normal. Allain and his identical twin elbowed their way through the crowd standing behind the bar, angling toward where he could see Kharis had already nabbed a booth. Business everywhere in New San Francisco had been picking up steadily over the past few months. What with the Valaraldans and people streaming up from Earth's surface, it was a wonder the city could contain them all. Everyone wanted to see the marvelous constellation of floating cities.

Allain couldn't exactly blame them.

"Anything new?" Allain asked, sitting across from Kharis. Allain2 sat next to him—a bit too close. Allain pushed him away, giving him a glare. His twin was already getting annoying.

Kharis took a long pull from his beer. Then, instead of responding, he just nodded toward one of the televisions mounted high up on the wall. The bar had gotten three more of them installed, and they were very popular. Allain tried to listen to the broadcast over the din of the crowd.

"The Space Agency is reporting that they are training all

available instruments on the phenomenon," the reporter was saying. It was the cute reporter he'd seen earlier—Ellarian, if he remembered correctly.

"So far not much is known," the reporter continued. "Ilyrion University leadership is staying tight-lipped about the investigation, and officials from the Senate are equally unresponsive. I'm here today with Fyliaster Magnus, High Historian for the Ilyrion Council of Mages. Fyliaster, you claim Iliaster Magnus is one of your ancestors. Viewers may recognize Iliaster as the writer of many great historical works, including *Dawn of an Empire*, which is still taught in schools throughout the world."

She pointed the microphone toward an elderly-looking gentleman wearing a long, black robe.

"That's correct, Ellarian," Fyliaster said. "The question on everyone's mind today is a simple one: is this the 'Fall' that early researchers predicted? And, if so, are we in any danger?"

"Can you tell us anything about the Fall?" Ellarian asked.

"Certainly," Fyliaster said. He had a deep voice and a magnanimous air, as if he were used to addressing crowds of people. He almost seemed to be *enjoying* this. "The Fall was uncovered over twenty thousand years ago by a researcher named Tarathiel. He found mentions of it scattered throughout ancient writings that had been discovered in the excavations under Nekhrumet. According to his findings, the Fall was purported to reoccur every hundred thousand years."

"That's quite a long timeframe," Ellarian noted.

Fyliaster nodded. "Indeed it is. Moreover, the Fall is expected to be a widespread extinction-level event."

The reporter pursed her lips. "But if that's true, wouldn't we all have been wiped out eons ago?"

"Not precisely. Events such as the Fall would have

survivors, small remnants of elves that live on in hiding, outlasting whatever destruction is going on around them."

"But what *is* the Fall?" Ellarian asked. "How does it destroy the world? And why does it keep coming back?"

"All very good questions, but I'm afraid we don't have the answers right now. I can assure you that the Council of Mages is doing everything we can to look into this threat." He looked into the camera. "We hope the Senate will lend their support as well."

"Riveting stuff, isn't it," Kharis said. His eyes were bleary and his words were slurred. How long had he been drinking today?

Allain2 snorted. "Boring stuff, is more like it."

Allain nodded. For once he agreed with his twin. "I'm tired of all this Fall crap."

Kharis didn't respond. A flustered server came by and asked if Allains wanted anything. They both ordered beers, then turned back to the TV. The news report had moved on to a different story.

"Now we come to our featured Isilya segment: A Survey of Mar." Isilya was like Wednesday on Valaralda, Allain had learned. They had different words over there for a lot of things.

"Scientists from all over Valaralda have been entranced by Mar, which is called Earth by its local inhabitants. Today we'll be showing footage of the Mediterranean region, thought to be near the origin point of the human species."

Allain tuned the TV out. He had no interest in remote locations on Earth. The planet was largely uninhabited now, after the Sundering three hundred years ago that had killed ninety-nine percent of the population. The old Council Leader from his home town had been in charge of that particular ritual. But now Silanar was dead, murdered by a vindictive elf named Quynn.

One life for billions. Doubtlessly a fair trade.

The beers arrived, and Allain let his thoughts drift onto other things. More important things, like his ever-present question: how did Allain2 come into being? And, more importantly: how the hell could he get rid of the bastard? He took a drink as he considered his options for the thousandth time. Maybe he just needed a change of pace, some new scenery. Maybe he should get out of the city.

The news package finished with some sweeping shots of the Mediterranean Sea, and Allain yawned. Then the program cut back over to the anchor.

"That was A Survey of Mar," she said. "Tune in every Isilya night for more. And, speaking of Mar, we have breaking news coming to you now from the Space Agency."

The news program changed to a shot of a harried-looking reporter. The man was wearing a suit made in the style of Earth; human culture seemed to be bleeding into Valaraldan culture at an astonishing pace. The elves seemed hungry for new and interesting things. He supposed it made sense.

"Thank you, Sarya," the reporter said. "I'm here with Arkiem Brightwing, Director of the Ilyrion Space Agency Research and Exploration Division. Director Arkiem, thank you for being here."

"My pleasure," Arkiem said. He was a very thin elf with long, blond hair.

"Can you tell us what you've discovered?"

"Certainly. As I'm sure you know, the ISA is very active on Mar. We know the planet was brought into our solar system for a reason, but we haven't uncovered the exact cause just yet."

"You're speaking of the Defense Mechanism," the reporter said.

"Indeed. Rumors abound—not just in our ancient writings, but also amongst the elven culture on Mar—that this 'Fall' can only be deterred by a very old device: the Defense Mechanism. We believe a piece of it may be hidden somewhere on Mar."

"And have you made a new discovery?"

"We have," Arkiem said. "Just today, we uncovered a signal of some kind, emanating from deep beneath the Mediterranean Sea."

"What type of signal? Like radio waves?"

"Without getting into the specifics, the signal appears to be caused by *dúathmain* emissions."

The reporter looked taken aback. "Can you elaborate? Our viewers may not be familiar with this."

Arkiem's expression became guarded. "We don't want to go into too many details on this program," he said. "*Dúathmain*, of course, refers to darkprime magic." The reporter opened his mouth, but Arkiem continued over him. "Yes, the Esaran government outlawed darkprime wood over ten thousand years ago. But Mar is a different planet—almost, as humans would put it, the 'Wild West' of magic. Even so, we were surprised to find *dúathmain* emissions coming from underneath the ocean."

"And will you be investigating?"

"We will indeed. As we speak, a team is being prepared to dive beneath the water. We'll be sure to let you know anything we find."

"Director Arkiem, thank you so much for your time," the reporter said. Arkiem smiled and nodded, and the reporter turned back to the camera. "We here at News One would like to remind our viewers that darkprime wood—and especially gatesending—is strictly forbidden on the continent of Esara and most other municipalities throughout the world. Any elves wishing to be tested for Alignment are encouraged to report to your nearest Department of Magical Research office. Please remember that magic use is a privilege, not a right: mages must be properly licensed and insured. Thank you."

Legal boilerplate, on a news program? Allain found himself snorting in derision. He'd thought the elves in Sylrantheas were strict, but imagine requiring a *license* for magic? It was crazy.

He took another drink of beer.

"So, Kharis," Allain2 said from his position next to Allain, "you got any plans? I mean, other than getting fat and drunk."

Allain glared at his twin. Allain2 always seemed to be saying the wrong things. He was far more aggressive and confrontational than Allain was. Allain wondered why that might be.

Just then, he noticed something unusual: there was a mole on Allain2's right cheek, underneath his eye. Allain could have sworn it hadn't been there before. He frowned, looking away. Perhaps he was just imagining things. He'd have to check his own face in a mirror later.

Kharis was looking at Allain2 with heavily lidded eyes. "This city can go to hell," he slurred. "I'm going back to the ground."

"Oh?" Allain said. "What will you do?"

Kharis swung his gaze over to him. "Pano Sylrantheas," he said. "Maybe they need an archery teacher."

"You might want to lay off the beer if you plan to shoot arrows," Allain2 said.

"Just one more," Kharis said. "Just one more."

Allain looked around at the crowd filling the bar, jostling

each other, talking loudly. The mass of people made him uncomfortable. Yes, a change of scenery was definitely in order. But he wouldn't go to Valaralda—he didn't want to get in trouble for using magic without a permit. Maybe Pano Sylrantheas. Or maybe New Paris.

With a wry grin, he drained his beer and slapped Allain2 hard on the back. "Let's go, chump," he said.

"Don't call me that," Allain2 said, but he finished his beer and followed Allain out of the bar.

Just before they left, Allain turned back to look at Kharis. The older man was staring deeply into his mug of beer, tears glistening in his eyes. The man had lost a lot, Allain knew. His son Fenian and his brother Lhoris were both dead, killed by Cothellon. The man deserved some sympathy. If he found it at the bottom of a bottle, so be it.

Allain hoped he would land on his feet.

TWELVE

ALLAIN LOOKED at the ground far below his dangling shoes. From his vantage point atop the New Eiffel Tower, he could see all of New Paris. The sky city sparkled at night, glowing with old-world charm. The Cothellon architects had done a masterful job replicating Paris up here in the sky. There was even a Seine of sorts: a thin band of water wound its way through the city, cutting through the Arrondissements with something that almost approached the romantic glamour of its namesake on Earth's surface. It was a closed system—the water was continuously recycled and purified, flowing across the city in endless loops.

The original city of Paris was a ghost town, of course. Allain hadn't visited—why would he?—but he knew what it probably looked like. He'd been to Old San Francisco. Derelict buildings would rise like infernal monuments to an age long forgotten. Weeds and trees and torn up roads and abandoned cars would be everywhere, and the only sounds would be those of nature, who had come back to claim her home.

It would be far too depressing to visit.

But New Paris—New Paris was a delight. Allain loved it

up here atop the New Eiffel. He and Allain2 came up here often, just to sit and watch and think. He found it relaxing.

He could see all the way out to the edge of the city, where the New Golden Gate Bridge joined New Paris with New San Francisco. It was ironic, in its way: San Francisco had sometimes been called the "Paris of the West". It was somehow fitting that it would be physically joined to Paris now. With the old Earth dead and returned to nature, these United Sky Cities were the only real reminder of what humanity had achieved, so long ago.

Lights suddenly flashed on the tower, shining brightly in the night sky. The New Eiffel Tower did this display every night, and people came from miles around to picnic in the lawn below, drinking wine and watching the lights. Allain found himself wishing that Arra could be here to see this. She'd never been to New Paris, not that he knew of. She'd never seen its beauty. He longed to take her up here sometime.

Allain smiled faintly to himself, thinking about her. He visualized her—stunning, strong, deadly. The most beautiful girl he'd ever seen. But then he pictured her in Trey's arms, and his mood soured. Trey: the bastard who'd stolen Arra from him.

No, no, that wasn't right. Trey wasn't bad. Allain saw Allain2 glaring at him, as if reading his mind, and Allain felt the anger slip away. It was almost as if his twin had taken it from him, in that one look. Allain took a deep breath of the crisp night air. The stars sparkled as if to match the tower, and all was right with the world for a moment.

Trey was a nice guy. Allain could admit that, at least. And Arra didn't love Allain. Never had, if he was being honest about it. He sighed wistfully and swung his legs up onto the platform. It was time to give up on her. Time to move on.

Time to go home.

"THE BROS ARE BACK!" Shot shouted as Allain and Allain2 walked into Shock Crew headquarters.

"Ho," Allain said. Allain2 was glowering, as usual, but Allain wasn't fooled. He knew his twin loved it down here in the Under.

Shock Crew had expanded. With the Department of Civil Service gone, the kids had been able to break down some walls and take over several neighboring rooms in the Under. The story of the last battle against the Cothellon had become legend, and Shock Crew had found itself inundated with underkids from all over the United Sky Cities. Everyone wanted to be part of the Crew that had helped overthrow the oppressive government.

At first, Allain had wondered why the kids didn't move out of the Under. It didn't take him long to realize why: there was a certain camaraderie down here, a certain feel to the place. Kids were everywhere—self regulating, self-subsisting, and generally just free. They liked not having adults around to supervise, and Allain agreed. He felt more at home here than he ever had in Sylrantheas.

"Anything new?" Shot asked as they walked through the water treatment plant, ducking as underkids threw stuff at them.

"Just this Fall thing everyone is talking about," Allain said.

Shot grunted. "Just when we thought we'd saved the world, here comes another disaster. Do you believe it? Will the Fall destroy the universe?"

"I don't know anything about it," Allain said. "But after

everything I've seen these past few months, nothing would surprise me."

Someone whistled at them, catching Shot's attention. A tall, spindly teenager ambled up to them, all elbows and knees.

"What's up, Stick?" Shot asked the kid.

"Got some new ones in from New Sydney," Stick said. "Where should I put 'em?"

Allain wondered if there were any girls in the new group. Sydney girls were different from the ones he was used to. They were more raw, more energetic, with hair in places he didn't expect. He'd managed to sack up with a few of them, and he wouldn't have minded another go.

Shot pursed his lips. "We got no more room down here, dammit," he said. "This keeps up any longer, the whole goddamn Under will be one Crew."

"Would that be so bad?" Allain asked.

"Might not be, but where the hell am I gonna get enough space for all that?"

Allain shrugged. It wasn't a bad problem to have.

"Put 'em over in Power Storage Four," Shot said. "And see if we can extend the scaffolding in there further down. Any luck with the mystery rooms?"

"We can't get in," Stick said. "Not even with the welding torches we stole. Those rooms are sealed up tighter than a virgin's bunghole."

"Nice, Stick," Shot said. "Way to keep it clean."

"You know we're in the Under, right, boss? This place is *anything* but clean."

"Keep trying," Shot said. "Nobody knows what those damn rooms are even *for*. I bet if we could crack the lid on them, we'd have more than enough space for all these incoming kids."

"You got it, boss," Stick said, turning and loping away.

Shot watched him go. "I swear," he said, "that kid eats more than any two of us put together, but he's still the skinniest damn thing I ever met."

They continued walking down the center of the room. A piece of wadded up paper hit Allain in the chest. He caught it and threw it up into the rigging. That earned him a whistle.

"How long you planning on staying this time?" Shot asked as they walked. Two kids were playing catch with an old ball of some kind. The thing was so dirty it was nearly unrecognizable. Allain ducked as the ball hurtled through the air, right where his face had been.

"Maybe for good," Allain said.

"And you?" Shot asked Allain2.

"Whatever he wants."

"You two always gonna stick together?"

Allain2 shrugged.

"Alright," Shot said. "You been down to Pano Sylrantheas lately?"

"Nope," Allain said. "Why?"

Shot shrugged. "Just curious is all. I hear lots of humans are settling there."

"Getting tired of dirty boys and cement?"

"Nah," Shot said. "Well, maybe. I can never get it out of my head. The forest."

"It's not all it's cracked up to be," Allain2 said. "Spend fifty years there and get back to me."

"What are you talking about?" Allain asked. "You haven't even been alive two months."

Allain2 glared at him. "I have all your memories, idiot."

"Don't call me that," Allain said.

Shot laughed.

They arrived at their destination: Dill's old tent. Shot had taken it over now that he was in charge of Shock Crew. His team of officers had grown. The logistics for feeding four thousand kids was a massive job, even with government handouts. Shot had the kids farming down here in the Under, growing stuff in hydroponic gardens. It kept them mostly out of trouble, and helped with the food problem.

The tent had been enlarged, too. Shot and Allains stepped inside to a whirl of activity. Grime was there, directing operations. A small team of "engineers"—the kids liked to call themselves that—were huddled over a table, discussing plans to enhance the vast scaffolding in the battery rooms. Spike was speaking urgently in a radio, spiky hair bobbing as she yelled and gesticulated.

"Business is good, I see," Allain said.

"If you can call it that."

"Heard from Dill lately?"

"Nah. He's over on Valaralda, doing Under-knows-what. Last I heard, he was going into some kinda desert."

"Why would he do that?"

"Beats me," Shot said. "All good?" he asked Spike, who had gotten off her radio.

"Buncha untrained idiots," she said, but she was smiling.

"You weren't much better yourself a few weeks ago."

"I'm a quick study. Quicker than the damn kids you keep giving me."

"We fighting a war I don't know about?"

"I know you think these new underkids are all fine," Spike said, "but I guarantee you some of them will be trouble. This kinda peace won't last."

"Always looking on the bright side, eh, Spike?"

"Shut up." Her radio blared again and she turned away.

Shot grinned at Allain. "She loves it," he said. She had a funny way of showing it.

Spike turned back to them suddenly, a concerned look on her face. "Someone's coming, boss."

"More underkids?" Shot didn't seem particularly concerned.

"No," Spike said, "someone else. An adult. An *elf*." She glared at Allain as if it were his fault.

"Battle stations!" Shot said, and Spike began speaking rapidly into her radio. Shot turned to Allain, a wide grin on his face. "I've always wanted to say that."

THIRTEEN

TREY AND ARRA had almost made it off campus when a stranger approached them. Trey stopped, unsure if he should be concerned. Ilyrion had seemed safe so far—almost unnaturally safe. Trey was waiting for the other shoe to drop. He continued holding Arra's hand as the man walked up to them.

"I apologize for the interruption," the man said. "Do you know where the Religious Studies building is?" The man seemed nervous about something—or maybe that was just how he always held himself. He was wearing an ugly purple robe with a belt around his waist. The belt was interesting: it looked like some kind of black material entwined with gold, twisting back and forth in intricate patterns.

"Religious Studies is over there," Arra said, pointing to a large, dark building just across the lawn from them.

"Oh, thank you," the stranger said, "thank you so much."

Suddenly Trey felt Arra pulling at his hand. She started slumping over, her eyes rolling up into her head. Before Trey could react, the stranger had caught her, keeping her from falling. Arra's eyes fluttered a few times, then she gasped.

"I'm—I'm okay," she said, but her voice betrayed her weakness. "I can stand on my own." The stranger was still holding her up.

"Are you sure?" the man asked.

"Yes," Arra said. "Thank you. I don't know what came over me."

The stranger released Arra and she stood. Trey noticed a leaf fluttering to the ground, having fallen from her hand. He looked up, but there weren't any trees above them. Weird.

"I apologize," the stranger said. "She looked like she was going to fall."

"Thank you for your help," Arra said. "I am fine."

"Very well," the man said. "Good evening to you both." He strode away, heading toward the Religious Studies building.

"What was that about?" Trey asked, watching him go.

"No idea."

"You sure you're doing okay?"

"Let's just go."

THEY TOOK A GRAVCAR HOME. The taxi was like the fallcars the Cothellon had back on Earth, except it wasn't powered by magic. The Esaran government had outlawed darkprime Trees—a pretty smart decision, since making them required murdering people. Luckily, technology was able to replace many of the things darkprime magic did. Trey figured Orym must be in paradise here, what with all the toys and gadgets to play with.

The ride home was a silent affair. Trey and Arra shared the taxi, but they didn't live together. Trey had wanted to, of course, but Arra had refused. Her memory wasn't recovering as quickly as Trey's, so she'd wanted to take things slow. It chafed at him, but Trey had agreed.

Orym was a very rich man on Earth, thanks to centuries spent as the Cothellon Scientist General. Earth money wasn't much good on Valaralda, of course, but Orym had other things. Commodities. Gold, silver, jewels—these things were wanted on Valaralda, so Orym was able to secure a pretty hefty fortune in local currency. But it was his bourbon collection that had fetched the highest price—apparently a few elves here had developed quite a taste for it.

Orym had been generous with his money. He'd set Arra and Trey up with two tiny apartments, giving them both a stipend to work with. It was enough to get them started on Valaralda.

The Esaran government had been remarkably receptive to all these new people coming in from Earth; between the low population on Valaralda, and the elves' good stewardship of the planet, there were plenty of resources to go around. Elves from Earth were pretty much given free reign. Magic usage was still subject to the Department of Magical Research licensing system, of course. Trey hadn't gotten around to getting licensed yet, so any magic he performed was technically illegal.

But screw them. Who needed a *license* for magic?

Trey looked out the window as the gravcar sped through the city. It was now full night, brightly-lit office buildings and restaurants passing by in a blur as they moved. This close in, Ilyrion looked a lot like New San Francisco, or at least how Trey imagined it would have looked if there had been more trees.

The gravcar angled upwards, and soon they were flying hundreds of feet up into the air. Trey looked ahead through the windshield and saw that they were coming up on a massive Prime Tree. Ilyrion had four of them, and this one was the biggest: a gigantic Prime Oak. This close, the Tree was almost hard to make out—the trunk and crown filled Trey's entire vision.

Just when it seemed they might crash into the tree, the driver banked to the right, skirting smoothly around the trunk. They sped past the wood, just feet away from it. Trey had a powerful urge to reach out and touch the Tree, to feel its warmth and life. Instead, he reached out for Arra's hand. She leaned up against him.

"It's beautiful, isn't it," she murmured.

Trey nodded, his chin resting on her hair. "I wonder how old it is?"

The taxi driver spoke. "This Tree dates back to the Great Awakening," he said.

"Remind me what that is?" Trey asked.

"The Great Awakening? How can you not know what that is? It's the first thing every kid learns."

"It's a long story," Trey said. "We're from Earth. Mar."

"Oh, you're one of *them*." The driver looked into his rearview mirror at them. "Never thought I'd meet one. You one of them that was there for the Sending?"

"We were."

This got the driver really excited. "You really twenty thousand years old?" Trey nodded. "But that's *incredible!* What's it like being alive that long?"

"We can't remember most of it," Trey said.

"You *can't?*" the driver asked, swerving to avoid a massive tree branch that had appeared in front of them. Then they were past the tree, hurtling through the air, angling back down toward the city. Evidently the driver enjoyed taking the scenic route, no doubt to rack up the meter. Trey wished they'd gotten an automated taxi instead of this manual one. It would have involved less talking.

"Like I said," Trey said, "it's a long story."

"Gatesickness, eh?" the driver asked. "That a real thing? Man, I read about all this stuff growing up, but I figured it was just something someone made up to keep us entertained. The Sending, Prime Mages, gatesending. It's all real?"

"It's all real," Trey said.

"Wow, man," the driver said. "Just wow."

The taxi settled down to street level. Trey saw that they had arrived at their destination, a seedy neighborhood in one of the less-affluent parts of the city. Ilyrion was just like any city: there were rich people, and there were poor people. There were good places to live, and there were bad ones.

This neighborhood was somewhere in the middle.

Trey paid the driver using the little electronic thing he'd been given. Apparently it was how the middle-class paid for things. The device was keyed to his thumbprint, at least—it'd be less likely to be stolen that way.

"Do you miss Sylrantheas?" Trey asked Arra as they got out of the gravcar. His shocksword clattered against the car as he moved through the door. He was going to have to get used to carrying the thing around.

She looked around blankly. "Sometimes."

"You okay?"

She seemed to shiver for a moment. "I just need some food."

Trey put a hand on her back, steering her toward his house. "I'll fix you something," he said. "I think I've still got some good veggies."

Arra didn't say anything—she just trudged toward his front door. Trey hoped nothing was wrong with her. She'd been acting strange all day, and those fainting episodes had him worried. He hefted the Book of Amplification, wondering if he should try healing her. Maybe that would be a good idea.

"Nice night for a walk," a voice said from directly behind him.

Trey jumped, spinning around to look at who had spoken. A short, graying man stood there, wearing an odd-looking gray robe that was cinched tight around his waist with a multicolored belt. The man's skin was shriveled, as if he'd spent too long underwater and never recovered. He held his hands out as if to show he wasn't carrying any weapons.

"Good evening," the man said.

"Who are you?" Trey asked.

The man thought about that for a moment. "I don't know," he said.

"How can you not know?"

"Nelenor holds me," he said. As if that was supposed to make any sense.

"Do you know what he's talking about?" Trey asked Arra.

She stepped forward to address the robed man. "What do you want?" she asked.

The man thought about that, too. "The Book," he said, pointing at the Book of Amplification in Trey's left hand.

"I'm not sure who you think you are," Trey said, "but you can't have the Book."

The man thought for another second. "Very well," he said, and made a little gesture.

Five more gray men materialized out of thin air. They surrounded Trey and Arra, looking like clones of the first man.

"We will take the Book now," the men said in unison.

"Shit," said Trey.

FOURTEEN

SHOCK CREW immediately went into action. Allain stood in the tent with his twin, trying to stay out of everybody's way. Shot had darted over to his command table, issuing orders. Spike was dispatching extra guards to man the doors. Allain couldn't see what was happening outside the tent, but he could hear kids shouting at each other and jumping from place to place on the rigging overhead.

"We're good," Spike yelled at Shot. "Just the one elf."

"Let him in," Shot ordered, turning to Allain. "Want to come meet our unexpected guest?"

"Sure." It might be nice to have another elf around.

Shot pulled the tent door aside and stepped through, Allains following right behind. The three of them stood in front of the tent, flanked by Crow and Wrench, Shot's two bodyguards. Underkids were spreading out above them in the rigging, makeshift weapons at the ready.

The stranger walked towards them.

It was a female elf. She walked carefully through the gauntlet, looking around as if in wonder. It must be her first time in the Under, Allain realized. Amazingly, the underkids in the rigging withheld their throws, letting her pass underneath them unmolested. They *never* did that, not even when Shot went through.

As the woman drew closer, Allain realized why. He had always thought of Arra as the most beautiful woman he'd ever seen in his life.

He'd been wrong.

This woman was *far* prettier than Arra.

She had long hair that was dark, verging on black. She was filled out in all the right places, hips and breasts moving enticingly as she walked. But Allain found himself staring at her lips more than anything else—they were thick and luscious, incredibly kissable. He didn't think he'd ever had a reaction this strong to a woman before. There was something *different* about her. Something poignant.

But who *was* she?

"Ho!" Shot called out to her as she approached.

The woman looked at them with an air of confusion. Her eyes were green, Allain noted. They only enhanced her mysterious beauty.

"Hello?" the woman said. She seemed unsure of herself.

"Who are you?" Shot asked. Allain found his mouth getting dry.

The woman looked down at herself, as if trying to figure out the answer to that question. Her clothing was dirty, but it looked like it might have been red, once. Now that she was closer, Allain could see that her hair was messy, too. What had this woman been through? Why was she here?

And why could he not take his eyes off of her?

"Lara," the woman said, her eyes unfocused. "No. Lora. Lora...lie? Lorelei. Yes! Lorelei." She looked at Shot, an innocent smile on her face. It was as if remembering her name was the greatest thing that had ever happened to her.

Something was clearly wrong with this woman.

Shot pulled a gun from his waistband and leveled it at her. "We should kill her," he said fiercely.

"Why?" Allain asked, shocked.

"You don't know?"

"No. Who is she?"

Shot glared at the woman. "This is the person who killed Elanil. She was the boss of the whole Cothellon operation. She's responsible for thousands of deaths. Fenian, Lhoris, Silanar. Her armies killed hundreds of underkids, too."

All that violence from this one woman? Allain found it hard to believe—Lorelei didn't seem dangerous at all. She just stood there, rocking side to side, smiling brightly at them. She seemed empty, like her brain was gone.

Allain stepped forward, raising both hands out to her, palms up. Lorelei placed her hands in his and looked at him. She was dirty and unkempt, but she was still intoxicating. Normally being this close to a beautiful woman would cause Allain to clam up, to go crazy. But not this time. This time he was calm. Peaceful. As if he'd finally met his match.

"My name is Allain," he said.

"Hello," Lorelei said. Then she blinked, and her eyes became sharper, more dangerous. She looked around the room, quickly scanning everything, as if assessing her combat situation. Then she stepped closer to Allain, leaning in until her face was just inches away. "Gatesickness," she said. Then she stepped back, eyes going blank again. She seemed to have completely forgotten what she was saying.

"So it *is* true," Shot said. "Trey mentioned he'd seen her on the streets, wandering around. He said her mind was gone, and he didn't have the heart to turn her in. I can see why."

"She's harmless," Allain said, although he was sure that wasn't true.

"I highly doubt that. But she's no longer the person she was—that much is clear." He smacked his lips. "Do you have anywhere to stay?"

"Stay..." Lorelei said. She lapsed off, becoming distracted by something. The room was remarkably silent—only the ever-present sound of the water recycling machines could be heard. The kids in the rigging were still. There was a kind of tension in the room, as if everyone was waiting for something terrible to happen. They had the Cothellon leader in their midst, and that could only lead to trouble.

"She's clearly lost her mind," Shot said.

"She can stay with us," Allain said.

Shot looked at him severely. "I'm not sure that's such a good idea."

"Why? I'll look after her."

Suddenly the room erupted into shouts. A ball of blue lightning shot through the air, narrowly missing Lorelei's head.

"Down!" Shot said. Allain threw himself on Lorelei, pushing them both to the ground. More lightning whizzed by, and gunshots erupted from somewhere near the main doors.

"Spike!" Shot called. "Battle stations!"

This time he meant it.

FIFTEEN

THE SIX IDENTICAL men just stood there, as if they were waiting for something. Were they illusions? Trey had been tricked by mistweaving before—he wasn't going to fall for it twice.

He struck at one of the clones, expecting his hand to fly through the image. Mistweavers couldn't create solid objects, only illusions made of light and sound. Trey figured if he demonstrated his lack of fear, the strange man might pack up his tricks and leave.

But his hand hit a real, warm person. The six clones were *real*. Trey was so surprised, he lost his balance and almost fell.

In unison, the assailants struck. Not with magic, but with their fists and feet. Two of them focused on Trey, punching him hard in the stomach and slapping his face. The slap stung like hell. Weren't fist fights supposed to involve...fists? In all the books and movies Trey had seen, the combatants struck each other in perfectly choreographed attacks, spinning and blocking and hitting with well-executed precision.

This fight was not like that at all.

Trey tried a kick, but one of the men blocked him, using a hand to stop his foot and push it down. The movement threw Trey even more off-balance, and he felt himself falling. Stumbling, he managed to catch himself just in time to get a fist to the face. He felt something snap and warm blood gushed out of his nose, splattering all over the pavement. He twisted and tried to strike back, hitting the attackers randomly, just trying to do anything to keep them away. But it was no use—he couldn't fight. He had no idea what he was doing.

Wait! He was a Prime Mage. How could a few Mundanes in robes defeat *him?* And his sword! Why hadn't he gone for that first? With the shocksword in hand, the strangers would surely be afraid of him. They'd cower in fear, cringing and crying. Oh yes, he'd have the upper hand then. He'd—

A fist hit him in the face again, and the whole world went dark.

THE SENATE WAS IN SESSION. They'd granted Tarathiel a seat next to his wife on the Senate floor—an unusual dispensation. Perhaps they felt it would mollify him.

It didn't.

They were assembled in the formal debate chamber, a vaulted room lined with white pillars and floored in marble. Light streamed in from the floor-to-ceiling windows on both sides. They'd been opened today, letting in the balmy weather. A light breeze carried with it the faint hint of the sea. Senators sat at white desks arrayed on the marble floor, facing the podium where Leriaar stood. The Speaker of the Senate looked as regal as she was beautiful, but Tarathiel knew that underneath that beauty was a ruthless spirit.

A large balcony overhung the rear of the room, and today

it was filled with people—onlookers from the public. There were even a few news reporters back there, tiny cameras mounted to their shoulders. Tarathiel had initially been grateful for the media coverage, thinking it would help his cause. But now he saw that it was more likely to hurt him.

He felt himself growing furious. It had only been a few minutes, and already everything was against him. He forced himself to take a deep breath, hoping it would calm his nerves.

It didn't.

"In short," Iliaster was saying, "there simply isn't enough direct evidence to support Tarathiel's theory. We need more time to study the texts he unearthed, to compare them against the existing historical record.

"Akhenaten was notoriously unreliable. He was even worshipped as a God during the final years of his life. What kind of man would allow that? He was unhinged. His only writings that remain are written in the pictographic Nekhru-mite language, a language that remains stubbornly resistant to translation, even to this day.

"It could be a hoax. It could be a mistranslation. I'm not necessarily saying that Tarathiel is trying to fool us—it's Akhenaten I'm worried about. His writings are ninety to a hundred thousand years old. They must be studied carefully.

"My opinion, as High Historian, is that they cannot be believed."

Tarathiel felt himself shaking with anger. His life's work, a hoax? A mistranslation? What could he possibly have to gain by perpetrating such a falsehood? Yes, he'd probably get some fame and glory out of it, and a vastly increased budget. But he didn't care about that—the fate of the *world* was at stake! Why didn't anyone else believe him?

He started to stand, but the conversation was already continuing without him.

"Thank you for your assessment, Iliaster," Senator Selenia said. "Will the Council of Mages continue to deliberate?"

"Yes, Senator," Iliaster said. "We will convene a committee to study Tarathiel's findings in great detail. We will get to the bottom of this within the year."

Within the *year*? With utter doom impending, with the Fall advancing, these mages wanted to waste a *year* evaluating the texts? Tarathiel had already spent years on it. He'd already proven to himself that the texts could be believed. Perhaps he should have involved the Council sooner. But they would have just gotten in his way.

Leriaar turned to Tarathiel, a look of barely contained amusement on her face. "Well," she said, "you've successfully convinced both branches of government to mount full-scale investigations into your work. This after your own Anthropological Society has already dedicated years of time and significant resources into the research. I believe this is a satisfactory outcome? It is certainly far more than *I* expected." She blinked at him demurely.

Tarathiel felt bile rising in his throat. He opened his mouth to respond, but Alleria beat him to it.

"Certainly, Speaker," she said, "we thank the Council of Mages and the Senate for their time." Leriaar smiled at her, but it was a thin smile with no warmth in it. There was no love lost between the Speaker of the Senate and Alleria.

Not as long as Tarathiel was involved.

"Very well," Leriaar said, "we will consider the matter concluded. Now, if there are—"

"Just a moment," Alleria said. Leriaar shot a glare at her for the briefest second, then forced a smile back onto her face.

"Yes?" Leriaar asked.

"We would like to put the matter to a vote," Alleria said.

Leriaar let out a deep sigh. "If you insist," she said quietly. Then, louder: "Senators, the motion on the table is to grant Tarathiel additional funds to pursue this...research."

"No," Alleria said, "that is not the motion."

Leriaar stared at her for a moment. Tarathiel could see her mind working furiously. Finally, she relented, motioning for Alleria to continue.

Alleria stood. She was resplendent in a gown made of cream-colored lace, snug around the bodice and full past the waist. Her long, auburn hair was loose, cascading down her back in luxurious waves. Tarathiel found himself momentarily distracted by her beauty, his anger forgotten. He knew the other men in the room were equally as entranced by her. But Leriaar was looking elsewhere: at him. Her eyes communicated desire and longing, and a hint of jealousy. She wanted him.

Tarathiel shivered.

"Tarathiel has already aptly demonstrated the correctness of his claims," Alleria said, "insofar as it is possible to determine at this time. His evidence suggests a pending conflict that could destroy the very planet itself, and everyone on it. The time for debate has passed."

Leriaar opened her mouth, but Alleria continued. "I'm not finished. The motion I propose is this: the Senate will authorize a special dispensation of funds to create a group of elves to combat this threat. We will proceed as follows: seven groups will use gatesending to travel to the planets indicated in the texts. The Space Agency has already located the planets, has already performed the exploratory gates, and can provide the proper parameters for this Sending. Tarathiel will be given special executive power to nominate individuals of his choosing for this mission."

"That's a tall order," Cresius said. "It'll never pass."

"It's a one-way trip," Selenia added. "You can't force anyone to do this."

"I'm still not finished," Alleria said, and the room became quiet again. There was a new tension in the air. "I exercise my right to a final motion."

The room erupted in chaos, Senators shouting at each other. Onlookers in the balcony whispered amongst themselves excitedly. The two news reporters were standing, cameras angling towards him.

Tarathiel leaned over to Arra. "Are you sure about this?" he whispered.

"Trust me," she whispered back.

Once a motion was seconded, it was ordinarily put up for immediate vote. The motion was passed based on a simple majority. It could then be called to appeal, whereupon the Senate would vote again. Votes were allowed two appeals, with a statute of limitations of one month. Then the motion would be introduced to the Council of Mages, where they would have an opportunity to veto it. It was a good system of checks and balances, and had proven to be a reliable, if slow, way to run the government.

But that was for a normal motion. Once per term, a Senator could invoke the right to a final motion. This did three things: it delayed the vote for one week, it made the results of that vote ineligible for appeal, and it prevented the Council of Mages from vetoing the motion.

All of this power came with a catch: the Speaker of the Senate—which, for this term, was Leriaar—would have to approve the motion personally.

They would get one chance to win the vote. If the motion

passed, it would be binding. If not, they'd never be able to bring it up again. It was all a big risk, and an unexpected one. Tarathiel and Alleria had discussed their strategy at length, and she'd never mentioned this.

But she'd asked him to trust her, and he would. He sat back in his seat as Leriaar called for order and the room quietened. The Senators returned to their desks, many of them with sour expressions on their faces.

"Do I hear a second?" Leriaar asked.

Nobody answered. Tarathiel looked around the room at the fourteen senators. Selenia was looking at nothing, as usual, her posture stiff and upright. Cresius looked downright angry, but that wasn't unusual. He'd been one of Tarathiel's fiercest opponents when he'd first introduced the Fall to the Senate. Gaelin and Vander were studiously trying to avoid looking at Tarathiel. Yshael was staring right at him, her gaze unnerving.

Nobody spoke up.

Embrae was sitting at the desk on the other side of Alleria, looking at Tarathiel with a curious expression. He wondered what was going through her head. Embrae was a friend of theirs. She and her husband, Galan, had spent many evenings at their house in Errenmel, sitting on the back porch looking at the garden, or going horse riding, or having tea. Tarathiel had sometimes balked at the time it took, being social with them. It was time taken away from his studies, time that could be spent saving the world.

But now he was starting to understand why Alleria had always insisted on it.

Embrae swallowed. "I'll second the motion," she said. The room was silent.

Leriaar banged her gavel. "The motion is seconded."

Next came the hard part: would Leriaar approve it?

Normally the Speaker had no say in such things, but this was a final motion. She held all the power.

Tarathiel met her eyes from across the room. Her green eyes reflected the sunlight, flashing at him with something approaching mirth. What would Leriaar want for this? He knew she wouldn't approve the vote without getting something in return. What would it be?

Her eyes flicked to Alleria.

Then she banged the gavel again. "The motion is approved. Delayed vote set for one week from today. Alleria, have the details on my desk within two days. This session is adjourned. Enjoy the weekend, Senators."

Everyone stood, chattering amongst themselves. Tarathiel saw the two news reporters making a beeline out the door. They were coming downstairs to accost him, most likely. He looked for another way out. Maybe through one of the open windows.

He was about to make a move when someone grabbed his arm. Startled, he swung around to see Cresius glaring at him.

"Why do you insist on pursuing this ridiculous course?" Cresius asked. "You know it will be shot down."

"Will it?" Tarathiel asked.

"Are you willfully trying to do us harm," Cresius asked, "or are you actually that stupid? Ilyrion does not have the funds to pursue every wild goose chase you dream up. And you *certainly* cannot take anyone with you." He stepped closer to Tarathiel, speaking quietly. "Mark my words, *foeg*, this will be the last time you ever appear on the Senate floor."

Tarathiel felt his face flush. *Foeg* was an old insult, an ancient word that nobody ever used anymore.

"Really pulling out the dictionary now, aren't you, Cresius?" Alleria said, stepping up to them and placing a hand on Tarathiel's arm. "I thought you had more intelligence than that." She sniffed. "Oh well, I suppose not all of us can carry ourselves respectfully on the floor. Come, Tarathiel, let's go."

Cresius grabbed Alleria's arm. Tarathiel could see that his grip was hurting her. "Say that again," Cresius hissed.

"Bad move," Tarathiel whispered.

He stepped toward Cresius, his fist darting in quickly to land on the taller man's neck. Cresius made a choking sound and started to lift his hands, but Tarathiel followed up with two swift punches to the man's face, taking care to avoid the jaw. Then, before Cresius could react, he stepped around the man and elbowed him hard in the kidney.

Cresius fell to the ground, gasping in pain. The whole thing had only taken seconds, and the room was slow to react to the fight. Alleria bent over Cresius, checking to see how he was doing. Gaelin and Iolas were running towards him, and Tarathiel caught sight of the news reporters closing in. Leriaar was just sitting at her desk, a wry grin on her face.

She was enjoying this.

Tarathiel felt disgusted. Nobody laid a hand on his wife— not if they wanted to survive the day. He felt adrenaline coursing through him, and he instinctively kept his hands up near his face to ward off any attackers. Everyone was closing in, taking all the space out of the room. All he saw were glares, glares and frowns and flashing eyes. They hated him. They hated his ideas, his research. They hated that he'd married so far above him.

They hated that he had just downed a Senator in four hits.

Should he run? Should he fight? Should he bellow and scream, or hide behind something? No. He could defend himself. He could stand up to a group of old politicians. They thought him a researcher, with his nose in books all day. But they were wrong. He'd trained for this. He was ready to show them what he could do.

He felt a hand on his shoulder, and he spun, ready to fight. But it was Alleria, looking at him with concern.

"Easy," she said quietly, stepping forward and drawing his arms around her. "You're okay."

Tarathiel felt the room expand again. His breathing slowed as she laid her head against his chest. He looked around, seeing the fear and anger and disappointment in everyone's faces. But Alleria was in his arms—nothing could go wrong now.

"My apologies," he said loudly, freeing one arm to gesture magnanimously. "It was an involuntary response. I will ensure Cresius is cared for."

Leriaar stepped down from the podium, her eyes only seeking him. "You have a fighter's instinct," she said as she approached. She traced a finger lightly over Tarathiel's arm, seemingly oblivious to Alleria. "Impressive, for a scholar." She patted his butt twice before walking away.

He owed her now, and he had a sinking feeling that this was only the beginning.

"I hate that woman," Alleria breathed into his chest. "Come on, let's get out of here. We have a vote to garner."

TREY GASPED, suddenly aware again. He was on the ground, and a bunch of people were scuffling above him. His thoughts swam for a moment before resolving: a stranger had attacked him and Arra. A stranger with five identical copies of himself. Trey had been hit; he'd been dropped. Because he didn't know how to fight.

But now memories were returning.

Now he remembered his training.

Now he could actually *fight*.

He got to his feet, everyone else a blur around him. Arra seemed to be doing fine for herself—she was darting in and out, jabbing and kicking with obvious skill. It must have been yet another thing she had learned in Sylrantheas.

But now it was Trey's turn. He waded in, preparing to drop one of the clones with a swift kick. He started the move —at least, his *brain* started the move. His muscles didn't react properly at *all*. He found himself flailing, unable to keep his balance. The kick went wild, weakly hitting the shin of one of the assailants. Nice.

What the hell? Trey *knew* what to do. He remembered his training now. He'd had years of it as a younger man, learning how to box and kick and various other kinds of martial arts. It had been a hobby of his, something to distract him from the more intellectual tasks he so often found himself doing. Something to get him outside. He had craved the outdoors, as a boy.

But apparently the memory alone was not enough. His *muscle* memory was shot. It had been thousands and thousands of years since he'd done those things, and his body had forgotten.

He needed practice.

Nevertheless, he tried again. But before he could even get his hands up, he'd been decked. One of the clones hit him in the face, and another kneed him in the crotch. He went down amidst a flurry of limbs and pain.

He was useless.

"*Enough!*" Arra shouted suddenly.

A low bass sound rumbled in the night air, and the six strange men were suddenly flung out in a circle. Trey saw a blast wave of magic fly through the air, pushing the men away with incredible force. They flew dozens of feet, then winked out one by one, until there was just the first man remaining. He got to his feet as Trey watched, a bloody smile on his face.

The man pulled the Book of Amplification out from under his robes and, still grinning, disappeared.

Trey felt a headache coming on.

SIXTEEN

RYLAN SHIFTED on his stool uncomfortably. "Why are you telling us this story?" he asked. He didn't like where it was going. All the violence—it reminded him too much of the Under.

"It be an important story, little ones," Mirra said. "You be learning many things from it." She bustled over to the window, peering outside. The sun was still raging above, but it was oddly cool in Mirra's little house.

"Just let her tell it," Dillon said. "Maybe she's right."

"Fine," Rylan said, "but I'm hungry."

"You're always hungry."

"Don' you worry, little ones," Mirra said, coming back over to stand by them. Small was off to the side playing with something again, but Mirra ignored him. "I be fixin' ya supper soon enough."

She settled in to continue her tale.

CARIEL POURED THE SKONDUL CAREFULLY, trying to keep her pitcher poised over Hloldr's glass as he waved it around. He was drunk a bit earlier than usual tonight. He was celebrating, and rightly so.

He had been the one to kill the great cavek.

Her eyes darted around the fire, taking stock. All around her, the grunts and growls of rylak filled the night, ferocious men and savage women shouting at each other uproariously, cheering Hloldr on. The fighting would start soon, by the look of things. Rylak always fought when they drank. And tonight, after a Hunt, things would be a lot worse than usual.

She caught Svalya, the packleader, looking at her from across the fire, her eyes veiled. Cariel nodded at her, and Svalya nodded back. She would be watching, Cariel knew, making sure nothing terrible happened to the elves this night.

She managed to refill Hloldr's glass without spilling too much—Hloldr hated to waste any of the milky liquor. Cariel had harvested this batch earlier that day, climbing high up into the palm trees surrounding the village. Once tapped from the tree's flowers, the palm sap fermented naturally in just a few hours. It didn't have a lot of alcohol content, but the rylak consumed enough of it to get drunk anyway.

Her master sated for the moment, Cariel stepped away from the fire ring, outside the grasp of the rylak's reach. When the fighting began, she wanted to be as far away from it as possible.

"He's going to be a problem," Ghilanna said, nodding at Hloldr. The other slave was working the fire with her, trying to slake the endless thirst of the rylak villagers. Cariel grimaced, looking down at her skondul pitcher. It was already empty, and she'd refilled it twice.

"You might want to give him some food," Ghilanna said. "Blunt the effects."

She was right. Cariel nodded to Ghilanna and set off for the kitchen.

The village had a central kitchen that fed everyone. Svalya, the packleader, preferred it that way. The rylak did all the hunting, but their kills were brought to the kitchens for distribution to the three hundred or so citizens of Skallgr. The kitchens were staffed entirely by elven slaves, and the area was strictly off-limits to rylak unless they were dropping off fresh meat. It would be a welcome respite after the roaring fire, and a relatively safe place for Cariel should the fighting start.

She looked up at the sky as she walked. Argul, the red moon, was alone in the heavens: a bad omen. Cariel shivered as she made her way to the kitchens—something evil was afoot tonight. She hoped she would be fortunate enough to avoid it. The shouts and growls of the rylak began to fade as she got further away.

A cloud of bekal swarmed up around her. She walked through them, keeping her mouth shut and breathing out slowly through her nose. The insects were still in their spawning stage—it would be a day before the bugs would truly be out in force. Cariel would be busy tonight, lowering mosquito nets and shuttering windows. The village would hole up indoors for the week it took the insects to complete their cycle—spawning, eating, mating, and dying by the millions. Tonight, they were still relatively harmless.

Velatha looked up at her briefly as she entered. The kitchen master was a slave like all the others, but she at least had some measure of authority here.

"Already?" Velatha asked, bending back down over the dough she was kneading. Cariel realized she was talking about the skondul. She shrugged.

"This will be his third pitcher," she said.

Velatha grunted. "And not even an hour in. Well, best see that he gets something else in his belly."

Like a hot iron poker? Cariel envisioned it, how it would feel to thrust it through Hloldr's chest. In her mind's eye, she watched him writhe in agony, clutching at the poker, trying to pull it out of him. Blood and viscera were everywhere. His eyes dimmed.

"Cariel!" Velatha snapped, and she realized she'd been daydreaming.

"Sorry," she muttered.

Velatha frowned at her. "The cavek is still roasting in the firepit," she said. "Give him some bread." She nodded toward the shelves running across the back of the room. Rows and rows of fresh-baked bread were lined up neatly along the shelves, waiting for eager rylak mouths with their sharp, snapping teeth. Cariel put the skondul pitcher down on a table and grabbed a loaf of crusty brown bread.

"Better fill that, too," Velatha said, looking at the empty pitcher. Cariel nodded mutely. There was no sense going out there without more skondul. She'd just be sent back to the kitchens again, probably with claw marks on her skin.

Putting the bread down, she grabbed the pitcher and went over to the basin where they kept the skondul. The open top of the basin allowed wild yeast to enter the liquid, encouraging further fermentation. On nights like this, a skin of dead bekal would form on top. They were drawn to the sweet palm sap like flies to honey. Most rylak would make her skim the bugs off, or even filter the skondul through a sieve before serving it to them, but Hloldr didn't mind the bugs. He said they added texture to the drink. Cariel grimaced at the thought.

But when she got to the skondul basin, she saw that it was empty.

"We're out," she called over to Velatha. "Where is everyone?"

The place was oddly empty. Usually the kitchens were bustling at night, with at least two or three other girls doing their best to stay ahead of the rylak's ravenous appetite. Tonight it was only Velatha, and the kitchens were quiet as a result. Too quiet.

"Outside, tending to the cavek roast," Velatha said, leaning into the thick slab of dough she was working. "There's something in the air tonight. They went through that skondul like it was water."

"Argul is up."

"I know. And the bekal are out, and only five of them died in the Hunt today. But it's more than that. You mark my words—something is coming."

"What is?"

Velatha stopped and straightened, her hands still deep in the sticky dough. "Child," she said softly, "just be careful."

Perhaps there was something to what she had said. But what could possibly happen? Tonight was like any other night in Skallgr—wild and hot, full of sweat and violence. Sure, this was a cavek night, a night of celebration, but she'd been through those before. Many times. She'd make it through this one, too.

Velatha turned back to her bread making. "You can fill your pitcher from the reserves in the cold room."

Nodding, Cariel turned and walked briskly out of the kitchen, heading through the back door into the hallway beyond. The cold room was in the back of the building and one floor down, buried underneath feet of earth and brick in order to keep it cool in the oppressive jungle heat.

The halls were deathly silent. Normally kitchen sounds echoed out here, bouncing down the stone corridors. But not tonight. Tonight, nothing stirred. Nothing spoke. Not even the bekal flies had penetrated this far—at least, not yet.

She had almost gotten to the stairs that led down to the cold room when she heard it. She paused, standing still, a shiver running down her spine. Had she heard a girl screaming? Now the hall was silent once again. Maybe it had just been her imagination.

But then the screams returned, more urgent this time. It was an elf's scream, which meant it was a slave. There was someone down here, and that person sounded very much in trouble.

And the screams sounded familiar.

Cariel set the pitcher down and took off running down the hall. The screams sounded again, louder. Something terrible was happening. She didn't think; she just ran. She had to stop whatever it was, if she could.

She skidded around a corner and found herself looking at a scene from a nightmare. It was the thing all female slaves were frightened of the most. The thing that was always there, hanging in the back of their minds. The thing that *would* happen, inevitably, inexorably. All it took was one moment with Svalya's back turned.

Tilla was in there. Her best friend was sitting spread-eagled on the floor, her back up against the shelves of the storeroom. What little clothes she still had on were ripped and torn and she was scrabbling at the ground, trying in vain to get away from the three large rylak men who were in the room with her. The rylak were standing for the moment, just looking at the naked elf. Tilla's screams had subsided into sobs as she sat there, breasts heaving. She didn't try to cover herself. There was nothing she could do.

The three rylak stepped forward slowly, erect penises bobbing as they moved. Cariel could see that the hackles on their neck had risen, indicating their level of arousal. Their claws were still sheathed as they stepped forward, towering over the poor girl.

Cariel should leave. She should leave right now, as quietly as possible. There was nothing she could do to save Tilla. Her friend was lost, and Cariel should run.

Svalya kept her males in line most of the time. They weren't allowed to touch the slaves, weren't allowed to mate with them. But Svalya's Enforcers couldn't be everywhere at once. Tonight they were occupied with keeping order outside, around the fire. Tonight was the perfect opportunity to escape attention, to get what the rylak wanted and craved.

Elven flesh.

Cariel should run.

But all she could do was stand there as the first rylak bent over Tilla, pawing her groin roughly with his hairy fingers. Like all rylak, he was fascinated by the relatively hairless body of the elven girl. The other two rylak crept up behind him, saliva dripping from their jaws as they watched, playing with themselves. Poor Tilla had screamed herself out—all she could do was sit there as they had their way with her.

Cariel should run.

But she couldn't just leave. She had to help her friend. Ever so quietly, she stepped into the storeroom, her hand running along the shelf to pick up a ceramic jug full of something—grape wine, probably, or maybe water. Hefting the jug, she lifted it over her head.

And struck with all her might.

The jug shattered over the head of one of the rylak, spattering red liquid everywhere. The rylak yelped in surprise, whirling to face her. She could see anger in his eyes, but he hadn't unsheathed his fingerclaws yet. She still had a chance.

Before he could do anything else, Cariel lunged toward

the shelves on her left, sweeping her arm behind the other jugs sitting there, pushing them as hard as she could. The vessels flew toward the three rylak, sailing a few feet into the center of the room and cracking against their heads and chests. Wine exploded out of the ceramic containers as they broke, and the rylak stumbled, surprise written on their faces.

One of them reached out for her, but Cariel ducked, keeping low as she darted under their grasp, heading toward Tilla. The slave girl was sitting motionless on the floor, panic frozen on her face.

"Come on!" Cariel shouted at Tilla, pulling roughly at her. But the girl didn't move, and Cariel couldn't lift her. And now it was too late.

The rylak struck.

One of them grabbed Cariel by the arms, his strong fingers digging painfully into her skin. He turned her force-fully, and she lost her balance, falling to the floor in front of Tilla. The rylak held her there, leering down at her. She could smell his rancid breath, see the froth already forming on his black lips.

She struggled against his hold, but he was far too strong. The other two rylak crowded in behind him, growling softly. Cariel looked around the room frantically, hoping for some kind of escape. Should she scream? Maybe Velatha would hear her. Maybe someone would come to rescue her.

Or maybe she was alone.

The first rylak unsheathed one fingerclaw and pointed it at her face, a wicked smile on his lips. Then, in one swift motion, he slashed her dress from top to bottom, ripping it away from her body and leaving her in just her undershorts. She felt the sudden air on her skin and instinctively tried to cover her breasts. The rylak in the back had begun touching themselves again, and she could hear them panting as they looked at her.

Cariel felt a wave of revulsion flood through her. She had to get away; she had to escape. There must be some way! She looked around the room, hoping for something—anything—that could aid her.

The first rylak licked his lips, leaning in and roughly fondling her left breast. His touch was sickening, and Cariel felt goosebumps on her skin. What could she do? The rylak's hand trailed down her stomach, coming to rest on the edge of her undershorts. Cariel slapped at him with her free hand, pushing at him, but it was in vain. He was far too strong.

The rylak pulled her undershorts down, and Cariel finally screamed.

The big men pressed toward her as she screamed, their stink and hair and sweat filling her senses. The first rylak still held her tightly in his grip, his grin widening as her shrieks continued. She could see his sharp teeth, could feel his breath on her. Cariel struggled against him, scratching at him, trying anything to get out of his grip. Behind her, Tilla was still paralyzed against the shelves.

The shelves. Cariel might be able to use them to her advantage. If she could just get her right arm out of this horrible rylak's grip, maybe she could...

The rylak released her arm. Yes! Cariel twisted, trying to reach the shelves behind her. But then the rylak grabbed her waist with both hands, lifting her as if she were a doll to play with. Cariel tried to keep her legs closed, but the other two rylak reached in, grabbing her feet and spreading her. The first rylak held her tightly, his penis pointed up at her, throbbing with anticipation. He was ready. And no one was coming to save her. The rylak lowered her, his hands around her torso, moments away from piercing her.

But Cariel had other ideas.

She leaned directly backwards, arching her back and reaching up over her head to grasp the shelves behind her. They were mounted against the wall, but not strongly—she just needed the right amount of force. Before the rylak could react, she pulled with all her might.

The shelves wrenched free, toppling down into the room like a house of wooden cards. They hit Cariel first, but she threw her arms up over her head, trying to shield herself from the worst of it. Jars and containers flew from the shelves as they fell, slamming into the rylak and causing them to lose their grip on Cariel. Liquid and flour splashed everywhere, coating everything. Cariel's skin grew slick with the wine and she used that to her advantage, twisting roughly from the rylak's grip. In his surprise, he dropped her.

And she was free.

There was no time to save Tilla—her friend was still lying there, unmoving. Cariel had gotten herself into this mess because of her, but now she needed to save herself. The rylak were yelping and yowling, pushing the heavy wooden shelves away and scrambling around for her. She only had moments to escape.

Cariel ducked to the left, skirting under the first rylak's long arm. Heedless of her nakedness, she ran towards the door. The floor was slippery—ceramic shards crunched into her feet, shredding her skin. But Cariel gritted her teeth and ignored the pain, stumbling and sliding and gasping as she moved. The small room was full of wild limbs and hair and teeth and the howling of angry rylak. Cariel moved as quickly as she could, trying to dodge everything at once.

She'd made it all the way to the door when she heard it: the rasp of unsheathing claws. It had only been a few seconds since she'd pulled down the shelves. She only needed one more lunge to get out of here alive. The rylak would be on her at any moment, but all she had to do was jump. She could do it. She could escape these brutal savages and their insatiable lust. She could run to Svalya, and the packleader would punish these men. Then she could escape, could leave this village for good. She'd find a way to make it on her own. She'd—

Claws pierced her arm, whipping her swiftly around. One of the rylak, the one who'd been lifting her, leaned in.

"Got you," he growled in his horrible language.

She spit in his face.

The rylak reacted immediately, slashing at her once, twice, three times, claws out. Cariel felt pain burn through her in a million places, and she screamed. She felt blood rushing to her head, and the world threatened to collapse around her.

The rylak jabbered something in his language, but she had lost all concentration and didn't understand. He looked at her for a second, as if deciding whether she was still worth toying with. Evidently his decision was easy to make.

He slashed her across the face, and Cariel saw no more.

PART
THREE

SEVENTEEN

ELANIL DREW IN A DEEP BREATH.

The world was all violet and black and silver and crazy. Lines didn't stay straight. Curves went impossibly far, warping around Elanil's vision as if possessed by some devil. The ground—if you could call it that—rose up steeply in one direction, forming a massive hill that never seemed to end. Above her, the sky was purple, with brilliant streaks of white arcing through it. Strange shapes darted here and there at the fringes of things, ghosts and shadows she couldn't pin down. And everything was deathly, eerily silent.

"Arra!" Elanil tried to shout, but her voice was gone. She'd driven herself hoarse. How long had she been there? She shivered, clutching thin arms around herself.

She was hunched on the ground beside a Tree. At least, it *seemed* like a Tree. It waved as she looked at it, like steam rising from a pot on boil, like a hot stone shimmering in the sun. Nothing in this cursed place stayed *put*. She constantly felt like she was going to be sick.

How long had she been here? She thought she'd seen Arra for a minute, sitting down beside this Tree, a book in her hands. The ghostly apparition had turned when she called, as if her sister could hear her. Elanil had called and called, but it had done no good—Arra hadn't been able to see her or help.

And now her voice had given out completely. Elanil collapsed on the ground next to the ghostly Tree, tears falling from her eyes. She was so helpless, so confused. She knew she was dead. She'd felt the bullet tear through her, hot blood seeping from her skin. And then she'd been sent here. Here, to this hazy world with its violet sky.

Was she dead? Was this heaven or hell? Or was it purgatory, a lifetime alone with her regrets?

She looked up.

In the distance, she could see two massive Trees: one starkly black, one bright gold. They shone against the purple sky, bright streaks of light shooting out of them to mingle with the stars. She could almost *feel* their malevolence, wracking the sky with derision and scorn.

The ground around her was green. It was a flat green, as if someone had painted the world but forgotten all the texture. She saw other Trees here and there, dotting the landscape as far as she could see. Some of them were ghostly, some of them were solid. And that was it: green ground and ghostly Trees, with two Trees looking down from up on high. Nothing else to break up the space. No rivers or houses, no farms or people.

Just Trees.

She swallowed hard. She was going to have to figure out a way out of this place, somehow.

ELANIL GAVE up on the Tree.

Her sister wasn't there. It was time to move on. Time.

Time? She looked around, looking at the stars above. They waved and shimmered, looking strangely wrong here, as if they were an image projected on steam.

But Arra wasn't there. Elanil put her hand on the Tree, feeling its warmth, its life. She felt something pulling from her soul, as if the Tree were feeding from her. But that couldn't be right—could it?

Could the Tree be *her*?

No. She couldn't think about it. She had to move on.

She turned and set out, trudging through the strange land, all curves and waves and grass and purple things.

She walked for what seemed like ages. She could see Trees around her, far off in the distance. There were a lot of them, actually. They were beautiful, if a little strange. Strange to see Trees so insubstantial, so ephemeral. So...

She lost the thought.

Ahead of her was a hill. And beside her, to her left and right, were Trees. A gauntlet of them, running in a little row. But these Trees looked different, somehow. They were more solid, more real. More frightening. They reached out to her, crooked arms plying through the air, as if they hoped to grab her and steal her very soul.

Elanil shuddered.

She kept walking. She didn't know why. She just knew that ahead of her, up the hill, through the gauntlet of Trees, was her destination. The Trees were blocking her view now, but she remembered what she'd seen at the top of the hill.

The two Trees.

They were there, waiting for her. Watching her. Judging her. Pulling her inexorably forward.

She reached the first Tree on her path. It was gnarled, frozen and strange. It wasn't waving in the wind like the ones she'd seen before. This Tree was fully here, fully real. And somehow it seemed angry.

"The gates of change," the Tree said.

Elanil jumped, startled. Had the Tree just *talked* to her? She peered up at it. It was an elm tree, but it was hunched over strangely. Elm was *her* tree, her wood, her magic. Leafrunning magic. She should feel an affinity for it. But something was wrong with it.

"Hello?" she asked. Her voice sounded plaintive in the purple air.

"The gates of change are here to stay," the Tree said. "The gates of memory are in its way."

The Tree *had* talked! And apparently it was a poet. Elanil looked around, wondering what was going on. Should she continue up the path? It led up the hill, toward where she'd seen the two big Trees. She felt a calling toward those Trees, as if her very soul depended on it. But this Tree was blocking her path.

"What do you want?" Elanil said. "Is this a test?"

The Tree didn't move, but she felt it change.

"The Masters' calls are black and gold. To which will your allegiance hold?"

The Masters. Black and gold. It must be talking about the two Trees at the top of the hill. One was black, and one was a strange white-gold. But what did this elm Tree mean by her allegiance? Was she supposed to *choose* one of them?

She didn't know what to say. The old elm Tree looked down at her, its twisted branches shivering slightly. It looked sad, standing there. Around her, she felt the other Trees in the gauntlet closing in. The purple sky was fading, becoming darker. She felt the air grow colder.

Acting out of instinct, she stepped forward and laid a hand on the Tree.

Suddenly she could see it. Not the Tree—something *inside* of it, a vision of some kind, filled her mind. It felt like a person. Like a person's soul. She saw an eye, looking at her from within the Tree. It glared at her, trying its best to frighten her.

But Elanil felt pity for the soul trapped there in the Tree.

"How can I help?" she asked it softly.

The eye glared at her for a moment longer. Then its expression softened, and she could see one, shining tear emerging from the eye. The tear splashed down onto her hand, and the vision faded. The Tree withdrew, pulling away from her hand.

"The Master's calls are black and gold," the elm Tree repeated. "To which will your allegiance hold?"

Elanil felt the single tear on her hand, and suddenly she knew the answer. Something came upon her, some force she couldn't understand.

"The binding dreams, myself, I call," she said, not knowing what it meant, "and then I splinter, leaves and all."

That literally made no sense. But the Tree turned back, peeling its branches and leaves upwards, moving away from the path.

If it had been a test, she had passed. She just didn't know why.

ELANIL STEPPED FORWARD TENTATIVELY. The purple world was dark now, so dark she could barely see. The path she was on was narrow—Trees of every shape and size encroached upon it, moving in tightly as she walked. Trapping her on the path.

She had tried once to duck to the side, to get off the path.

But the Trees had immediately reacted, twisting together, almost pinning her between them. She had yelped and jumped backward, narrowly escaping.

She hadn't tried that again.

The Trees wanted her to continue down the path. For what reason, she couldn't say. But she knew where the path lead: to the two big Trees of black and gold, standing high on the hill at the end of the path. She could see them now, glowing strangely in the unearthly night.

They gave her the creeps.

She made it several hundred feet before an Oak Tree dipped in front of her, its entire vast crown of branches bowing and scraping on the road, blocking her path.

"Hello, Oak," she said.

The Tree creaked and cracked, settling into position. Then it spoke:

One Tree
breaks, cut to the core
One soul
wakes, emerging once more
One Tree
found with enmity's eye
One soul
bound to the purple sky

It was a very nice poem, but Elanil once again had no idea what it meant. Was this whole strange world full of poetic Trees? The Oak twisted a little, as if waiting for an answer.

Elanil did what she'd done the first time: she stepped forward, gently touching the Tree. She couldn't get to the trunk, so she grasped one of its slender branches, taking care not to break it.

An eye looked into her mind. It was a different eye; she

could feel the soul behind it was different. Kinder, but equally sad.

Somehow she knew the soul was trapped forever.

"Hello," Elanil said softly. "I feel your pain. I would get you out of there, if I could."

The eye in the Tree closed, and a tear dropped out of it, landing on her hand. She stepped back as the Tree repeated its poem. Elanil was surprised to find that some of the words had changed:

One Tree
shorn, cut to the core
One soul
born, emerging once more
One Tree
blessed with enmity's eye
One soul
pressed to the purple sky

The Tree's tear sunk into her skin, and once again the response came to her:

Your Tree
calls to the heart of gold
Your soul
falls in the days of old—

Elanil stopped suddenly, a new idea coming to her mind. "Wait a minute," she said to the Tree. "This isn't right. I can get you out."

She touched the Oak again, and once more the eye regarded her. It was just in her mind, just a vision from the Tree. But somehow she knew it was real—that there was a soul trapped in there. A person. The eye looked at her, and she could see its anguish. She desperately wanted to help whoever it was.

She quested inward with her mind, tunneling into the

Tree. The eye flinched and tried to close, but she held it there, somehow forcing it to remain open. She traveled further with her mind, tunneling into the wood, feeling its grain and its life. The cells of the Tree were like a prison—a prison made not of iron, but of wood. Wood that had been perverted, twisted, changed into something else. She could break the wood, if she was strong enough. She just had to twist her mind in a certain—

ENOUGH!

The force of the word threw Elanil backwards, blasting her away from the Tree and sending her hurtling painfully to the ground. The sound echoed, rattling around the world, rumbling through the Trees and over the path. She could feel the intensity of it in her bones.

She suddenly found herself very frightened.

The Oak Tree withdrew into itself, shrinking and crumpling, splitting and cracking and turning to dust before her eyes. Within moments the Tree was no more, and the way was open.

Was it dead? She hoped not. She had wanted to save that Tree, not kill it. She felt a tear of her own drop out of her eye.

Where had that voice come from? It had sounded strong, evil. Something had power in this place, power beyond anything she could muster. Power to destroy; power to imprison.

Shuddering, Elanil got to her feet and continued down the path.

EIGHTEEN

SLOWLY, painfully, Trey got to his feet. He looked around, wiping blood from his mouth and nose. The six attackers—or had it just been one?—were gone. And with them, the Book of Amplification. The priceless, irreplaceable artifact had been stolen. If Silanar had still been alive, he would have been furious with Trey.

Arra didn't seem very happy about it, either. She glared at him, not bothering to help him stand. "Nice performance, there," she said.

"I'm not much of a fighter," he said, knowing the words sounded lame. What did she expect, exactly?

Arra turned away. "Clearly," she muttered, before walking up the stairs to her house. That was it? She was just going to leave him there?

"Hey!" Trey called, and she turned. "Do you at least want to have dinner with me?"

Arra blew out a breath. "Fine," she said. "Fifteen minutes." Then she turned and stalked into her house, slamming the door behind her.

"ARE YOU OKAY?" Trey asked, after they'd both settled at the table. They were in his house, with a simple dinner of vegetables and broth. Ilyrion elves weren't much for eating meat.

"I'm fine," Arra said. She seemed very out of sorts, but Trey couldn't pin down why. He laid a hand on her arm.

"I'm sorry I wasn't more help out there," he said. "I'm sorry I let the Book get stolen."

Arra looked at him for a long moment, then sighed. "What happened to you? You were out for a few minutes. I was worried about you." She had a funny way of showing it.

"I had a memory," Trey said. "I remembered...us, in the Senate. It was before the Sending. When we were trying to convince them to do it."

Arra nodded. Had she been experiencing memories of her own? "That stupid vote," she said, stirring her soup idly. She looked back up at him. "Trey," she asked, "if the tables were turned, if I was the one in trouble, would you have saved me?"

"You seemed to handle yourself just fine out there. Hell, your combat skills are far better than anything I can seem to muster."

"That's not what I meant, Trey."

"Then what?"

"If I needed help—if I was *truly* in trouble—would you help me?"

Trey leaned toward her. "Of *course* I would! How can you even ask something like that?"

Arra looked back down at her soup. "I don't know," she said. "You're just...never mind. Let's eat."

Trey watched her, wondering what he should say. He wanted to hold her, to kiss her, to assure her that he would always be there for her. He could *feel* it—his love for her transcended the ages. It sounded stupid in his own head, but there it was: he'd been in love with this woman for millennia, and he wasn't about to stop now.

But something about it wasn't clicking.

He took a bite of soup, hoping he would find a way to fix whatever was going on between them.

THEY SLEPT in their separate houses, as usual. Arra was gone the next morning, off to a Senate hearing or something. She hadn't bothered to say anything to him. Trey ate a quick breakfast of eggs, tomatoes, and cucumbers, thinking.

He went back to the Anthropological Society after breakfast. It was a new day—time to try again. The offices looked different in daylight. Not better, necessarily, just different. Brighter.

Maybe he was being optimistic.

Myrddin was holding open office hours this morning, so Trey thought he'd try his luck a second time. There was nobody at the office when he arrived; the Anthropological Society was almost like a ghost town. Nobody was interested in history anymore. Their lack of funding was a travesty, to Trey's mind. Maybe if he were a Senator, he could figure out a way to change it. Maybe he could get Arra to do something. Maybe.

The Society deserved more respect.

"Hi," Trey said to Myrddin as he walked in.

"Good morning," Myrddin said, nodding to him.

Trey plopped down in one of the office chairs. "Cresius," he said.

"What?"

"Cresius. He was on my team back then. He was a Senator, but he had an interest in archaeology. He was with me when I discovered the writings about the Fall."

Myrddin frowned. "I fail to see what relevance that has."

"You asked me who was on my team. He was one of them. But he turned on me, you see. He disavowed any knowledge of the Fall, said I'd mistranslated the texts."

Myrddin flicked his eyes back and forth, apparently accessing information via his ocular monitor. Trey had heard of those—only certain people had them. Richer people. He had no desire to stick something in his eye, no desire to plug a computer into his brain. Books and pages were enough for him.

Myrddin evidently found what he was looking for. "Cresius was a vocal opponent of the Sending," he said. "Voted against it, even managed to sway several others to do so. It says here that he was indeed a member of the expedition that uncovered the artifacts. Very good." He crossed his arms, focusing his eyes once more on Trey. "Of course, you could have looked this information up for yourself."

Trey glared at the man. What was it going to take to convince him he was Tarathiel? Maybe he should have brought his shocksword with him. But no, that probably would have just gotten him arrested.

"Where's that Book you had with you yesterday?" Myrddin asked suddenly.

"What?"

"That Book. It's a magical artifact, is it not?"

"How did you know that?"

Myrddin smiled thinly. "I have my sources. Can you bring it in? I'd like to look at it."

"No."

"Why not?"

"It was…" Trey paused. Should he tell him the truth? He couldn't think of any credible lies at the moment. Deception wasn't something he was very good at. "It was stolen."

Myrddin laughed, a loud guffaw that echoed in the small office. "Really? You were just here last night, and already the Book is stolen?" His eyes narrowed. "Or do you just not want to let me see it?"

Trey shook his head sadly. "A bunch of guys jumped us last night. They were like…clones, or something. Identical copies of each other." He shivered, remembering it. "It was creepy."

A look of alarm flashed briefly over Myrddin's face, but he quickly masked it. "And these…clones…stole the Book?"

"Yes. I tried to fight them—I even remembered how!—but it didn't work. They got away."

Myrddin snorted. "That doesn't surprise me. You don't look like a very tough guy."

No, Trey supposed he did not. Perhaps it was finally time to start working out. To start retraining the knowledge he'd used to have, many millennia ago.

"Look," he said, "if you'll just give me access to my old records, that's all I want. You don't have to pay me, you don't have to fund any more research. I just want to see the old texts, to see if there's anything I missed."

"I told you, we lost those records. And even if we hadn't, we don't have the funds to pay for your research."

"I was hoping you were lying about the records."

"What would I gain by doing that?"

"You'd keep me away, for one. I think you still have them."

"Do you want to know what I think?" Myrddin asked. "I think you're a fraud, and not a very good one. I think you're pretending to be a man who died tens of thousands of years ago. I don't know why you want access to those records, or how you had that Book in your possession, but clearly you're an imbecile. Now get out of my office."

"So you admit you have the records?"

Myrddin stood, suddenly menacing. "The records are gone. Now leave, before I call security. And don't return."

The rejection stung. Trey opened his mouth, but couldn't think of anything to say in reply. He'd worked *hard* for the Society, back before he'd gone to Earth. He'd been a good researcher, a good archaeologist. Hell, he'd been a good fighter, too. He wasn't an imbecile. He was *right* about all this —the Fall, the writings, the danger. Something was coming, something with the power to destroy all elvenkind.

But nobody would believe him.

He stood unsteadily. Myrddin's glare followed him as he left.

NINETEEN

OUTSIDE THE ANTHROPOLOGICAL SOCIETY BUILDING, Trey was stopped by Lashel. Trey almost didn't recognize him, almost walked on by, but then he remembered: Lashel was a big fan. His *only* fan. And he could use a fan right about now.

"I brought a copy," Lashel said when he saw Trey. He was waving a paperback book. "I can sign it if you want!" Trey frowned at him, and he looked down, abashed. "No," he said, "that's silly. *You* should sign it. Sign one for me, I mean. I mean...here."

Trey was confused. What the hell was Lashel talking about?

Then he handed Trey the book, and he remembered. *Tarathiel: Age of Discovery*, the cover said, printed in flowing script. Behind the title was a painting of the Thesserin Desert, replete with the great city of Nekhrumet in the background. And there was Tarathiel, looking very small in the foreground, bending over to pick something up from the ground.

It brought back sudden memories.

TARATHIEL PUT the photograph down on the table. "It's not very flattering, is it."

Alleria laughed. "You say that about all your photos," she said. She was right.

They were eating dinner: white rice and beans, a bit of chicken—which was a treat—and a salad of tomatoes, cucumbers, and peppers, with strawberries on the side. Tarathiel took a drink of mead before replying. The golden liquid was sweet and just slightly effervescent. Tarathiel liked the way it tingled on his tongue.

He leaned over and kissed Alleria on the neck. "I just don't like the spotlight. Unlike *some* people." He poked her waist, where he knew she was ticklish.

She squealed. "Hey! Trying to eat here. And besides, *someone* has to hog the spotlight. Otherwise you'll never get this motion passed."

Tarathiel took a bite of chicken. She was right, he knew. The Sending had to happen, or the elves were doomed. Why the hell had the ancient elves made things so difficult, anyway? What person in their right mind created a Defense Mechanism that spanned seven *planets?* Who could even *do* such a thing, for that matter?

The dawning of the Second Age was full of wonders like that, though. He'd read about some of them: animals that did the bidding of elves; mages who could work the magic without touching any primewood; great armies of mages, who subdued the northern continents, bringing unity to the world of Valaralda. And darker things: shadow forms, elves who shambled about as if dead; slaves, who existed only to provide power to whomever placed a bleed upon their hearts; great prisons, where evil mages were captured and held indefinitely. And stories of something more: a vast, purple world full of light and energy, where souls could commune with the very gods themselves.

But that was all fascination and mystery, legend and superstition. It had been called the Great Awakening. It had been the dawn of magic, after all. He could forgive the ancient elves for being overcome with awe. But magic was a pretty normal thing now. People were more realistic about what it could do. It must have been quite spectacular for those who had first discovered it, back so long ago when magic had first appeared in the world. Tarathiel almost envied them, the ones who had been the first.

But now was not that time.

He realized, with a start, that Alleria was looking at him. She had that look in her eyes, that look that he so relished seeing. Even now, with dinner on the table and important things to discuss, he found himself swept up by that look.

He put his hand on her leg, giving her a look of his own. She put down her fork and smiled as his hand crept up her leg.

THEY LAY in bed when they had finished, sunset streaming in from their bedroom windows. They had chosen this house in Errenmel partly because of those windows. He and Alleria loved lying here underneath the evening rays, just enjoying each other, just being in love. He could hear the faint tinkle of the water fountain outside.

They lived on a beautiful half-acre in Errenmel, the town of his birth. Even though Alleria worked in the city, she was content to commute every day. That gave Tarathiel the house to himself most days, working on his research.

Tarathiel traced a line up her stomach with his finger,

JEREMY THOMAS FULLER

admiring how the beads of sweat clung to her skin. He let his finger trail upwards between her breasts, then he reached up to tap her on the nose. She laughed.

"Having fun?" she asked.

"You know me," Tarathiel said. "It's the little things."

She looked down at her breasts. "Watch who you're calling little, buster."

Tarathiel grinned at her. Outside, the sky was turning shades of purple and orange. "So," he said, changing the subject, "one week."

"One week," Alleria echoed. "And it's going to be close."

"Tell me."

She turned on her side to face him. The setting sun streamed through her hair, making her glow. Tarathiel lost what she was saying for a moment, getting distracted by her beauty.

"...the majority," she said.

"Sorry," Tarathiel interrupted, "I got distracted." He leaned in for a kiss, and she obliged.

"You need to pay attention," she said.

"Yes, ma'am. I'll try."

"Let me start again. The Ertha party is likely to all vote for you, but they're the minority. Silma has the majority. Our job is to convince or coerce as many of them as possible to vote our way."

"Bribes, you mean."

"Think of it as concessions. Politics is all about give and take, quid pro quo. You don't get anything for free in the Senate."

"I see. So...who do we have, again?"

She smiled, tapping him on the nose. "If all the Ertha vote for us, we have five of them: Sakaala, Skalanis, Thaola, Yshael, and Vander."

"Five out of fourteen," he said. "That's not good."

"It's not. With nine Silma on the floor, we need to convince two of them to vote in favor."

"That's assuming Leriaar breaks the tie our way," Tarathiel said.

"You know she will." Alleria's tone made it clear she wasn't entirely happy with the situation.

Tarathiel sighed. "I've tried to get her to lose interest."

"Have you?"

"Well." Maybe he hadn't tried as hard as he could. "Anyway, we want her to vote for us."

"Indeed. So that leaves two Silma to sway. We don't have a shot in hell with Cresius."

Tarathiel growled. "That backstabber."

"Can you honestly say you're surprised?"

Tarathiel thought back to the last expedition. Cresius had been showing signs of malcontent for a while. He'd wanted to lead the dig, but Tarathiel had refused. Cresius was the junior man on the team, and Tarathiel didn't think he'd be a good leader.

He'd been right.

"You know," Tarathiel said, "Leriaar gives me an idea."

"Oh, she does, does she?"

He ignored that. "Gaelin. I've seen him looking at you. I wonder if we can use that to our advantage?"

"Tarathiel!" Alleria said, sounding shocked. "You're not suggesting what I think you're suggesting, are you?"

"What?" Tarathiel said. "No! No, I'm just saying you could —I don't know—put in a good word with him."

"A good word."

"Just a word." He grabbed her waist, pulling her close. She threw a naked leg over him.

"You think a word will be enough to sway him?" she asked.

Tarathiel looked at her face, at her body. "You can be very persuasive."

She frowned. "Seriously, though, I'm not using sex to get a vote."

"That's not what I'm asking. You know what? Never mind. Forget it."

She pushed him away, lying on her back and staring at the ceiling. She was silent for a long moment. Tarathiel watched the rise and fall of her breasts as she breathed.

"It's rather simple, actually," she said.

"Yes?"

"Senator Keerla has a bill coming up. She plans to introduce it next week. I'm not supposed to know about it, but Vander let it slip. I'll trade my vote for hers."

That did seem simple. "What's the bill?"

"Don't worry about it."

"Why not? I don't want to trade my goals for something I don't even know."

"What does it matter? If our motion passes, we'll be gone from here. It doesn't matter what other laws get passed once we leave."

"We?"

Alleria looked at him severely. "You didn't think I'd let you leave without me, did you?"

"Who says I'm even going at all?"

Alleria pouted at him. "You think I don't know you after all this time? You're going to volunteer for the Sending. I can see it in your eyes." She stared at him, blue eyes piercing into his soul. And for the first time, he knew she was right. He *would* go along with the Sending. It meant never coming back to Valaralda. It probably meant dying in the process. He was going to go, and he wasn't going to tell her.

"I'm going with you," she said, and he could tell there would be no arguing with her.

He reached out, clasping her hand. "I want you with me, darling," he said, squeezing her hand.

She smiled. "I love it when you call me that. Darling."

He kissed her. She tasted of strawberries.

"So," he said when the kiss was over, "what bill is Keerla introducing?"

Alleria sighed. "The bill cuts funding to the Anthropological Society."

"What! Why? Where does the money go?"

"To the Department of Magical Research."

"Why do they need the money?"

Alleria shrugged. "They must have some reason. I'm sure Keerla will go over that when she introduces the motion."

"Does the Council hate the Society that much?"

"Nobody hates the Society. People just think the money can be spent on...other things."

"Is that what you think?"

She frowned at him. "No, silly. Of course not."

He laid back on the bed. This whole politics thing was too much for him, too unnatural. He felt a sudden longing to get back to his books. The sun was almost set now, and the room was getting dark.

"So that leaves one more vote," he said after a while.

"Yes," Alleria said quietly.

"TREY!" Lashel was saying. "Trey!" He waved his hand in front of Trey's face.

"What?" Trey asked, annoyed.

"You went blank there for a minute. You okay?"

Trey looked around. It was still morning, and he was still on the University campus. He could still taste Alleria, still feel the sweat on her skin. The memory began to fade, and he found himself growing wistful.

"Trey?"

"I'm fine. What do you want?"

Lashel looked crestfallen, and Trey realized he was being too harsh. "Sorry. I've been through a lot lately. Memories keep coming back to me, and…"

"Gatesickness must be terrible," Lashel said.

"It is. Anyway, I'm sorry for being a pain. Did you need something?"

"I just wanted to give you an update," Lashel said. "I spoke with some people at the Society. I did my best, but…"

"They won't help."

"I'm sorry, Trey."

Trey sighed. It seemed the Anthropological Society was a dead end. "We have to get the Mechanism activated."

"I know. We'll keep working on it."

"We?"

Lashel looked hurt. "Sorry. I didn't mean to assume. I just thought maybe we could work together on this. I've been doing some research of my own—"

"You're in," Trey said.

Lashel stopped, his mouth still open. "Really?"

"Sure," Trey said. "I could use all the help I can get."

"Great!" Lashel said, excitement on his face. "Where do we start?"

"We need my research. The Society said they'd lost it."

Lashel thought about that for a minute. "Have you gone back home yet?"

"There's nothing in my apartment that'll help."

"No, I mean home. Where you used to live, in Errenmel."

"You know about that?"

"I wrote the book on you, Trey."

"Oh, yeah. But why would I go there?"

"Maybe you'll find something. Maybe some memories will come back."

It would be nice to see his old home. "Is it still there?"

"It is. There's another couple living there now, but I'm sure they'd let you take a look."

Trey looked around campus, weighing his options. He'd hit a dead end here; maybe getting out of the city would do him some good. "Fine," he said. "We'll go to Errenmel. You coming?"

"I'd love to!"

"Let me see if Arra is around," Trey said. "She might like to see this."

TWENTY

QUYNN WAS LOSING a lot of weight in this dungeon.

Maybe it wasn't a dungeon, but he had started thinking of it like that. Dungeons were dark, cold places buried underneath castles. This jail cell was the same, except instead of being underground, he was somewhere in the New San Francisco Under, high up in the sky. Either way, it was still dark. And cold.

Very dungeon-like.

And they weren't feeding him enough. Quynn wasn't even sure precisely who his captors were. They were elves—he knew that much. Probably some of the elves from Sylrantheas, or maybe the ones from that new coalition, the United Sky Cities. Everyone had been so quick to jump all over the Cothellon the moment their plan had been completed. Everyone had been so quick to imprison *him*, without any sort of due process.

He probably deserved it, though. He hadn't exactly been charitable the last time he interacted with the Eldrim. He'd tried to kill Trey and Arra. He *had* killed Silanar, Callan, and plenty of others, and ordered the deaths of hundreds more.

Oh, and he'd also destroyed their entire city. Sure, he'd taken a wicked slice to the gut for his troubles, but nobody cared about that. They'd just healed him up and shipped him down to the jail cells under the city, next to all the shit and refuse and dirty children who called this place home.

The Under.

It was disgusting.

But none of that was even the biggest problem. Sure, he was losing weight, probably getting sick from all the nasty bacteria down here. He was cold and depressed and miserable and a little bit afraid. But that wasn't the worst part.

The worst part was how fucking *boring* it was down here.

He shuffled his feet, making little figure eights in the dust, his back up against the cold stone wall. He tried to keep his mind awake by asking himself questions. Why had they failed? By all accounts, the Cothellon's plan had succeeded. The planet had traveled through the gate, just as Lorelei had wanted. Everything had worked out according to the plan. So why, then, was there no happy ending? Shouldn't the Cothellon be ruling now? Shouldn't Quynn be lording it over everyone from high atop some throne, with Lorelei by his side? Shouldn't whatever the hell she'd been planning resulted in some kind of *happiness* for them? Why had they even needed the gate? Why had they needed to move the planet?

And why the hell had it taken him this long to question her?

It was like she had some sort of power over him. Could it be mindmaster magic? No—Quynn discarded the notion. He'd been a mindmaster for hundreds of years. He'd know if someone else was in his head like that.

No, it was probably just plain old-fashioned lust that had driven him to Lorelei. Women always had been powerful like that to him, and Lorelei was the best he'd ever met at using her body to get her way. It had been worth it, though. He pictured her, lying there naked on her stark white bed.

Yes, it had definitely been worth it.

He blew out a breath. He was thinking in circles again. There was no solution here, no answer to his endless questions. He needed to get *out* somehow. Sitting here alone was eventually going to kill him.

Just then he heard a shuffling sound outside his cell. Was it that strange man again? Quynn's clone? He had only shown himself that one time so far, but it had been very unsettling. Quynn wondered if perhaps he had hallucinated the whole thing. There was no other explanation for it—copies of yourself didn't just spring up out of nowhere. It had to be a hallucination.

The shuffling sound came again, and a face suddenly peered in at him from the shadows. Whoever it was poked its nose through the bars in his cell, peering at him with eyes that glinted strangely.

"Little splinter, all alone," the man rasped. His nose was angled sharply downward, almost like a hook. It lent him a malicious appearance. Quynn was sure that whoever this was, he was up to no good.

"What do you want?" Quynn asked, his voice coming out garbled. It had been weeks since he had spoken. He cleared his throat. "Who are you?"

"Who in violet's sky is shown?" the man asked. It made a strange sort of poem.

What was he going on about? Somehow the man seemed imminently dangerous. Quynn wondered how he should respond.

"Little splinter, here to die," the man continued. "Will you join the violet sky?"

Again with the violet sky. None of this was making sense.

"Um," Quynn said, still unsure what to say. What did the man mean? He'd never heard of a violet sky. Sure, he'd *dreamed* it before...wait. He *had* dreamed of a violet sky. Why hadn't he remembered that until now? What had it meant? He racked his brain, trying to remember.

Evidently the stranger decided on a different tack. He brought his hands up, poking spindly gray arms through the bars in the cell, palms up. In the dim light, Quynn could barely see that each hand held a coin. The coin in the man's right hand was a pale gold, with the image of a tree on it. The coin in his left hand was dark, almost completely black, with a gray tree embossed within. The metal of the dark coin glinted strangely, almost as if it were made out of darkprime wood. Could both coins be made out of wood, polished to look like metal? That would be a very strange use for primewood.

"The Masters' calls are black and gold," the stranger said in his raspy voice. "To which will your allegiance hold?" A different poem, but equally confusing.

Quynn looked at him, trying to discern his intent. The man's whole face was pinched, and his hair was wispy, kind of a dark gray. The whole man seemed gray, in fact—skin and all. He almost didn't seem alive. Quynn shivered. Where were the guards? How had this stranger even gotten in here?

"Choose now," the stranger said, "and be gone from here." This time it wasn't a poem. The man seemed anxious, worried, like his time here was limited.

Quynn got to his feet painfully, limbs sore from sitting against the wall for so long. He padded over to the door and looked once more at the coins. One was light, and one was dark. It almost seemed like he was being made to choose between magics. But that was ridiculous—his Alignment had already chosen for him. He could use both types of magic, as he'd proven during his fight against Trey. He could no more choose a type of magic than choose an arm—it was a Sophie's choice, impossible.

The stranger was waiting patiently now, no longer repeating his question. Now that Quynn was closer, he could see the man's pointed ears. He was an elf, albeit a very sick-looking one.

He looked again at the two coins. The gray tree in the black coin disturbed him—it seemed to stare at him, daring him to choose it. The black coin almost seemed to throb, as if trying to draw him in. He felt suddenly repulsed by it.

But still, he couldn't deny its draw.

So, without a word, he grabbed the black coin from the stranger's hand. The coin felt warm, almost as if it were alive. He thought he heard someone speaking to him for an instant, someone in the coin. He jumped, surprised. But he must have been imagining it, for the coin just sat there in his palm, shining. So he stuck it in his pocket. It felt heavy there, as if it didn't want him to forget about it.

The gray man clapped his hands together suddenly. "The choice has been made," he rasped, then clutched the cell bars with both hands. Instantly the whole door fuzzed away into semi-transparency. "Come," the stranger said.

Quynn wasted no time, stepping through the cell bars and out into the hallway. The stranger released the bars, and the door faded back into being, as solid as before. The man was a mergemelder, Quynn realized. He could see dust falling from his hand.

The stranger turned away from him and started ambling down the hall. He moved in an odd fashion, sort of hunched over, as if there was something wrong with his back. The stranger didn't look behind; he just beckoned to Quynn as he left.

"Come," the stranger said. "Come."

Quynn shrugged to himself. Whoever this person was, he seemed to be Quynn's ticket out of here. He set off down the cement tunnel, following the odd gray man.

He hoped he wouldn't live to regret this.

TWENTY-ONE

"WHAT IS THIS?" Orym asked, looking at Arkiem's glass desk. Displays had come alive all over it, showing various maps and diagrams and video views. One of the displays appeared to be a map of Valaralda rendered flat, with Ilyrion right in the center. He could see the lushness of the forests north of Ilyrion, the ocean to the east, and the desert to the west.

Half a dozen red lines were arcing out from Ilyrion, heading in smooth curves toward the edge of the desert. But there was nothing in that part of the desert, Orym knew. The lines weren't pointing anywhere near the great city of Nekhrumet. They were pointing to the middle of nowhere. How strange.

Then Orym realized where the lines were originating. It was the neighborhood Trey and Arra were living in. He felt his blood run cold as he looked at the map.

Arkiem stepped over to inspect the display. "That's funny," he said. "We don't normally have the *dúathmain* monitors active for Ilyrion. No point, since nobody uses it."

"Someone's using darkprime magic, right?" Orym asked. Someone in Trey's neighborhood.

"Looks that way," Arkiem said.

"But why does it lead to the desert?"

"You got me," Arkiem said. "Maybe the sensors need calibrating."

Druindar stepped forward, swiftly tapping the desk. The red lines went away. "Probably an instrument glitch," he said. "I'll have them checked out tomorrow." He tapped the desk again and the displays disappeared.

Orym looked at the man, wondering if he was telling the truth. It seemed awfully strange that darkprime magic would suddenly erupt right where Trey and Arra were staying. Maybe they'd been the ones using the magic. After all, they did have large stores of the wood. But that didn't explain why the lines were leading out to the desert. One more mystery to solve. Or maybe the instruments really did need calibrating.

"Let's get back to this," Druindar said, walking back over to the holographic map of Earth.

ALLAIN SCRAMBLED ALONG THE FLOOR, pulling Lorelei with him. Gunshots continued to blaze, ricocheting around the room as they crawled past a heap of blankets and behind one of the big machines. Allain2 had gone the other way, dodging to the north end of the room with Shot.

Allain peeked his head out, trying to see who the attackers were. He caught a quick glimpse of someone in a gray robe, hurtling balls of lightning one after another. Whenever the lightning hit the rigging overhead, fires sprung out. The rigging was made up mainly of ropes, hammocks, and blankets—it wasn't designed to handle lightning. Underekids were struggling desperately to keep the flames under control, passing buckets of water up from the water reclamation machines below. They had a system all worked out, but the magic was coming too fast.

"Stay here," he hissed at Lorelei. She nodded at him blankly. Even hunched on the ground, bedraggled and confused, she was still gorgeous. Allain found himself resolving to keep her safe, no matter what it took.

He got to his feet and crept around the machine they were hiding behind. It was whirring loudly—probably part of the water treatment plant that surrounded this area of the Under. There were big, open tanks of water in the next chamber. Maybe he could draw the attackers over there, use that to his advantage? He discarded the thought. It wouldn't do any good.

He didn't have a weapon, and the only magic he had was mistweaving. Could he use it to distract them? That might work. He stepped out from his hiding place, looking around for the enemy. The attacks had stopped.

He felt in his pocket, pulling out his latest carving: a giant bumblebee. Taking a step, he flicked at the wood with his tiny carving knife. Almost immediately, he felt Prime magic Invest in the wood, bursting through it like the sun coming out from the clouds.

Underkids swarmed the rigging above him, frantically throwing water on the flames. A bucket of it splashed down on Allain, but he ignored it, wiping his face with his arm and looking around the room. Where had the gray-robed man gone? How many attackers were they facing?

Suddenly the man appeared out of thin air, right in front of Allain. Allain yelped in surprise, lifting his knife reflexively and pointing it at the man. The guy was wearing a long robe made out of some kind of rough-looking dark gray fabric. He had a multi-colored belt around his waist, made up of bright pieces of yarn. It looked like a little rainbow around his waist. How strange.

The man appeared to be unarmed, and he had an almost vacant expression on his face. He was just standing there in front of Allain, doing nothing. Hadn't he been attacking them a moment ago? Allain was confused.

Shot and Allain2 walked up beside him.

"What do you want?" Shot asked. He was pointing his gun at the stranger.

The gray man paused a moment before answering. "A woman," he said finally. "Lara. Velion desires her."

Lara? Velion? What was this man going on about? Then Lorelei came out, walking unsteadily toward the man, and Allain realized what he wanted.

It was Lorelei.

"You want her?" Allain asked, gesturing toward Lorelei.

"Velion desires her," the man repeated, as if it made any more sense the second time.

"Sorry, bud," Allain said. "You can't have her."

The man shrugged, taking a step forward.

"Back off, man!" Shot said, jamming his gun at the robed mage's chest. "He said you can't have her."

Allain was wondering where the other attackers had gone. Hadn't there been more than one? Somebody had been shooting bullets, not magic. He looked around the room, trying to spot anyone else. There were a lot of places to hide.

Then he saw it. "Get down!" he shouted, grappling Shot and pushing him away. They ran into Allain2, all three falling to the ground in a heap of limbs.

Three lightning balls flew through the air, right where they'd been standing.

The boys crawled behind the nearest obstacle. It was a

flimsy-looking metal box of some kind, draped with dirty sheets. It wouldn't provide much shelter. Allain saw four gray-robed men descending through the rigging, intent on Lorelei. She was still standing in the middle of the room, looking at the first man. There was no fear in her eyes. Her mind was gone.

A fifth man showed up from the direction of the main entrance. That made six of these guys. Three of them held guns, and the other three were unarmed. Allain had no doubt they were all mages of some kind, and at least one of them was a shockstriker. Then he noticed something strange: all six robed men looked alike. No, it was more than that. They looked *identical* to each other. How could that be?

But there was no time for that now. The six men circled Lorelei, reaching their hands out as if to grab her. He had to do something, and he had to do it now. But what?

Suddenly he had an idea.

He lifted the bumblebee carving, flicking a couple scratches in it to add texture. The skilled action caused magic to flare up once more in the wood, Investing it with power. Mistweaving power, the power of illusion.

Time to see if his idea would work.

Using his mind, he Willed an illusion to life. But this wasn't just any sort of illusion. It wasn't a bear or a snake or a rat or a rabbit. It wasn't even a dragon. No, this illusion was something new, something different.

Something unexpected.

He cast the illusion, and Lorelei disappeared.

Allain felt joy course through him. It had worked! Instead of creating a new thing using mistweaving, he'd created the *absence* of a thing. He'd Willed Lorelei to be gone. And she had disappeared.

Of course, she was still there, probably wondering why

she suddenly couldn't see herself. The six gray mages looked confused, turning this way and that, looking to see where she'd gone. It was probably only a matter of time before one of them got the bright idea to touch her, to put his hand where she'd been just a moment ago. Or maybe one of them would accidentally stumble into her. Either way, the invisibility wouldn't do much good for long.

Time for another trick.

Allain flicked the bumblebee carving again, enhancing its shape ever so slightly. His Sculpture Talent poured life into the wood, and he immediately put it to work. Only this time, it was *himself* he made invisible.

Immediately the world went haywire.

Everything became hazy, almost as if it had all turned to steam, wafting up from the ground. Allain found it very disorienting—he stumbled, struggling to maintain his concentration, keeping the illusions going. Both he and Lorelei were invisible now. It took a lot more concentration to do both of them at once, but he could manage it.

He turned to look behind him, and the motion almost made him sick. Everything was swaying and indistinct, hard to see. Everything except Allain2, who was staring right at him, perfectly solid.

Allain felt a shock roll through him. His twin was standing several feet away, but Allain could see him *through* everything. It was like the whole world wasn't real, and Allain2 was the only real thing left. His body was brightly colorful, standing out sharply against the hazy background. Then Allain2 turned to look at him, and Allain felt his stomach drop.

Allain2's eyes were glowing brilliantly white, his mouth a dark slash. He looked angry, as if there was some latent power inside him, waiting to come out. It was frightening.

"Help her," Allain2 said, but his mouth didn't move. *Creepy*.

Okay. Yes. Help her. That's why he'd done this, to help her. Allain shook himself out of his fright, willing himself to ignore the ghastly form of Allain2. He could see Lorelei now, even though he was sure he was still maintaining her illusion of invisibility. She had turned toward him, and he could see fright in her eyes. Did he look as strange to her as Allain2 did to him?

The six identical mages were beginning to move, spreading out to search the room. They hadn't walked through Lorelei yet, which was good. The illusion was holding. Allain stepped through the widening circle of men, grabbing Lorelei gently by the arm. Her look of fright softened at his touch, and she allowed herself to be guided away.

They skirted between two of the mages and made their way back to Shot and Allain2. Shot was looking around with confusion—to him, Lorelei and Allain had simply disappeared.

Allain stepped behind the hanging sheets and released the magic. He and Lorelei popped back into being, in front of Shot. Part of the bumblebee carving turned to dust, its magic exhausted. Shot let out a small yelp.

"Where the hell did you go?" he whispered, looking past them at the six robed men. Two of them were heading their way.

"Magic," Allain said, grinning.

Shot glared at him. "Can you get us out of here?" he asked. "Or kill those mages?"

"Afraid not," Allain said. He turned and saw Allain2 giving him an odd expression. With a start, Allain realized his twin's hair color had changed—it was lighter now, almost blond. What the hell? His nose was a little bigger, too. They no longer looked like identical twins. Was Allain2's appearance decaying over time? Would they eventually look nothing alike?

"Where the hell is Spike?" Shot muttered. "I can't take them all with this one gun."

"What if you made one of those robe guys invisible?" Allain2 asked.

"Why?" Allain responded, keeping his voice low. "What good would that do?"

Allain2 shrugged. "Maybe confuse them?"

"Worth a shot, I guess," Allain said. "Go ahead and try it."

"Me?" Allain2 asked.

"Yes, you. Why not?"

"I...don't think I can."

"Really? But I thought you were my clone. You can't mistweave? Have you tried?"

"Give me that," Allain2 said, grabbing the carving and knife. He made a few marks in the wood, but he dug too deeply—a chunk of wood came out, deforming the bumblebee.

"Ow," Allain2 said, holding his hand up to his head. "That hurts."

"You can't even carve," Allain said, dumbfounded. All this time, he'd thought Allain2 was his twin in every way. How had they not tried this before?

"It hurts when I carve," Allain2 said. "Really bad."

"Well, I guess that won't work, then," Allain said. "Give me that back." He grabbed the carving and the knife, quickly making some changes to the bumblebee to smooth out the mistake Allain2 had made. As he worked, he felt magic Investing into the wood. And *his* head felt fine. Strange. For whatever reason, only one of them could mistweave. It must have something to do with whatever had caused them to split in the first place.

"What the hell are you two doing?" Shot whispered. Two of the mages were almost on them. "Get ready to fight!"

Suddenly a shout rang out from above. "The cavalry has arrived!" Spike called, swinging down through the rigging, accompanied by a dozen underkids.

And just like that, the fight was on.

Allain tried to stay out of the way as Spike's kids swung down, guns blazing. They'd been practicing for weeks, and most of them were pretty good shots—but their opponents were mages. One of them counterattacked, shooting bolts and balls of blue lightning from his fists. Another mage flew upwards through the air—clearly using fallfoiling—catching one of the overhead underkids by surprise. A third mage threw up a forcefield, protecting himself. They were all using different kinds of magic. It was almost like they'd been sent here as a team, specifically designed to cover each magical ability.

Or as if a Prime Mage had been split into six components.

But that was impossible—right?

Allain didn't know what to do—he didn't have a weapon, and mistweaving wasn't of much use. His invisibility trick was cool, but he didn't see how it would help.

All around him, the room was in chaos. The six mages were clearly skilled, fearsome warriors. And some of them had guns. Allain saw one underkid go down in a spray of blood, shot in the chest. Another got hit in the face by a bolt of lightning that singed his hair, dropping him a dozen feet to the floor. One of the robed mages got hit by a bullet, but he shrugged off the attack, the hole closing as soon as the bullet hit. That guy must have been a soulsoother.

Allain frowned. The fight had only been going on for a

minute, and already things weren't looking good. He crouched behind the hanging sheets, one hand holding Lorelei's arm, the other holding his bumblebee carving. He hoped nobody would notice him.

Allain2 nudged him. "Try it," he said. "Make one of them invisible."

"Why?"

"They're coordinating their attacks," Allain2 said. "Look."

He was right. Now that Allain was paying attention, he could see the mages making eye contact and giving each other subtle hand signals. They weren't telepathic—they just had a very efficient system of communication worked out. Turning one or more of them invisible would screw with their plan, at least. It would probably confuse the hell out of them.

Unless they knew that trick too.

"Worth a shot," Allain said. He had nothing else to contribute—might as well try it.

Flick, flick. He made quick work with the carving knife, hollowing out a small section near where the bee's wing would meet its thorax. Power flooded the carving, and Allain opened his mind, concentrating on the trick he'd used before. It was like making any other illusion—envision what you wanted to see, fix it firmly in your head, and it would appear. Only this time he wanted something to *disappear*. It was the same principle, just in reverse. He focused on the shock-striker.

Blink. The mage disappeared.

Then something very strange happened.

The five visible mages stopped in their tracks, turning as one to look directly at the sixth—invisible—mage. Four of the mages flickered, like a bad TV signal, their bodies wavering ever so slightly. Then, one by one, each of the flickering mages sort of *sucked* inward, blurring rapidly through the air toward the one who hadn't flickered. They didn't move—they just flew silently, each one disappearing as they hit the first.

Allain felt the sixth mage, the one who was invisible, fly inward as well—and then he, too, disappeared. This wasn't an illusion—this was reality. The clones were gone, leaving just one mage left.

And that mage collapsed on the ground, senseless.

TWENTY-TWO

"SO LET ME GET THIS STRAIGHT," Orym said. Director Arkiem and Chief Magitech Officer Druindar turned to look at him. "Something—or someone—is under the Mediterranean Sea on Earth. And whatever that person or thing is, it's sending out an unprecedented stream of darkprime magic directly to us on Valaralda."

"That's correct," Arkiem said.

"Has the signal always been there? Has it been streaming between the two planets for a long time? And if so, why didn't you notice it?"

"It hasn't," Druindar said. "We would have noticed. The signal started up when Mar entered our solar system."

"But why?"

Druindar shrugged.

"Is it pointing anywhere?"

"Yes," Arkiem said. "It's pointing to a place in the Thesserin Desert."

"Show me."

Arkiem fiddled with the desk controls, bringing up Valaralda on the big holographic display. The planet rotated, then abruptly zoomed in. Orym felt his stomach lurch as the image moved—it was very realistic. He recognized Ilyrion, on the south end of the continent of Esara. To the west of the city was a vast desert—the Thesserin Desert. The red line curved in from outer space, coming to rest at a spot only a few miles into the desert.

"Wait a minute," Orym said. "That location looks familiar. Isn't that where we saw the other magic streams a minute ago?"

Arkiem frowned. "It might be."

"Whatever it was, it's gone now," Druindar said. "Can we get back to our topic?"

"I thought we *were* on topic," Orym said. "This signal. What is it? Why does it point here?"

"We don't know," Druindar said. "But we want you to find out."

Orym swallowed. "Me?" he asked. "Why?"

"Druindar recommended you," Arkiem said.

Orym turned to look at the Magitech Officer. He'd never met the man before today. Why had he recommended him?

"Your reputation precedes you," Druindar said. "And frankly, we can't spare anyone else."

"What do you have in mind for me to do?"

"We want you to lead a small expedition," Arkiem said. "Take a submersible under the ocean and investigate the source of this signal."

"What do you think you'll find?"

"We don't know," Arkiem said. "To be honest, I was against sending anyone. Our budget is stretched thin enough as it is, what with the telescope suddenly getting everyone's attention. But Druindar convinced me to go ahead with it, provided you can lead the mission."

It sounded interesting, but Orym wasn't sure this was how

he wanted to spend his time. There was so much to do here on Valaralda, so many technologies to see, so much time to catch up on. Did he really want to go back to Earth? He'd just gotten back here, back home.

Although it didn't really *feel* like home, yet.

"How long do you expect it to take?" Orym asked.

"Not long," Druindar said. "A week, maybe two. The flight over should take about twelve hours, and we can drop you near the submersible's entry point."

"Will you be coming?"

"I'm afraid I can't spare him," Arkiem said. "You'll be in charge of this one. But you'll have radio contact with us at all times, plus a full operations staff on this end. And I believe you'll find your team equal to the challenge. What do you think?"

Orym looked again at the holographic display. It had changed back to Earth, rotating placidly amongst the stars. The strange red line was still there, shooting out from the sea. He could almost feel it calling to him, beckoning him.

The Mediterranean Sea. Something about it was sparking a memory, as if that part of the world were somehow important.

Wait a minute. Orym cocked his head, narrowing his eyes at the display. The Mediterranean Sea flowed into the Ionian and Tyrrhenian Seas. There was a little island in the Tyrrhenian, the site of one of the world's many supervolcanoes. Or it *had* been, before Phoenix had gotten there.

Stromboli.

Could this strange signal be what Magona had been searching for five years ago? She had been close, but if this was what Orym thought it was, she hadn't quite been in the right place.

And that wasn't all.

"Did you know," Orym said, "that some scholars on Earth used to think there was a lost civilization under the Mediterranean Sea? Right where the signal is originating."

"Really?" Arkiem said. "Do you believe it's real?"

Orym laughed. "It couldn't be. The theory was soundly disproven, hundreds of years ago."

"Or maybe the humans just didn't know what they were talking about."

The humans didn't—Orym was sure of that. But Magona had been poking around there for a reason, and she didn't strike him as someone whose reasons were ever *good*.

"I'll do it," he said, leaning back in his chair.

Arkiem smiled. "Very good. We'll get started right away. Out of curiosity, what was this lost civilization called?"

Orym gave him a level stare. "Atlantis."

TWENTY-THREE

THE MAGE WAS OUT COLD. Allain helped Shot pick him up, tying a rope around him and bringing him into the tent. Lorelei followed them in, with Allain2 right behind. Allain2's hair was lighter than before, almost blond. It made him look even uglier, if that were possible.

"What should we do with him?" Spike asked. They'd placed the mage in a rickety metal chair.

"Anyone know who he is?" Shot asked.

Everyone was silent.

"There were six of them. Where'd the other ones go?"

Allain almost said something, but decided against it. The other five mages had disappeared when he'd made one of them invisible. He didn't know how to explain it, so he decided not to. He'd have to experiment more with invisibility illusions, see if he could figure it out.

"Well," Shot said into the silent tent, "we know what the bastard can do. The next question is: what should we do with him?"

Just then, the mage woke up.

He immediately fell off the chair, spluttering. "What—" he said, his voice gravelly. "Who—"

Then it seemed like he caught a signal from somewhere: his head turned in a specific direction, as if he were an antenna. He listened for a second, then turned back to the group. Everyone was looking at him with avid attention.

"Nelenor wants the girl," he said in that gravelly voice of his.

Who the hell was Nelenor?

The mage caught sight of Lorelei. "There!" he shouted, pointing at her. "The Twins shall be reborn! The Twins shall—"

Shot slapped him in the face, hard. "Shut up." The mage grew quiet. "Can you tell us who you are?"

The mage started crying. His body was shaking, and he was repeating one word over and over again. Allain leaned in to hear it.

"Ilyrion," the mage was saying.

"He wants to go to Ilyrion," Allain observed.

"Or he wants to get away from there," Shot said.

"Maybe we should just kill him," Allain2 suggested.

Lorelei stepped forward then, clearly agitated. "The gates of change," she said. "The gates of memory." She was clearly as loony as the mage. Then she turned, clutching Allain's shirt with her fist. "Take me," she breathed. "Take me to the Jewel of the South."

"Ooookay," Allain said, but he couldn't deny he was getting a little turned on. Lorelei was mad as a hatter, but her hand on his shirt was nonetheless welcome. Maybe he should take her where she wanted to go.

"Where is the Jewel of the South?" he asked.

"Ilyrion," she breathed, stepping even closer. She smelled

like garbage, but he found it intoxicating anyway. Something was clearly wrong with him.

"That's on Valaralda," he said, turning to Shot. "Well? Can we?"

"You can do whatever you want," Shot said, "as long as you get these freaks out of here."

Grime stepped forward. "There's a ship leaving in a few hours," he said, "bound for Ilyrion. They'll let you on it if you give them this." He handed Allain a piece of metal with strange markings on it.

"What is this?" Allain asked.

"Visit visa. It's electronic. Can't be forged, at least not by anyone on Earth. It'll get the four of you onto Valaralda."

"Where'd you get it?"

"Orym gave us several of them."

Allain turned to Allain2. "You game?"

Allain2 shrugged. "I don't care."

Allain glared at him for a second before turning to Lorelei. She was still looking at him, with something like longing in her eyes. He found it incredibly erotic, despite her smell. Maybe he could get her cleaned up along the way.

"We're going to take you home," he said.

She smiled.

THE SPACESHIP WAS unlike anything Allain had ever seen before. It was sleek, with a metallic hull that curved deliciously as it swept toward the back. The craft was as futuristic as he'd imagined it would be. He hoped it was safe.

The ship's clerk waved his metal visa across some device she had, then motioned them to proceed. Allain, Allain2 and

Lorelei entered the ship, shepherding the still-manacled gray mage. Allain had taken to calling him a "shadowmage." Something about his gray robes made him think of it. It seemed to fit.

The interior of the ship was as sleek as the exterior, all modern curves and metal finishes. The cabin inside was divided into four rows that were four seats wide—pretty narrow, but at least the seats themselves looked comfortable. They made their way to the front of the cabin, where their seats were situated.

Allain found himself getting nervous with anticipation. Would it hurt, traveling to outer space? Would they have enough air? Would the shadowmage suddenly attack them all?

Allain caught Lorelei looking at him, and he blushed. He'd found her a shower at a hotel in the city before they'd come to the ship, and now she smelled as good as she looked. He wished her mind wasn't so broken; it would have been nice to have someone else to talk to besides Allain2.

He settled himself in his chair as the countdown began.

THE STRANGER LED Quynn out of the jail and up to the surface of New San Francisco. The nameless man was silent the whole time, and they encountered nobody else along the way.

A shuttle was waiting for them on the surface, a sleek spaceship of metal and chrome.

Quynn looked at the person who'd freed him, trying to discern his intentions, but the man didn't return his gaze. He just walked into the spaceship's metal door, yawning open like the mouth of a cave.

Should he follow? He should probably run. He might even

get away. But something told him this savior of his could hurt him greatly if he tried to escape. He'd probably regret it if he tried.

Quynn looked at the city all around him. After three hundred years in New San Francisco, everything was starting to look the same. Dull and lifeless, a dead end. The Cothellon were gone, their plan complete.

There was nothing for him here.

So he decided to follow the stranger. Maybe there was a new plan, something to sink his teeth into.

Anything would be better than sitting in jail.

The inside of the shuttle was far more spacious than it had appeared from the outside. It was clean and modern, with space for maybe a hundred people in rows of uncomfortable-looking seats. Quynn took the seat that was indicated to him, feeling himself sink into the chair. It was far more pleasant than it looked.

The stranger still hadn't said a word to him after getting him out of the cell, and Quynn was growing tired of the silence. Where were they going? How long would it take?

Other passengers filed in, taking their seats throughout the shuttle. A scruffy-looking boy was looking at him from a few rows away. He was seated next to a dark-haired woman who looked familiar, but her back was turned and he couldn't see her face.

More and more people entered the cabin, and Quynn found himself getting annoyed. After spending so long alone in a cell, the presence of so many people was getting on his nerves.

"Good morning," a voice said over the sound system in the cabin. "I'm Captain Stilmyst, and I'll be piloting this Cairland 883 with service to Ilyrion. We're running at only 55% capacity today, so feel free to spread out throughout the cabin.

Our trip is expected to take eleven hours fifty five minutes. We'll be accelerating and decelerating at a nice and comfortable 1 G, so the gravfields in your chairs won't need to be activated. Subjective time on this trip does not vary meaningfully from point of reference on Valaralda.

"We'll be serving three meals and two snacks on this trip. The stewards will take over from here with safety instructions. On behalf of Ilyrion Space Transport Services, I'd like to wish you all a happy flight."

The captain sounded nice enough at least, even if Quynn hadn't understood half of what he'd said. Orym had always been around in the past to explain scientific stuff to him. Still, he understood the time. Twelve hours cooped up in this tin can with a bunch of strangers and the odd gray man who'd rescued him. He felt panic beginning to rise as three stewards appeared and began their safety demonstration.

"How does this thing even work?" a woman behind him whispered to someone next to her. "I didn't see any engines or anything."

Quynn turned his head just enough to see two human women talking.

"Sam told me it was some kind of magic," the other woman whispered. "Leaf something or other."

Leafrunning in space? Quynn suddenly grew even more nervous. Magic should never be used for spaceflight, as far as he was concerned. It was unnatural. He took a deep breath, trying to calm himself. He could do this. It would be okay. The women's whispers blended with the steward's safety lessons, a blur of words and faces.

The next twelve hours would feel like an eternity.

ALLAIN HAD twelve hours to kill in the spaceship, and there wasn't much to occupy his time. He'd brought a carving with him, but he wasn't sure how the captain would react to having wood shavings all over his floor.

So instead, he occupied himself trying to talk to Lorelei. She had moments of lucidity, but most of the time the things she said made no sense. He'd gathered that she was suffering extreme gatesickness—apparently she'd been through far too many gates in the past, and the planet jump had been one too many.

It had nearly made her go insane.

"Why are you splintered?" she asked him halfway through the trip. The screens along the sides of the ship were displaying video images of the solar system, panning and zooming beautifully as they crossed the interminable space between Earth and Valaralda.

"Splintered?" Allain asked. "I don't understand." Next to him, Allain2 perked up somewhat. He'd been dozing off.

"You are soulsplintered. Why?" Lorelei put her hand on his leg, apparently unaware of the effect it had on him. It seemed almost an unconscious action.

"I don't know what you mean," Allain said. "What is a soulsplinter?"

Lorelei frowned. "You don't know? It's when—" But the moment passed, and she lost the thought. "Stars!" she said, pointing at the screens on the edge of the ship. "Are you taking me to the gates?"

He didn't know what she was talking about, but this soulsplinter thing had him intrigued. "Lorelei," he said, grabbing her hand. She didn't resist—she just looked at him with her deep green eyes. "What is a soulsplinter?"

With her free hand, she pointed at Allain2. "Him," she said. "He's you."

Well, Allain already knew that. But what he didn't know was *how*. "Tell me more," he prompted.

She seemed lost for a moment, her eyes going blank. Then, miraculously, she continued. "He is a projection made real. You misted yourself, did you not? It is a simple thing. But why did you keep him?"

Allain thought back to the ancient stories, like the one Kythaela had used to tell—the one about Usunaar and his siblings, Talanaar and Koranaar. In the story, Koranaar made an illusion of herself using mistweaving. Allain's father had told him it was forbidden to do that. Allain had tried it once, but Orist had chastened him. "It is dangerous," he'd said, but never why.

Then Allain had done it again, in the Prime Forest. He'd been trying to escape some Cothellon soldiers, and he'd thought a projection of himself would do the trick. But the projection had flickered, so he'd made it stronger. And stronger.

And boom, Allain2 was born.

But Lorelei was acting as if it were the easiest thing in the world. What did she know? Had other mages actually done it on purpose? And why did she ask why he'd kept him? As if Allain had any other choice.

Or did he?

Suddenly the shadowmage next to Allain2 started convulsing. Allain2 grabbed the man, holding him down in his gravchair. Spittle was forming around the man's mouth, and he was making strange sounds. The other passengers were looking at them strangely. Allain grew worried—should he do something? But then the shadowmage fainted entirely.

Great. Now he had an insane woman, a comatose shadowmage, and a no-longer-identical twin that was apparently the result of some unexpected magic. And here he was, on the way to a new planet, about to meet a bunch of elves who'd been around for hundreds of thousands of years. What the hell was he doing? Was there some kind of *plan* in all this?

Allain shrunk down in his chair, itching to carve something.

THE TRIP to Valaralda was uneventful, once Quynn got himself calmed down. The food was good, too, although it was a bit spicier than he was accustomed to. They'd had to strap into their seats for the brief period of weightlessness in the middle of the trip, when the spaceship turned around to begin deceleration. The whole thing was disconcerting, but Quynn was proud that he had not been one of the five or so people to vomit during the experience.

Then they'd landed, and the door opened. The woman he thought he'd recognized left before he could get a good look at her, accompanied by that scruffy boy and his two friends. Then it was finally Quynn's turn.

He'd never been so happy to breathe fresh air in all his life.

Quynn followed the shadowy mage into the city. Memories began blossoming in his mind as he saw Ilyrion again for the first time. Wait—he'd been here before! But how? The memories were like shadows, beating on the surface of his mind. He knew they were there, but he couldn't quite see them. How could he possibly have been here before? There must be an explanation.

The city was big, and a lot more picturesque than anything he'd seen on Earth. Graceful curves and sharp angles met sweeping minarets and spindly towers. Sheer glass and slick metal collided with warm wood and rough stone, forming impossibly beautiful combinations. Here and there, massive Prime Trees were integrated right into the architecture of the city, buildings warping and swooping around the wood. He could see the ocean glittering in the distance. Various kinds of vehicles floated silently through the air, and everywhere elves walked or sat or sunned themselves on vast green lawns.

Quynn could see all of this and more from his vantage point on the spaceship landing pad. He stopped, taking it in. Ilyrion was breathtaking and strangely familiar. He still didn't understand how he could have any memories of the place— he himself was only seven hundred years old, give or take a few decades.

The gray man had stopped to let him look at the city, but now he became impatient, motioning for to Quynn to follow. Quynn was hesitant, but he decided to oblige. He'd gone too far to stop now. There must be *something* interesting at the end of all of this.

The strange man led him under the city, through a hidden hatchway and into a series of tunnels. It reminded him of the Under in New San Francisco. That city held secrets, and Ilyrion was no different. Quynn had always found that the most interesting things lay just underneath reality. He felt himself growing excited.

They walked through tunnels and halls, under doors and bridges. They must have walked for miles, and then they had to board a train and travel even further. Finally they got to where they were going, and Quynn found himself awed.

It was one of the most incredible rooms he had ever seen.

"Quynn," the man said. It was the first time he'd said anything after letting him out of his cell. "Welcome to Memory."

TWENTY-FOUR

"IS CARIEL GOING TO BE OKAY?" Rylan asked. "What happened?"

Mirra had paused in her story about Cariel. She was fiddling with one of the little Trees in the window. It looked like she was caressing the leaves. How could she be so calm after such an intense story? Rylan found himself anxious. Had Cariel been raped? Did she escape?

Mirra turned towards him slowly. Her face was hard to make out, but he could see a grin slowly widening on her lips.

"So ya *do* like da story!" she said.

Next to him, Dill shifted on his stool. "Are you sure this story is...appropriate?" he asked.

"This be a story about *life*," Mirra said, walking over to her rickety old stove. She had an odd walk, as if she had rehearsed the steps. She fumbled about, pulling out a pot and filling it with water from the sink. She placed the pot on the stove and turned it on before turning back to them. "Does *life* be appropriate?"

Dill frowned. "It's just that...it seems pretty violent. There are children here."

"You think I've never seen rape before?" Rylan asked.

Dill stopped cold. "Never in my Crew," he said, his voice quiet. "Never under my watch."

"In case you've forgotten," Rylan said, "I wasn't *in* your Crew."

"Did you ever..." Dill started, but then he seemed to think better of it.

"What?" Rylan asked. "Did I what? Rape anyone?"

Dill nodded soberly.

"Shit, no," Rylan said. "What do I look like, some kind of animal? But I saw it. Oh, yes, I saw it a few times, when I couldn't look away. Maybe if you'd paid more attention to the other Crews, you'd have noticed it. The Under is a harder place than you think."

Dill's face was almost blank. "You have no idea what I think," he said, his voice flat. "You don't know what I know. You weren't the first child born in the Under."

It took Rylan a minute to realize Dill's blankness was a mask for pain.

"You still miss Phoenix," he said.

Dill nodded.

"I miss her too."

"Hush now, chillens," Mirra said, and they turned to her. Steam was escaping from the pot on the stove. "Let ol' Mirra finish da story."

Rylan's stomach grumbled.

BLACK
   blood pain
   slash
   harsh claws.

THE FIGHTING and the surging will to breathe
    alone
    unaided
    so afraid. The harsh
    wet wind of purple slumber and
    the black deep claws
    and the red of leaves
    and darkness.
    Darkness.

CARIEL COULDN'T SEE. Everything hurt. Everything, but especially her eyes. She rolled over, retching on what she imagined was the ground. Her face was stinging, and she felt something wet dripping down her nose. Everything was black.

She tried to open her eyes.

Failed.

She turned her head, frantically trying to look up, right, left—*anywhere*.

She tried—*hard*—to open her eyes. But they wouldn't open.

Panic rising.

She stared upwards, feeling blood, feeling passion, feeling shame. She'd only been trying to *help*. She'd only been trying to get them to *stop*.

She'd only been trying to *see*.

Useless. Her eyes, her face. Useless. She cast about, striking the ground with her hands, feeling dry earth, worms, wood, bugs. *Feeling*, but not seeing. She lay back, hurting, trying not to make a sound.

Then she felt something else—wet—against her cheek.

Tears.

HOURS PASSED. Maybe days. Maybe years.

Cariel got to her feet. The world shook in her mind, but she couldn't see it happen. She could only stand, and step, and stand, keeping her balance as best she could. The stumble, the pain became too much.

She retched again. The sound was strangely loud, liquid bile and hot meat splattering on the flat ground.

She heard a buzzing sound in her ears. It was in her head, that buzzing sound—sharp, incessant, insistent. It was blood, buzzing in her veins, splitting through her brain. It was sweat, cracking from her legs, dropping from the trees.

Or it was bugs.

Bekal, swarming, biting, feeding. Bugs and bugs, in her mouth, in her ears, sliding up her nose and flying and swirling and flitting and—she spit them out, trying again to open her fucking eyes.

But the rylak had *killed* her eyes.

The rylak, with their claws and their fur and their cocks—they'd destroyed any chance she'd had at seeing again.

Faintness overtook her, the sweltering jungle overcoming her body. Blood and tears and spit she'd given: and now she was nothing but meat for the bekal flies to harvest. Nothing but hot, red meat and hair and skin.

She wept again, her face buried in the mud. The river she'd crawled to. It felt cool against her naked skin. It felt strong, like a rainforest after a storm.

She never wanted to cry again.

HUNGRY.

She was hungry. Twins, she was hungry. She gloried in the feeling, exulting in the pain of her stomach.

For it had finally overtaken the pain in her eyes.

But now Cariel had a real problem: she was blind and alone in the Kalmansa Wilds, a deadly jungle. She was defenseless. Scared.

And *blind*. Twins damn it! *Blind*.

She'd just been trying to refill the skondul. She'd just been —fuck it. Stop. Stop thinking of what had been. Stop thinking of the wretched rylak and their wretched claws.

She could hear their growls, even now. She could hear their *words*. She could feel them inside her, feel them slashing her face.

But she'd never be able to see them again.

Good fucking riddance.

The river water was brackish in her mouth, but she drank it anyway. There must have been a backflow from the Kaja Ocean, to the south. It wasn't that bad. It wasn't enough to kill her, she thought. She hoped.

The water felt good.

The blood had dried on her face. Her eyes were swollen and gone: sliced beyond recognition. She knew that now. She could feel it. She could feel the anger burning in her soul. She could feel the hatred for the beasts that had done it—the beasts that had been drunk, and violent, and stupid. The rylak had no regard for the elves. No regard whatsoever.

Cariel vowed, in that moment, to repay the sentiment.

TWENTY-FIVE

TREY'S BUTT hurt from all the bouncing. They hadn't wanted to spend the money to hire a gravcar all the way out to Errenmel, so they'd had to settle for an old-fashioned horse-drawn cart. The animals weren't quite the same as horses on Earth: they were larger, with thick lower legs and wide, flat faces. They didn't look especially friendly, but they pulled the cart well.

The cart itself wasn't much to speak of. It was made of wood, with plain wooden seats that were terribly uncomfortable. The driver had gone on and on about his horses, George and Bessie. Trey thought it awfully strange that a driver in Ilyrion would use names like that, but he brushed it aside. There were plenty of stranger things to worry about.

Lashel didn't seem bothered by the cart. He was staring at the passing countryside with rapt attention. Trey envied the man's curiosity.

Arra looked disgruntled, bouncing along on the wooden bench next to Trey. She had agreed to come along, but she looked like she was beginning to regret her decision. Trey reached out and took her hand.

"I'm glad you're doing this with me," he said.

"I lived there too, you know."

Trey squeezed her hand. "I know."

But the memories were murky. He had flashes of time spent together in their house, time spent arguing in the Senate. But he couldn't remember anything from before. How had they met? What was their life like before they'd been married? Pieces of the puzzle were falling into place, but it wasn't yet enough.

They passed the time silently, watching the hills and trees roll by. Despite the rough ride, Trey found himself growing drowsy.

"WAKE *UP!*" Alleria whispered, shaking Tarathiel's shoulder roughly. He started awake.

"Sorry," he grunted, looking around blearily.

He was in the Senate chamber, sitting at the desk he'd been given next to Alleria. The Senate was in session, and they'd been debating his motion for hours.

He was growing dreadfully tired of it.

Selenia—the senator from Thesserial, the city right next to the Thesserin Desert—had the floor. She was pacing up and down the aisle, her signature blonde braid swishing back and forth as she moved. Selenia was powerful; her influence within the Senate was startling. It paid to pay attention to what she said, or at least that's what Alleria always told him. Tarathiel had never quite figured out *why* she was so important, though.

He was never very good with politics.

"Fellow Senators," Selenia was saying, "we've argued this to death. None of us can prove that the Fall is real. If it's some kind of entity out in space, our long-range telescopes aren't strong enough to detect it yet. And if it's something else, well —it might be even harder to find, much less understand."

She was walking down the rows of desks as she talked, looking straight ahead. She had a curious habit of touching every desk as she went by.

"But let's assume, for the sake of the argument, that the Fall is a real phenomenon, that it means to do us great harm. How do we know that this Defense Mechanism exists? How do we know where it is, what it will do?"

Tarathiel ground his teeth. He wasn't allowed to speak up while she said her peace—all he could do was listen and fume.

There wasn't *time* for any of this.

"It is true," Selenia continued, "that during the centuries following the Great Awakening, there was great power on Valaralda. One could argue that the elves during that time were capable of creating a device such as this. They could have known about the Fall. They could have prepared us for this eventuality."

She reached the end of the row and turned, coming back the other way, tapping each desk as she passed. Her long, blonde hair was tied back in that braid she always wore, looking like a trio of serpents ready to pounce. Her eyes were a kind of strange milky gray.

"But why, we must ask, has that information been lost? Why was it hidden in the desert, under the sands? When Tarathiel found it, the words were written in a long-forgotten language, a language only the ancient priests of Akhenaten understood, few of which survive to this day. A language of pictures. Most of his work is a result of this translation."

Selenia turned, almost facing him, but not quite. She was looking past him, at the back of the room.

"But how," Selenia continued, "do we know that Tarathiel made the correct translation? How do we verify the veracity of his work? These, and more, are the questions we must ask before we can allow this vote to pass. Thank you."

Her argument finished, she headed back to her seat, tapping each desk that she passed.

"Senator Selenia," Leriaar said, "thank you for your words. Next, we will hear from Senator Cresius."

Selenia passed by Alleria's desk, and suddenly Alleria moaned in pain. Tarathiel looked at her with concern. She was hunched over, clutching her heart. Tarathiel stood, but Selenia was there first, her arm around Alleria.

"Are you okay, my dear?" she asked.

Alleria straightened, her breath coming easier. "Yes," she said. "Yes, I think so. Thank you for your concern."

"Make sure to drink lots of water," Selenia said.

"I will."

Selenia turned and left, tapping her way up the row of desks, braid twitching faithfully.

"What was that?" Tarathiel asked, leaning over Alleria. The other Senators hadn't noticed her episode, or were ignoring it. Cresius had begun to speak near the front of the room, but Tarathiel ignored him.

"I'm fine," Alleria whispered. "Just a little pain in my chest. It's gone now. I feel a little weak, but I'll be fine. Probably just need some food."

"When did you eat last?"

"Shh," Alleria said. "Listen to the debate. We need to know how to respond."

Tarathiel returned to his seat, frowning. He hoped she wasn't getting sick. The debate was not going well—there were just too many weaknesses, too many holes in his research. He should have waited until he'd developed airtight evidence of his claims. He should have had a second translation done, or a third. But did they have time for that? He shook his head, still tuning out Cresius. No, he'd done the best he could. Now it was up to the Senate, to Alleria's political skills.

He hoped it would be enough to save the world.

TWENTY-SIX

"TREY, WAKE UP. WE'RE HERE."

Alleria's voice was speaking to him. Trey opened his eyes and saw her there, looking down at him. The sun was streaming through her hair, her lips quirked in a slight frown. She was radiant.

"Come on."

Trey sat up painfully. "Ow," he said, stretching his neck from side to side. It hurt like hell.

"Serves you right for sleeping on this thing."

The Senate was gone, swept away like the dregs of a dream. They had finally arrived in Errenmel, the town of his birth. The town he and Alleria had lived in, before the Sending.

Memories flooded back to him, but the experience was different this time. It didn't feel like a vision or a flashback— the memories were just there, once again taking up space in his mind. It was a comfort to know they were there.

Errenmel was small and quaint, full of character. Beautiful houses formed the town proper, old buildings made of wood and stone, meticulously maintained over tens of thousands of years. Roofs were thatched or made from clay tiles. Windows were ornate, set in cast iron frames or built directly into the stonework.

Elves walked here and there, making their slow way along the streets. A few carts rolled along, their drivers nodding a greeting to everyone they passed. A dog barked in the distance. Birds chirped. It reminded him of the villages he used to read about in all those fantasy novels—except this was the real thing.

There was a church in the center of town, a towering, three-story building. The church featured tall stained glass windows along the front, depicting the Twins: one black Tree entwined with one gold Tree, their branches reaching outward upon a field of purple and green. Trey could remember going to that church as a child. He'd liked it there.

Trey's gaze moved outward, to where the houses thinned, fanning out and dotting the countryside. Farms covered the hills, a patchwork quilt of crops. Everything was green and golden and fresh and vibrant. Trey remembered loving it here.

It had been so long.

"It's beautiful," Arra said.

"Do you remember any of this?" Trey asked.

Arra shook her head sadly. "I feel like the memories are there, underneath the surface somewhere. But they won't unlock."

"You'll get them back. I know you will."

"I hope so."

The cart stopped, and everyone got out. "It's this way," Lashel said. Trey and Arra followed, hand in hand.

When they got there, the house was exactly as he remembered. The walls were brick, with wooden tiles on the steeply-sloped roof. Small windows poked out here and there, little metal strips separating the glass into grids. There was a flower garden out front, and a beautiful wooden door with a little arch on top, cut right into the brick. Smoke was coming out of the chimney at the back of the house. It was all delightfully low-tech.

"Reminds me of Sylrantheas," Arra said to him as they walked up the curving path to the front door.

"This was our home," Trey said. "Do you remember it?"

Arra shook her head. "Not really. A few fleeting memories, but nothing concrete. It feels like someone else's life."

"I wish I could help bring it back for you."

"Well, you can't."

"It's still a cute house, after all these years. Amazing they've kept it this well maintained."

"There's more technology here than meets the eye," Lashel said. "Most of the house has probably been replaced with synthetic materials by now."

"At least it doesn't look it," Trey said.

"Indeed."

"Do you know who lives here now?"

Lashel consulted the little leather-bound notebook he always had with him. "Family by the name of Eveningfall," he said. "Kids grown and gone. It's just the husband and wife now. They've lived here for five hundred years, give or take."

"Sounds like a lovely couple," Arra said.

"Do they know we're coming?" Trey asked.

"They do," Lashel said. "I called ahead. They sounded excited to meet you."

"Let's hope we live up to their expectations."

He knocked on the wooden door, the sound bringing back memories. They had used to love entertaining guests here, he remembered. The breeze brought the scent of lavender as they waited.

The door creaked open, and a friendly-looking elf appeared. He was wearing a brown knit sweater and pants, a small pair of glasses perched on his nose. He looked 700, maybe 800—Trey's gauge of elven age was still a bit shaky.

"Hi," Trey said. No need for a formal greeting, he hoped. "My name is Trey, and this is Arra. We used to live here, long ago."

"Greetings," the man said, making the sign of the Twins and bowing slightly. "My name is Laurenar. Please, come in."

They stepped inside. It was darker indoors, and it smelled of cherry wood and old varnish. Laurenar led them down a hall and into the living room. It was like walking through a memory. Trey kept seeing shadows of things on the walls, faces and pictures. Laughter ringing, the sound of silverware clinking on porcelain.

Arra caught his mood and smiled at him as they sat on a soft leathery couch. "Our house was beautiful," she said.

"They've made some improvements." Trey's head was filled with a kind of double vision; memories colliding with the here and now.

Laurenar had a worried look on his face. "You okay?" he asked.

Lashel replied first. "Trey and Arra have recently been through a high-powered Sending," he said. "Their memories are fragmented."

"I'm so sorry," Laurenar said. "That must be terrible."

"Have you ever been through a gate?" Trey asked.

Laurenar looked shocked. "Why would I ever want to do such a thing?"

"Never mind."

A lovely older woman entered the room, carrying a tray of drinks. Her graying hair was braided, and she was wearing little earrings that made a tinkling sound as she moved.

"Tea?" she asked, setting the tray down.

"Thank you, dear," Laurenar said. "My wife, Naevys."

Trey stood, giving a traditional greeting: the sign of the Twins, two fingers crossed together, and a slight bowing of the head. "Thank you so much for having us, Naevys," he said. "My name is Trey—Tarathiel, originally. This is my wife —er, I'm sorry. This is Arra." He hoped Arra wouldn't be too offended by the slip. "And this is Lashel, from the University."

"We spoke on the phone," Lashel said.

"Pleased to meet you all," Naevys said, returning the sign of the Twins. "Who would like tea?"

They all said they would, and Naevys set about pouring it. Trey could have gone for some good coffee, or even some bourbon, but you couldn't get any of that on Valaralda. So he munched on candied chestnuts—he was sure they weren't called chestnuts here, but they tasted the same—and drank the hot herbal tea. Something about the smell of the tea triggered another cascade of memories, and he lost touch with reality for a long moment. When he came back to himself, Arra was regaling them with tales of Earth.

"It sounds delightful, dear," Naevys said. "I'd like to visit, someday."

"You must go to Pano Sylrantheas," Arra said. "The redwood forest is incredible."

"I'd like that very much."

"So, Trey," Laurenar said, "what brings you here? I suppose you'd like to get a look at the rest of the house?"

Trey nodded. "The University lost my research," he said, "and they won't give me my job back. It was Lashel's idea to visit. Maybe he thought we'd find something here. I don't know."

"I thought it might be helpful with your gatesickness," Lashel said. "Is it?"

"Yes," Trey said, at the same time Arra said "No." They looked at each other.

"We can go," Trey said to her.

"No," Arra said, "stay as long as you like. I would love another cup of tea while you boys do your thing." She was avoiding him, avoiding his face. He knew her well enough to know that something was wrong. He'd have to tackle that later.

"I'll take the tour," Trey said, standing.

Laurenar took them out back first, going through the kitchen and then through a sliding glass door. Trey hadn't seen a backyard ever in his recent life. It struck him as wrong: shouldn't there be another building here, or a road? But gradually, other versions of himself integrated in. He'd had other houses, even farms. An actual castle at one point in feudal England. That took him by surprise—it was the first time he'd remembered *anything* from before New San Francisco.

"Need a moment?" Laurenar asked, eyes full of concern.

Trey was gasping, trying to get a handle on everything. The people he'd been—they were so distant, so murky. Then it all went blank somewhere around the 1800s.

Trey stumbled, had to lean on Laurenar for support.

He remembered dying now. He'd—oh, God—he'd been shot in active duty during the War of 1812. It had been somewhere up in the American-Canadian frontier, and he'd been shot dead by an elf over a matter of fifty cents. It hadn't even been related to the damn war at all. The coward had waited until they were outdoors. He'd gotten Trey out under some false pretense, and shot him in the forest where nobody would find him.

What a dick.

But if he could remember that, how was he still alive? His

head started hurting. Something had happened after that, something involving a tree. But that part was blurry, still.

"...get him to a doctor," Lashel was saying.

"I can help carry him," Laurenar said.

"No," Trey said, trying to straighten and mostly failing. "I'm fine."

It was clear the other men didn't believe him, but Trey persisted anyway. He wasn't going to faint—not here. He thought he might throw up, but decided against it.

"Can we go inside?" he asked. Maybe it had been the lawn and the trees around it. Maybe they'd put something in the tea.

Laurenar led them back inside. "Still want the tour?" he asked.

Trey's head was feeling better, if only a bit. He'd go lie down when this was over, but for now he wanted to see it through. This house was unlocking more memories than he'd ever expected.

He wondered if he would survive the trip.

"Yes," he said, hearing the cowardice in his voice.

Apart from the living room and kitchen, there was a hall and three rooms and a bathroom. Room number one was Alleria and dressmaking, her hobby of the year, one year. That didn't stick—she'd traded in the dresses for a bow and arrow after that, impressing Tarathiel with her physical forti-tude. She'd trained hard on that bow; she'd loved it. But it didn't stick either, not for long. She'd cleared the room many times over the years, trading one thing for another, always interested in something new. She was like that, then.

She was still like that.

Room two was lovemaking, a great large bed with lace pillows—her idea of a joke that they hadn't gotten around to changing yet. Big windows looked out on the yard, out west where the sun would set every night and they'd lie there together after dinner, content in each other's arms.

Trey wasn't even seeing the real house now, with its real things. He was living in memories, lost to the here and now.

Laurenar took them to the last room, the room at the back of the house. The one with the little quirky window that was too high up, that looked out on the raised street above where neighborhood kids used to play and once a goat stayed there all day and ate all the grass in front of the window. Tarathiel had sat there watching it eat, contemplating goat things. Alleria had had to pull him away when it came time for dinner. She was always doing that, pulling him out of his studies when it had been too long, seeing to his needs. His mind was always off thinking big things, while hers was focused on the task at hand: hunting, or gardening, or any of a thousand other things she did.

Did they ever do anything *together*? Tarathiel had always thought they would. He'd thought marriage would be like an endless game of house, or dress-up, with the world as a plaything. But he was no good at playing with things. He was too serious, too focused on his projects, too wrapped up in theories and speculation.

They'd had the outdoors together, in the earlier days. Tarathiel hadn't always been a bookworm. Before his fateful dig under the tomb, before his translation of the ancient texts written by the Moon God, Akhenaten; before his discovery of the Fall, Tarathiel had been a very different person. They'd camped together under the stars, or fished, or taken a sailboat out on the lake. They'd tried archery together, he remembered, before she had really tried to master it. They'd drank and laughed and danced and played. He remembered romping through a field of grain. Playing with the cat her parents had. Running up a bill at the tavern with her, singing along badly with that band, Leaf Strip.

He'd lost her in here, in this office, first. He'd lost himself, but it amounted to the same thing. Then he lost the woman too, lost her for good, and it had taken twenty thousand fucking years to find her again.

She was still somewhere in there, in her head or his.

He hadn't found the key to unlocking her.

He leaned on Tarathiel's desk, which wasn't a desk at all, but actually a bookshelf. His mind broke apart, the pieces flying off into space. Trey felt hot tears in his eyes as he tried to put it back together, grasping at remembrances and feelings and things.

The bookshelf was a desk, and the room was his prison. He'd ended the world from this very room, before he knew what he had done.

He grabbed a handful of books, suddenly wrenching them from the shelf, scattering them along the floor. He was heedless of the hands grasping at him, the voices shouting for him to stop. Salty tears fell down his cheeks as he reached through the shelf to the wall beyond. They were really pulling at him now. He had gone mad; he was insane. He touched a certain spot on the wall, not even knowing what he was doing, just running on memories. A compartment opened, creaking outwards like the door of a tomb.

Trey stood, tears drying on his face, as Laurenar and Lashel stopped struggling. They each had one of his arms, but they no longer pulled at him.

Their mouths were open.

Inside the hidden compartment was a thick, dusty book. It had wooden covers and an engravement on the front, carefully labeled in the way Tarathiel had always done it during his time at the Anthropological Society.

Study Journal
of Tarathiel Riverbow
vol. 23; started 29 Gwirith, 79983 AA

"Twins," Lashel breathed. "Do you know what this *is*?"

"It's one of my journals," Trey said.

Obviously.

"If this is what I think it is," Lashel said, "it contains your original research on the Fall. No one but you has ever seen this before."

"Will it help?"

"It'll do more than help. It'll get you back into the Society."

"I guess that's good."

"Good?" Lashel was beside himself.

But Trey was still reeling with emotion. That world—his life—it had been so *near*, so immediate. And yet it had been so long ago. Twenty thousand years. How could anyone remember that long? How could you *exist* that long? His life back then was but a dim memory, if he could remember it at all. Trey couldn't reconcile it, didn't know how to integrate the thoughts. It was everything and nothing, truth and false-hood and life and death all wrapped up together.

But he had his journal now. His twenty-third journal, the one that contained his most critical discoveries. Now he could re-read his thoughts. Now he could resume his research. Now he could find the Defense Mechanism, and save this sorry planet from a threat none of them wanted to believe existed.

It was all on him.

The end of the world was nearer now. Might as well see it through.

PART
FOUR

The defeat of the weapon and its two bearers brought about the largest transition this world has ever known. Called the Great Awakening, it was the dawn of culture and the dawn of magic: the Second Age.

There were those who resisted the change, who were terrified of this new power that suddenly pervaded the world. These dissidents cried out against the use of magic, claiming that it was born of evil, that it would cause a greater evil still. Yet they were soon silenced by the marching of time. For who can deny the great pleasures and progress that the Awakening wrought?

Look unto Ilyrion, that shining jewel of the south. Look unto it with joy—for we have Awakened.

Introduction from
    "Dawn of an Empire"
    by Iliaster Magnus,
    High Historian,
    Ilyrion Council of Mages
    18401 A.A.

TWENTY-SEVEN

ELANIL CONTINUED through the gauntlet of Trees.

She wasn't hungry or tired, even though she must have been in this place for what—hours? Days? Her wrists hurt from when she had fallen, when the voice from the sky had shouted *enough!* and she had been thrown to the ground. But that was the only pain she'd felt in this place, so far.

She encountered eight more Trees, answering their questions as she went. Each Tree was a different type, each one representing one half of the seven woodpairs. So the pattern was clear: she would be forced to pass through fourteen Trees before she was finished. There were other Trees along the gauntlet—hundreds of them—but only some of them blocked her way, challenging her with a poem.

There was no going backward. Every time she went a few feet further, Trees moved into position behind her. They were dour-looking, tightly placed, with barely enough room to squeeze by. She had thought about trying, but something kept her from it. When she looked into the darkness between the Trees, she thought she could see death itself.

And so she continued ever onward, heading toward the black and gold Trees at the end of the path. She caught glimpses of them from time to time, through breaks in the leaves. They didn't scare her as they once had, even though she was pretty sure one of them had spoken to her earlier, throwing her to the ground. She should fear them, but she did not. Perhaps someone was trapped inside of them, too. Someone who was tired and sad, who just wanted to go home.

Someone like her.

Each of the Trees she spoke with had a different poem in a different form. The words were meaningless to her, but there were many similarities. Most of them spoke of souls and binding, of memories and death. One mentioned a Key, another a weapon in the sky. Elanil tried to remember the things they said. Perhaps it would come in handy later.

She was approaching the eleventh Tree when she saw something new: another person! She started running, joy overcoming her. She was no longer alone in this cursed place!

But something was wrong. The person—a woman, by the looks of it—was stuck in something. She was struggling. As Elanil stepped forward, she felt her stomach wrench.

The person in front of her was more than just trapped—it looked like she was being *eaten* by a Tree. The woman's legs were gone already, subsumed by the wood. She was hammering the trunk with her fists, screaming and crying. Her chest heaved and her hair flew wildly as she struggled, but it was no good. She was already halfway gone, consumed by the dark wood.

Elanil picked up speed, running toward the hapless woman. As she got nearer, the woman turned to look at her.

Elanil screamed.

It was her mother! Melenora, her dear, sweet mother, was in front of her, being eaten alive by a monstrous Tree.

"Mother!" Elanil cried. "What happened? Why are you here?"

Tears were streaming down Melenora's face. She looked haggard, scared. Elanil grabbed her hands, trying to pull her out of the tree.

"My Elanil," Melenora said, her voice weak. "Oh, no. Not you, too. Not you." She wept.

Elanil pulled and pulled, but her mother was stuck. She grabbed the trunk, trying to feel where it connected to her mother's legs, but the join was seamless.

"What happened?" Elanil asked, scratching the bark, trying to break it apart.

"I strayed from the path," Melenora said. She had ceased her struggling. As Elanil watched, her mother sank another inch into the trunk.

"No!" Elanil screamed. "Let her go!"

She scratched and scraped, her hands raw and bleeding, but it was no use. The Tree would not let go.

"Speak to me!" she shouted at the Tree. "Ask me your question!"

But the Tree was silent. Melenora watched her with sad eyes. "If you're here," she said, "it means you're dead."

Elanil was crying now. She sank to the ground in front of Melenora, unable to think of anything else to do.

"Oh, my poor baby," Melenora said. "Do not cry for me. We are both dead, here, but you must continue. Do not be caught like I was! You are so close!"

"I can get you out," Elanil said, sobbing. "I know it!"

She got to her knees and started pounding on the roots of the Tree. She felt little flashes of pain in her mind with every hit.

"You must go on," Melenora said. Tears were streaming down her face. "Go on for me, my darling. Live for me. I will be alright here. I'll be safe in the Tree."

"No!" Elanil screamed. "You'll be trapped forever!"

She fumbled in her pockets, hoping to find some prime-wood. Maybe she could destroy the Tree with magic, push it over or break it in half. But there was no wood in her pockets. She was powerless.

"It is too late for me," Melenora said softly. "Go, my daughter. Live. Survive." Her expression turned fierce. "Live to destroy the bastards that did this to me!"

"I will not leave you!" Elanil cried.

She stood, leaning forward and placing her hand against the Tree trunk. She would get her mother out. She would kill this Tree, kill it and free her mother. Then they would get out of this accursed place. Together.

She quested with her mind, trying to find the eye in the Tree. Maybe she could reason with it, or threaten it. But there was no soul in the Tree that she could find. Not yet. And suddenly she understood.

Her *mother* was the soul in the Tree. Or she would be, soon, if she wasn't freed.

Elanil felt bitter anger burn through her. Her mind turned, focusing on the material of the Tree, concentrating on the wood. She could see the latticework of cells with her mind, feel how they connected and chained, forming a prison for her mother's soul.

A soulprison.

And Elanil knew that she could break the prison, if she just twisted her mind like so—

NO.

It was the same voice as before. It felt like it was speaking directly to her mind, making her head hurt with its power. This time there was no blow, no force throwing her to the ground. But the voice was just as strong, just as commanding.

Just as malevolent.

"Who are you?" Elanil shouted at the sky. "Let my mother go!"

IT IS TOO LATE FOR HER.

Elanil felt coldness enter her heart.

"Then I will free her myself," she said, and she *twisted* her mind.

YOU WILL NOT.

Elanil was suddenly flung backwards. She flew through the air for dozens of feet, landing on the hard ground in a crumple of limbs. Pain flashed all over her body, and she screamed.

"No!" she cried, struggling to get to her feet.

But up ahead, the Tree was accelerating, consuming her mother's body inch by inch.

"No!" Elanil screamed again, but it was too late.

Melenora's body was nearly gone. She looked at Elanil with sadness in her eyes. "Do great things, my daughter," she said, and then she was swallowed and gone.

Gone.

Elanil screamed and thrashed, pounding the ground in anger, tears rolling down her face. Her mother was gone. Imprisoned by a Tree. And she had been unable to save her.

"Why?" she sobbed toward the sky. "Why did you do this?"

COME FORWARD, LITTLE ONE.

She will make an excellent subject, yes!

A new voice had spoken, piercing into her brain. It felt like needles in her mind, like sleet in a winter storm. Elanil rose shakily, her crying done. Anger took its place, filling her bones, firming her step. Whatever was going on here, whatever force had taken her mother, Elanil knew that these voices were somehow responsible. If they wanted her to come forward, she would do so.

And she would destroy them.

TWENTY-EIGHT

ALLAIN STEPPED OFF THE SHIP, Lorelei in tow. She'd eaten and used the restroom just fine during the trip. She seemed normal, until you tried to talk to her. Then you could see that her mind was vacant. Ruined.

They stepped out into a beautiful, sunlit day. The vast city of Ilyrion spread out before them, spires and arches and towers almost glistening with reflected light. Allain found himself gaping. He'd never seen anything like it before in his life. Even Allain2 was impressed—he was actually smiling. The expression looked strange on him.

The Trees were the best part of Ilyrion. Allain could spot four of them from his vantage point high up on the space transport platform. They were integrated right into the city, buildings and bridges looping around the wood. It was remarkable. It was no Eiffel Tower, but it was remarkable just the same.

Lorelei stood beside him stoically, unmoved by the city. She was muttering something under her breath, something about the Fall. Allain2 was hanging on to the shadowmage they'd captured in the Under. The gray-robed man was capable of walking just fine, but he never said anything approaching intelligence.

This is what it had come to. Allain was surrounded by insane people.

"So," Allain2 said, "why did we come here, again?"

"This guy," Allain said, pointing at the shadowmage. "He kept talking about Ilyrion. Plus Grime got us a free trip. Might as well see where the elves came from, right?"

Allain2 grunted. "Might as well. So, big leader, we're here. Now what?"

Allain had no idea. He probably should have thought things through a bit more before jumping on an interplanetary spaceship, but forethought had never really been one of his strong points. He had hoped the shadowmage would point the way, but he wasn't doing anything.

Someone was approaching. It was a man in a gray robe; he was heading right for them, ignoring all the other disembarking passengers. The guy's head was shaved and he had a belt around his waist, black with bits of gold in it. Allain compared him to the shadowmage they'd brought with them. The two men's outfits and hair style were similar, but their faces were different. Not clones, then. Not this time.

Nevertheless, he steeled himself for a fight.

The new man smiled as he approached. "Greetings," he said, holding his hand out in the human custom. "My name is Lionar. I see you've found another one of us. Thank you for bringing him back safely."

Allain shook the man's hand tentatively. He felt something crinkle in his palm, and a leaf fell to the ground as he released his grip.

He ignored it.

"This man attacked us," Allain said, gesturing to the captive shadowmage. "We want to know why."

"Oh, dear," Lionar said. "I feared as much. Some of our members have become...lost, of late. When Mar—forgive me, Earth—entered our system, they just snapped. It's been quite the job rounding them up. I do hope he wasn't too much trouble."

"He almost killed dozens of us."

"That *is* terrible," Lionar said. "I assure you, his actions will be appropriately dealt with. Was anyone hurt?"

"We're fine," Allain2 said. "Who *are* you people?"

Lionar smiled. "We are an ancient order of priests and mages, worshippers of the Twins."

"Does your group have a name?"

"We do, indeed! We are called the Eglaria. Our order has existed for a hundred thousand years."

"And do your members always go around shooting people?"

"Of course not," Lionar said. "We are a peaceful order. We deeply regret the actions of the few, and hope it does not reflect upon our order as a whole. But tell me: who are you?"

"I'm Allain2," Allain2 said.

"A very interesting name," Lionar said, shaking Allain2's hand and turning back to Allain. "So you must be Allain."

Allain hadn't given the man his name yet. How had he known? Allain2 and him didn't look anything alike anymore. There was no way he could have known that they were magical clones of each other.

Lionar seemed to sense his confusion. "I felt it when I shook your hands," he said, holding one of his hands out, palm upward. He was holding a maple leaf. Allain instantly recognized it as a leaf from a Prime Tree. It had a distinctive look—more vibrant, more colorful.

"What is the leaf for?" Allain asked. He had only thought

the *wood* of a Prime Tree was useful. He'd never considered the leaves might have some power.

"It allows me to see into your soul," Lionar said. "An ability passed down by the Eglaria over the generations. We call it soulspecting."

"And what do you see?"

"I see a soulsplinter that is decaying rapidly." He pointed at Allain2. "You two used to look alike, did you not?"

"We did," Allain said. "Exactly alike."

"Yes. Over time, the connection worsens. Why do you leave the splinter in place?"

"Do we have a choice?"

"You happened upon it by accident, then. I see." He giggled as if it were the funniest thing he'd heard in a while.

"Can you put us back together?" Allain2 asked.

"Only *you* can do that," Lionar said. "But I haven't met this lovely lady yet! Tell me, what is your name?"

He reached out to shake Lorelei's hand. Allain could clearly see a Prime Leaf in his hand—Lionar wasn't trying to hide it. He grasped Lorelei's hand warmly, peering into her eyes. She looked back at him, but didn't respond.

"Oh, dear," Lionar said. "Oh, dear, dear me. This poor woman is suffering from extreme soulblinding. What in the names of the Twins has been done to her?"

"We found her like this," Allain said. "We were hoping someone here could help her."

"Oh, we can, we can. Come. It just so happens that my order is very skilled with this sort of thing. It is fortuitous that we met today. I will take you to our facilities, and we will see what can be done."

This was all a little too convenient. Allain found himself skeptical—Lionar had clearly expected them to be here, arriving in this ship. How had he known? And what did he want with them? The shadowmage they'd captured in the Under had said he wanted Lorelei. Could it be that by bringing her here to Valaralda, he was playing right into their hands?

Allain was suddenly sure that Lionar wasn't telling them the whole truth. This thing with the leaves—soulspecting—it made him nervous. He didn't like someone prying into his soul. What other things had the man uncovered? How did he know so much?

Lionar must have seen the expression on Allain's face. "I promise you, you'll be perfectly safe."

"I don't believe you," Allain said.

"Neither do I," Allain2 agreed.

Lionar laughed. "Good! Nothing wrong with a little healthy skepticism. Honestly, if you *had* trusted me right away, I would have been concerned."

"So where does that leave us?" Allain asked.

Lionar held up another Prime Leaf—maple, again. "Take it," he said. "Try it on me."

Hesitantly, Allain took the leaf. "What do I do?"

"Soulmagic is all in your mind," Lionar said. "With soulspection, you just need to be touching my skin somewhere, and also be touching a Prime Leaf."

"Does the type of leaf matter?"

"No."

"Will I be able to read your mind?"

"Try it and see."

Allain hesitated. This was a new type of magic, something he'd never heard of before. But hadn't he always wanted to take risks, to work outside the lines? Everyone had always limited him—his father, the Mentors, everyone wanted him to play by the rules. Here was a chance to do something new, something interesting.

He decided to take that chance.

He clasped Lionar's hand, like a human handshake, but with the Prime Leaf between their palms. He held the position, wondering if anything was supposed to be happening. He thought he felt something, something small opening in his mind. But he wasn't sure.

"Now what?" he asked.

"Do you feel it?"

"I think so."

"What do you feel?" Allain2 asked.

"It feels like something—some*one*—else is in my mind. Like a flower waiting to bloom. But that sounds silly."

"Not at all," Lionar said. "It's a very apt description. Now all you need to do is open the flower."

Allain tried to visualize it in his mind. He couldn't see the flower, but he could feel it there, taking up space. Closing his eyes, he Willed the petals to open.

It was as easy as that.

As the flower opened, he felt Lionar's presence blossom in his head. It wasn't the man's thoughts, exactly. It wasn't even really his personality. It was deeper than that. Lower. As if he were peering into the man's very soul. He held his eyes closed as things began to swim into his vision.

He could see it now, Lionar's soul. It was round, like the center of a flower. Allain could see cracks on the soul, like dry mud in the sun. The cracks made a circle in the middle, with branches of cracks leading out from that center, like a pie cut into rough slices. Six slices, and a circle in the middle. It was very strange.

It looked like there was some kind of blight on the soul—black stuff, like mold. There wasn't much of it, and it was mostly centered on one of the pie slices. Allain didn't know what it was, but it didn't look good.

Then something else caught his mind's eye: there was a tendril of some sort, like a green stem, or a rope. It led away from Lionar's soul, gleaming in his brain. Glowing in the dark.

He opened his eyes, and he could still see the green tendril of light, as if it had been burned into his retinas. He tried to look for it, but it faded.

He let out a breath.

"Interesting, isn't it?" Lionar said.

Allain could only nod. He was still trying to come to grips with what he'd just seen. It had felt so strange, and yet so—intimate. He shivered.

"I wish I could go back to my first time," Lionar said, looking wistful.

"I want to try," Allain2 said.

Lionar smiled. "Maybe later. Did you see any reason not to trust me?"

"I have no idea *what* I saw," Allain said. "It was weird, all cracked into pieces."

"The seven Aspects of the soul," Lionar said, as if it were common knowledge.

"What does that mean?"

Lionar laid a hand on Allain's arm. There was no leaf there this time. It was just a kindly gesture, and Allain felt calmed by it.

"I would love to continue this theological discussion," Lionar said. "Perhaps you should consider joining our order. But might I suggest we move to a more hospitable location? The sun out here is getting a bit strong."

He was right—Allain could feel his skin beginning to burn under the bright sunlight. All the other passengers from the spaceship were long gone. Transport officials were looking at them strangely, but they appeared hesitant to interrupt Lionar. Maybe it was the robe he was wearing. They seemed afraid of it.

"You'll be safe," Lionar said.

"I think I believe you," Allain said. He wasn't sure why. Maybe it was the man's vulnerability—it took a great deal of trust to let someone else pry into your soul.

"Why does no one on Earth know about this type of magic?" Allain asked.

"It may be because of the gatesickness. Soulblinding, as my order calls it. Your people, the elves on Earth, they lost a lot of memories during the Sending. They probably forgot all about the ancient soulmagic."

"Or they remembered, but decided to keep it a secret," Allain2 said. Always the optimist.

"That may be the case."

"Okay," Allain said, "but it seems really easy. Can anyone do it?"

"Only Talented mages can perform soulmagic," Lionar said. "And only the Broken Ones—or the highly soulattuned —can access the more advanced forms. But for most, yes. Soulspection is quite easy. If you have a Prime Leaf, you just need to know what to look for."

Most of that hadn't made any sense. "I wonder if anyone ever figures it out by accident," Allain2 asked.

"Like your soulsplinter?"

"I suppose."

Lionar gave him a small smile. "It happens all the time," he said. "All the time."

TWENTY-NINE

CARIEL'S FACE hurt like hell. It was more than just the ruined eyes and the blood. Her forehead was hot, hotter than the jungle. It was a fever. She was sick. This, on top of her wounds, on top of her eyes. On top of her friend getting raped and probably killed.

Svalya had failed them. She had failed them all.

Cariel felt along her body, feeling the cuts and bruises on her naked skin. Nothing seemed to be broken—nothing but her pride and her face. But the fever would probably be the death of her.

And even if not—what? The jungle would kill her, even if she *wasn't* blind. She shuddered to think of the animals, of the insects, of the myriad ways in which she could die. There were wildcats out here, and cavek, and sakul. The bekal flies alone could kill her if they infected her with disease. Maybe they already had.

And she couldn't see.

She couldn't *see*.

How could she live? What could she possibly do to survive? She was weak and blind and starving and feverish.

She was broken, bereft. Her best friend, her only friend, had been destroyed. Her only protector had failed. And now she had nothing and no one.

She was no longer a slave to the rylak. She was instead a slave to the world—to the world and to her eyes.

But she was also angry. She was enraged, through the miasma of pain. She crawled through the mud, feeling sticks and leaves crunching beneath her bare knees. She was naked and alone and blind and *furious*. How dare they do this to her? How dare the rylak treat her kind this way?

What wrong had the elves ever done?

She grasped at grass, lifting it to her mouth, too hungry to care about the taste, about whether it would kill her. She cast about with her hands, flailing on the ground, trying to find something, anything, to eat. She scraped her fingers and her arms as she crawled. She felt bugs and maybe a lizard slithering away from her and underneath her knees. She felt the thickness of the jungle all around her, oppressing her, the weight of it heavy on her soul. She felt adrift, cast into an ocean of night, the only exit the pinpricks of the forest on the floor of her mind.

She couldn't see. But her mind took up the empty spaces, filling them with light from memory and imagination. She saw sparks and flashes, death and rape and wine. She saw claws, fur, masks of teeth bared against the pain. Shelves crashing down around her, the upturn of Tilla's breasts, how the girl's face had just looked, had stared, the light disconnected. The thoughts were distant, puppet-like, whirling about with the shrieks and broken ceramic of the captive night. The rylak were in her ears, her bones, her stomach, her eyes. They were on her tongue, a monster's tongue, and leaves and broken motion could do nothing to prevent the screams and shallow cries.

She was dead. Her Tilla was dead. Her life was dead.

Had been dead.

Had been for some time.

Elves.

Such useless things.

Such pretty things.

Such smooth and pretty, mindless girls, whose backs snapped like the slapping of an hourglass to the floor, a rylak's floor, bamboo and camphor tree, magnolia. Mangrove. Fire.

Fear. Flee. She could flee. She took a step, a fleeting step, a tottered step.

Her eyes a flame.

And the balance of the night moved, shifting at an angle to the sun, and the line of the horizon that was not there turned sideways, became untrue, became a villain, became the ground.

Whirling, tumbling, smoothing limbs and breasts and blood and heat. Fire. Free. Flee. Fall. She could fall. She could fall.

She could fall.

Cariel tumbled from a ravine she could not see. The invisible world whipped by her, speed increasing speed, and when she met the ground it was like a friend, a dear old friend, like Tilla on the ground, like a rylak's cock, a slaver's mouth.

It swallowed up the very last of her senses and she knew no more.

WHEN SHE WOKE, the world was still gone. Her ravaged eyes, her feverish face, her heaving stomach were still there. And she felt new pains, like friends she'd never known, joining with the litany. A twisted arm, a broken toe, a leg that wouldn't move. It couldn't move, because part of it was gone.

And she could feel her blood, feel it seeping out of her pores, from her veins, from her eyes. She could feel life slipping away, and she closed eyes that were not there and

let it go.

Death, the welcomeness of death, overwhelmed her.

And she let it come.

Something wet touched her.

She recoiled as if by accident, her hand jerking away. Her mind refused to jump, refused to stir at the provocation. It was already dead, her mind. She had already moved on.

It touched her again. Wet. Snuffling. Coarse.

Something rough licked her. Licked her hand, over and over. It liked her, or it was eating her. Cariel was past the point of caring. The tongue continued caressing her hand like sandpaper, dredging up the emotions and the fear.

Then she felt fangs on her skin.

She screamed. Felt lungs compress, painful too.

She had nothing left but thoughts now. The whole world was a mystery to her mind, lost to everything but touch and taste and sound and smell. She could feel the sun on her face, hear the bekal and their tiny wings. Taste the mud and salty water, the mushrooms and the ferns. Touch the rough bark of the tree, the sharp leaves beneath her. She could smell the blood, bitter blood, her blood. She could feel the roughness of the tongue and fangs against her skin.

A padded footfall. A rumble in the throat.

A wildcat.

It was there, touching her. It had a meal now. One last spark entered Cariel's mind as she realized that her body could feed something, help something, *be* something. She would die, but this cat would surely survive. Perhaps it would even kill a rylak, if it dared. Perhaps it would exact revenge for poor Tilla and for Cariel's eyes.

Perhaps.

And Cariel's body would go on, living on in nourishment. Perhaps in this fullness of death she would finally learn the purpose of existence. She lay back, awash in pain, and luxuriated in the thought of death's teeth and claws.

But the wildcat did not eat her. It was nuzzling her, teething on her—but not hard enough to break the skin. It didn't want her for a meal? Maybe it was just testing her, feeling her out. Surely soon it would take a nice gnawing bite from her arm, rip the muscle and skin away, carrying with it dirt and blood and tears and pain. Maybe it was biding its time.

Then the large cat rubbed on her, cheek hair and whiskers plump and coarse. The motion disturbed her arm, pushed it sideways and down. Her mind leapt, springing at invisible shadows.

She was dead. Surely she was dead? But the wildcat was so warm, so loving. Her synapses connected for one brief moment, drawing muscles closed, pushing arm and hand alive for one small second, reaching up and clutching the only thing she had. The only thing that was there for her in this warm, wet wilderness.

The cat.

It met her halfway, head grazing her fingers, butting firmly into her palm. She held her hand there as the cat moved, burrowing its fur through her fingers. She clutched at it weakly, feeling the life in this invisible creature. She pressed her hand into its head, its body, feeling the blood and warmth and rumbling purring it made. The cat was her only connection to the real world. The only companion she had. The only life in this lonely place.

She reached for it, not with her hands, but with her heart and mind. She needed its warmth, its soul. She needed a friend out there in the jungle. Her own soul leapt forward, lunging to meet this friend, this cat in the mire. She couldn't see, but she could feel its presence, its being, its spirit.

Something happened inside her.

She couldn't describe it, even to herself. A piece of her disconnected, had nothing to latch onto. Her sanity was frail, fraught with darkness. A strand of it moved, came out and floundered through her ruined eyes. It found the cat, twining with it then retracting, back into her face, back into her soul.

Merged. Bound.

And suddenly she was *aware* of the cat in a way she couldn't understand. Then something else blossomed, something she hadn't expected. Something she hadn't dared hope for.

Something that had been irrevocably lost.

Suddenly, she could *see*.

The first thing she noticed was the whiskers on each side of her face. Her field of view was different, elongated subtly. The color of the world was wrong, too—everything was blue and green, with hardly any red. The world was a little out of focus, but the gradations were incredible. And even though dusk was falling, she could still see quite well in the encroaching darkness.

She turned her head this way and that, feeling the rumbling in her body, feeling her tail wagging involuntarily in the air. Her whiskers picked up the breeze. She noticed smoke in the distance. The ferns to her right gave off a pungent aroma, but she tuned that out, focusing instead on the rank elf in front of her. The elf was dirty and sick, with savage red slashes across her face. And an arm, bent the wrong way. And a leg. Half a leg. Blood pooling to the ground.

The elf retched / Cariel retched. She turned / saw herself turn over, scrambling in the mud. Her paws / her hands felt like the mud / her claws opened instinctively, ready to pounce. The fur on her back rippled / her body tingled with realization. Her devastated eyes saw nothing / her eyes saw a vole poke its head out, see her, run like hell. Her muscles tensed, ready to run after it / her muscles tensed, ready to fight.

Realization came to her slowly, at first.

She *was* the cat.

The cat was her.

And the wounds and seething splinters of her body went away, invisible like the dusk inside her eyes, gone like the dust before the rain. She was whole / this cat was whole. She was strong / she was proud. She was pure.

She bared her teeth, hissing at the setting sun.

THIRTY

THE CIRCULAR ROOM Quynn found himself in was huge—at least twenty stories tall, and very wide. Elves scuttled around everywhere, running to and fro about their business. The room was full of noise: clattering metal and power tools; elves shouting and radios hissing; alarms beeping and mechanisms whirring. The whole place was alive with lights and sound, and the air held the acrid stench of burning electronics.

A massive device of some kind took up most of the center of the room. It was tall, with a central portion dominated by thick hydraulics and black circuit boards. A series of clear pipes erupted like a spiderweb from the middle of the device, fanning out high over Quynn's head. The pipes connected at various points along the outer wall. He counted fourteen pipes, and all but one was glowing with a strange, blueish light.

There were video screens and wires and other unidentifiable protrusions all along the massive machine. Catwalks led to and fro at intervals all the way up the twenty story height. Elves could be seen far above, leaning off the catwalks and making some adjustments to the machines. It made Quynn nervous just looking at them up there. Further up, some kind of smoky haze obscured the ceiling.

His gaze returned to the floor. Doors led off in various directions, most of them closed. In one section of the chamber, Quynn saw a series of mirrors. In another, a chair, with an elf strapped in like a prisoner about to be tortured. Another part of the room held a three-dimensional display showing some kind of schematic.

A flash of light caught his attention, over by the mirrors. As Quynn watched, a swirling gate appeared for a split second, vanishing as quickly as it had come. He thought he heard somebody scream. It was gatesending magic, which was illegal on Valaralda—making this a clandestine operation.

Quynn wasn't sure whether to be nervous or relieved.

An elf walked by, dressed in a gray robe that was an exact match for the one Quynn's savior was wearing. The elf did not acknowledge Quynn—he just walked right on by. As he passed, Quynn saw that he was carrying something. Something that he shouldn't have in his possession.

It was the Book of Amplification.

Where had the man gotten it? Last Quynn had heard, Trey was in possession of the Book. Had the man stolen it from Trey? Was Trey working for these people? What were they planning on doing with the Book?

The elf strolled away, oblivious to Quynn's sudden interest. Quynn watched as the man deftly climbed a ladder that led up the outer wall. Still carrying the Book with one hand, the man climbed up three stories until he reached the spiderweb of pipes. Then he slotted the Book into a receptacle on the wall, and the last remaining pipe lit up blue. Quynn scanned the wall, looking at each of the pipe connections.

His mouth dropped open in amazement.

Each pipe had a Book on one end, slotted into the wall. Fourteen pipes and fourteen Books, identical to the one Quynn had just seen. Quynn had thought that the Book of Amplification was unique, that only one of its kind existed in the world. But these strange gray elves had found more. A lot more.

Thirteen more, to be precise.

Quynn's mind spun, thinking of the possibilities.

"You must be Quynn."

He jumped, startled. A man was standing next to him. He could have sworn he hadn't been there a moment before. He was about two inches taller than Quynn and very good-looking, with a well-tailored suit and dark, short, wavy hair with a haircut that must have cost a fortune. His eyes were a strange golden color, almost unsettling.

"Uh," Quynn said, clearing his throat. "Yes. And you are?"

The man ignored him for a moment, turning instead to the mage in the gray robe. "Jacob," he said, pressing something into the man's hand, "you did well bringing him here. Return to the Master with my blessing."

Jacob bowed his head slightly, then turned and tottered off.

"Pleased to meet you, good sir," the tall man said, turning back to him. "I'm Talon." He reached out to shake Quynn's hand. His grip was firm.

"Talon?" Quynn asked. "That's a strange name."

Talon smiled, baring teeth that were exceptionally straight and beautifully white. "I get that a lot," he said. "Welcome to Memory."

"That's a strange name, too," Quynn said. "What *is* this place?"

Talon looked around the room, a proud expression on his face. "This place," he said, "is a memory of what once was. Of what once could be. Here is where we make dreams come true, if you can pay the price. You can find all manner of things down here—things of the *dark* persuasion." He smiled widely, teeth glinting.

"You mean darkprime magic."

"Darkprime, unlicensed lightprime, gatesending—you name it, we do it."

"But all of that is illegal."

"Is that a problem for you?" Talon's look suddenly became dangerous.

"No, no," Quynn said, holding his hands up. "I don't care, believe me. But how do you keep such a large place a secret?"

Talon barked a laugh. "We don't," he said. "Not really. Not from the ones that matter. You'd be surprised what a few bribes in the right places can accomplish. And besides, half the government uses our services."

"Your...services?"

"Oh, you know, the usual. Memory reclamation therapy, instantaneous transportation, black market delivery services, intentional memory loss."

"*Intentional* memory loss?"

"You'd be surprised," Talon smirked.

"Memory," Quynn said. "The name is starting to make some sense. But where does all the darkprime wood come from?"

"Vagrants. Miscreants. Losers. People in a lot of debt. Assisted suicide. Murder for hire. Never a shortage of bodies down here, old chap. Never a shortage of blood. I'm sure you understand." He grinned again.

Quynn did understand. More and more, this place was starting to sound like the floating cities on Earth. "You have fourteen Books of Amplification," he said.

Talon's expression suddenly became guarded. "You

noticed that, did you? Just something we're working on. Call it an experiment."

"What kind of experiment?"

Talon clapped him on the back. "Never you mind, good sir. It's not important."

"Why am I here?"

"A more relevant question. In fact, a lot of us around here have been wanting to meet you."

"You know who I am?"

Talon gave a sort of half smile. "That we do, good sir. That we do. We'll make the rounds shortly, introduce you to the chaps. But first, there's something I wanted you to look at."

Quynn frowned. "Okay," he said. This whole encounter had been strange, from the moment he'd been taken out of his cell. Who the hell were these people, and what were they planning?

"Follow me," Talon said, setting off into the vast chamber. Quynn followed as they threaded their way around various machines and platforms. There was a lot going on down here in the underbelly of the city. The one place darkprime magic was still allowed to flourish in Ilyrion.

"How long have you been a Prime Mage?" Talon asked as they walked.

Quynn started. How had he known? "Not long," he said. "A month or two."

"You were a mage before?"

"I was a mindmaster, yes."

"Let me guess," Talon said, stepping carefully over a bundle of wires on the ground, "something big happened to you, something emotional. You got either really angry or really sad. Or both. Am I right?"

Quynn stopped walking, his mouth hanging open. "How did you know?" he asked. It had happened the night he'd caught Lorelei in bed with Trey. He'd been overcome with rage, and something had *snapped* inside him. He'd gained his other powers in that moment.

Talon turned, regarding him with a kindly expression. "It's called a soulblock," he said. "Nearly every Prime Mage has one at first, if they emerge without a soulshaman to guide them. It's a shame, really. A lot of unrealized potential out there, just waiting for the right set of circumstances."

Quynn's mind whirled with questions. "What's a soulshaman?"

"Soulmagic flows through us all," Talon said, setting back out across the facility. Quynn had to run to catch up with him. "It's the underlying force behind the Prime. A soulshaman understands the raw power of the soul, can harness it and use it."

Quynn didn't understand a word. There was another power *behind* Prime magic? That didn't make any sense. And yet, it also might explain a lot of things. "What can you do with this...soulmagic?" he asked.

Talon ducked under a low-hanging steel beam. "Oh," he said, "you can do lots of things. I'm sure you'll learn about them soon enough. But we don't have the time for that now." He stopped in front of a bank of computers. "I was wondering if you could take a look at this," he said, motioning to a tiny screen.

Quynn stepped forward, trying to get a closer look. The screen appeared to contain a bunch of symbols—hieroglyphics of some sort, if he wasn't mistaken. It looked like ancient Egyptian pictographs from Earth. He couldn't read them.

"I don't know what these are," he said, turning around just in time to see Talon pressing a button on a nearby machine.

"Thanks so much for your help, old chap," Talon said, flashing him a toothy grin.

Something bright flashed over Quynn, zipping down from his head to his feet. He felt cold wash over his body, as if he'd been dipped in ice.

Everything around him disappeared.

THIRTY-ONE

LIONAR TOOK Allain and his group on a meandering course through the city, slowed a bit by the still-nameless mage who had attacked them in the Under. Allain2 was hanging on to the man, shepherding him through the streets. Allain had Lorelei in tow, and Lionar was at the head, cheerfully pointing out sights as they went.

It was a funny sort of tour group.

The city passed in a blur, and eventually their trip took a darker turn, heading into a series of alleys and then into an unmarked building. Then they passed a series of gates guarded by big guys with big guns. At each point, Lionar knew a password to get them through.

They found themselves in an underground area next, much like the Unders on Earth. It had clearly been purpose-built for whatever they needed, though—it wasn't city infrastructure repurposed for living quarters, like the Under was. So it had a markedly better appearance than where Shock Crew had its headquarters: nice stonework in the tunnels, modern lighting placed at respectable intervals, even some decorations here and there.

"You built all this?" Allain asked as they walked.

"Many of these tunnels existed long before Ilyrion was this big," Lionar said. "They'd been covered up and lost when we found them. So we enlarged and improved them, made use of them."

"But why here? Are you afraid of something?"

Lionar laughed. "Afraid? No. This place gives us the space we need to conduct our various businesses and operations. Some of the things we do are of dubious legality."

They encountered another door made out of steel. This time Lionar unlocked it with a keycard he had with him. The door beeped and slid open smoothly, and he ushered them in.

"You sure this is a good idea?" Allain2 asked under his breath as they passed through.

"Not at all."

"We're almost there, gentlemen," Lionar said. "And lady. Just a quick train trip, next."

"A *train*?"

Lionar took them through one final door, and Allain found himself staring at a sleek, silver train shaped like an elongated bullet. It was long and curvy, big enough to carry hundreds of people, made entirely of shiny metal with no windows. It looked like it probably moved *fast*.

"We're going on that?" Allain asked. "Where *is* this place you're taking us?"

"The trip will take but a moment," Lionar said, ushering them all through a narrow door that peeled open in the silvery train's shell.

Allain went through, ducking to avoid hitting his head on anything. The inside of the train was spartan and very modern, with black upholstered seats and glass tables and rows of crystal glasses hanging on the sides. Everyone found places to sit, staring at each other since there were no windows of any kind. The seats were far more comfortable than they looked.

"Everyone in?" Lionar asked. "Good. We'll be underway momentarily." He took a seat of his own, and the door cycled shut silently, sliding closed on hidden tracks.

"This is quite the operation," Allain2 muttered, "whatever it is." Allain nodded his agreement.

The train lurched, and Allain could feel inertia take him as the vehicle sped up. If it was on tracks—and Allain wasn't sure, having not had a good look at the area underneath the train—the tracks were silent. There was almost no vibration, no perception of movement once the train had accelerated. They were probably using magic, he realized, to make it go. Magic or some kind of high technology.

What was he getting himself into?

It was maybe five minutes—maybe ten—before the train stopped. Allain had no perception of how far they had traveled, but he figured they were probably still underneath Ilyrion. The train door cycled open and everyone exited, Lionar taking up the rear. Then the man took the lead again, bringing them down one more tunnel and up to one more door.

"This is it," he said. "We've arrived." He pushed the door open and they all stepped through.

Allain found himself in a massive room, circular and very tall. There was some kind of big machine taking up most of the space in the middle, with various ancillary stations all around on the floor. Allain paused for a moment to take it all in—this was more technology than he'd ever seen before in one place. He had no idea what any of it was.

Allain2 whistled softly. "That's one hell of a machine," he said.

"This is our headquarters," Lionar said. "We call it Memory."

Out of the corner of his eye, Allain caught a magical gate flash into existence, sliding over somebody and making them disappear. He thought for a second that he'd recognized the man who'd just been gated, but he hadn't seen him clearly. Maybe it was just his imagination.

Somebody approached them. He was tall and good-looking, with short-cropped brown hair and golden eyes. He was wearing a men's suit in human fashion, though his pointed ears made it obvious that he was an elf. Allain could tell that the man was very muscular. He wouldn't want to cross him.

The man smiled widely as he approached. "More visitors!" he said. "Fantastic. Welcome to Memory. My name is Talon. I see Lionar here has been taking good care of you. Lionar, please take our colleague"—he motioned to the subdued shadowmage—"and show him to his cell."

Talon was acting as if he already knew what had happened with the attack. How were these guys getting their information?

"It was a pleasure meeting you," Lionar said, turning to Allain. "I look forward to continuing our discussion." He grabbed the shadowmage's arm, steering him away.

"I'm told this woman suffers from extreme soulblinding," Talon said. "What you call gatesickness."

"That's right," Allain said. "But how did you know? We just got here."

Talon flashed his teeth in a smile. "Lionar told me as you were walking here. Our communication technology is really quite advanced, you know. Some of us are outfitted with subvocal transducers, allowing us to communicate without vocalizing."

So they could talk to each other without anyone knowing

it? That seemed like a very powerful technology. Dangerously powerful—like magic.

"Can you fix her?" Allain asked. Lorelei was just standing there, looking at nothing in particular.

"Do you mind?" Talon asked, stepping forward and holding up a Prime Leaf. He wanted to soulspect her.

"Fine," Allain said.

Talon gingerly reached out and took Lorelei's hand in his own, with the leaf between them. He stayed that way for a moment, his eyes closed. When he opened them, he had a pained expression on his face.

"This woman's mind is damaged almost beyond repair," he said. "Almost. We've been working on a new type of memory therapy, and there's a good chance it will work for her."

"Is it dangerous?" Allain asked. He didn't want Lorelei to be hurt.

"A certain percentage of patients experience catastrophic memory loss instead of repair," Talon said. "But in this case, the risk is negligible. She's already lost everything she has to lose."

He didn't ask them how it had happened. Not that Allain could have answered, but he found it curious nonetheless. How *did* Lorelei get this way, anyway? What had happened to her? And why did nobody else seem to care?

"Shall we proceed?" Talon asked. "The process only takes a few minutes. We can do it right now."

"We don't have any money or anything," Allain said.

"No need for that," Talon said, smiling. "We will consider it repayment for bringing back our fallen mage."

Something about all this wasn't ringing true for Allain. They wanted Lorelei for something, but what? He turned to Allain2. "What do you think?" he asked.

Allain2 just shrugged. "We've come this far."

Allain turned back to Talon. "Alright," he said, "let's give it a shot."

Talon took them around the room to the left, tracing his way over wires and around bits of machinery. The outer edge of the room was broken into sections, sort of like pie slices, like what a soul looked like through the leaf. Each section on the outside of the room seemed to have its own distinct purpose: some had drawers or desks, some had mirrors or machines. In more than a few of them, Allain saw gates being used. Apparently the prohibition on gatesending had no effect down here among the lawless.

They traipsed maybe halfway around the circular chamber before finally arriving at their destination. It was a small wedge of space like all the others, bounded on three sides by walls and open in the front, facing the machine in the middle. Talon ushered them inside the little space, gently nudging Lorelei up onto a silver platform.

A small control panel had been placed along the wall, and a gray-robed mage was standing next to it. He had a violet belt on, and his head was shaved. The man nodded to Talon as they entered, but he said nothing.

"As you know," Talon said, "gatesending is the seventh Light Aspect—the Prime power, the center of the soul. But gatesending interacts with memory in strange, often unpredictable, ways. Over the years, we've been researching the precise implications of this interaction. We found that certain types of power modulation, combined with quick repetition of a specific size of gate, can predictably cause patients to regain access to their memories.

"Picture a coin, tarnished after years of age. Used wrongly, gatesending can add to that tarnish, making the coin even more dirty, inscrutable. But used in another way, gates can act as a cleansing device, a way to remove the tarnish.

"The memories are never gone, you see. Just lost. The neural pathways to them break, but they can be repaired.

"Are you ready?"

Allain stepped up to Lorelei, taking both hands in his. She allowed it passively, looking into his eyes without much expression on her face.

"Is this something you want to do?" he asked her.

"The gates of memory," she whispered.

Maybe this is what she'd been talking about the whole time. It was as much of an acknowledgement as he was going to get. He released her hands, nodding to Talon.

"Stand back," Talon said, waiting until Allain did so. Lorelei stayed where she was, looking at him with something approaching puzzlement. He could get lost in those eyes.

"Proceed," Talon said to the mage with the violet belt. The man pushed a few buttons on the control panel, then raised his hands.

There was a low humming sound, and Allain felt the floor vibrate slightly. Then a shimmering gate appeared on the platform, passing up over Lorelei's body before winking out. Then a second gate appeared, doing the same thing. They made a buzzing sound as they moved. A third gate appeared, and a fourth, coming faster and faster. Soon there were dozens of gates, flying through the air faster than Allain could track. They coursed across Lorelei's body, light flashing and spinning. Her mouth was open in a rictus grin, and her muscles had all gone rigid.

She screamed.

Allain made a move as if to step forward, but Talon stopped him with a hand. "Wait," Talon said. "It's almost done."

Allain bit his lip. Her screaming continued, reaching a feverish pitch. It looked like they were hurting her, torturing her. The gates just kept coming faster and faster until they were a blur. He could still see Lorelei. She was looking at him as the screams racked her body.

Then it was done.

The gates went out all at once, and Lorelei slumped to the ground, breathing heavily. Allain darted forward, catching her just before she hit. Her skin was pallid, her body weak. He smoothed back the hair from her forehead, wishing he hadn't gone along with this. They'd nearly killed her! He held her, not knowing what else to do.

"Lorelei?" he asked. "Can you hear me?"

She opened her eyes. They were clear and focused, piercing into him like a knife.

"Who are you?" she asked. Her tone was different—calm and precise.

"Allain," he said. "My name is Allain."

She pulled out of his grip, struggling to sit up on the floor. "And where is this?"

"Greetings, my dear," Talon said, stepping forward. "You're beneath Ilyrion, in a place called Memory. How do you feel?"

She looked up at him, a frown creasing her face. "Did we make the Conjunction?" she asked. Allain had no idea what she meant.

"Earth did translate successfully to the Persephone system," Talon said. Did these two know each other?

"I see," Lorelei said, holding a hand up to her head. "How long has it been?"

"Since the translation? About a month."

"Since the Sending."

Talon's eyes narrowed. "Twenty thousand, fifteen years," he said. Allain still had no idea what was going on.

Lorelei looked like she was doing some math in her head, her mouth moving silently.

"Shit," she said, brushing Allain away and standing up. She tottered slightly, but managed to keep her balance. "I need to talk to Trey. We don't have much time left."

THIRTY-TWO

QUYNN'S EYES struggled to adjust to the sudden darkness all around him. A warm, sultry wind blew by, and the sounds of insects filled his ears. He smelled something pungent, something unrecognizable. A fly buzzed by his ear and he instinctively slapped at it.

Where the hell was he?

It was nighttime, wherever it was. A glittering array of stars shone overhead, brightening as his eyes became used to the darkness. There were *two* moons in the sky: one was blue, and one was white. They hung near each other, half way below the zenith. Quynn turned and saw a third moon—a red moon—hanging just above the horizon. It looked sickly, sinister.

A vast jungle was behind him, as far as he could see. He was standing on some kind of rocky promontory—there was a sheer cliff in front of him, several hundred feet high. Millions of trees were arrayed below him, and a river wound through them, sparkling in the starlight. To his right and below there was a massive obelisk, clearly made by some kind of intelligent life. It was a round ball on a pedestal, almost like the spinning globes they made on Earth. But part of it had crumbled inwards, and it was covered in dirt, moss, and ivy. Clearly nothing had touched it in quite some time.

Quynn took a deep breath and almost gagged. The scent out here was strong, sweet and spicy all at once. It must have been coming from the vegetation all around. Quynn spotted flowers and bushes and dozens of kinds of trees, none of which were like anything he had ever seen.

It was an alien world. And somehow he'd been Sent here. By Talon. On purpose. He'd been taken out of jail and brought to Valaralda, only to be Sent here—wherever here was.

What the hell was he supposed to do? Was he supposed to die? What was the thinking, exactly? His survival skills were rusty, to be sure, and with everything so unknown on this planet, he was likely to eat something poisonous and die on the first day. He was lucky he could even breathe here. It seemed an odd way to kill him, though. Why not just shoot him? Why not just leave him in jail to begin with?

There must be more here than he was seeing.

A gate flashed into existence next to him, unbearably bright. It disappeared as quickly as it had come, and a man stood there. A man in a gray robe, with a shaved head. He wore a pale blue belt and had a large backpack slung over one shoulder.

Quynn thought about tackling him, but stifled the urge. Hurting this man was not in his best interest right now. He might be his only lifeline. Better to question him, and figure out what was going on.

They stood facing each other for a long moment. Quynn cleared his throat suggestively.

"Greetings," the other man said. "My name is Saul."

"Greetings?" Quynn said. "*That's* what you're going with?"

"My apologies," Saul said. He was keeping himself carefully motionless, obviously trying to avoid antagonizing Quynn. But Quynn was already antagonized. He really wanted to kill this fucker, but he managed to restrain himself.

"Not an improvement," Quynn said. "Try again."

The man was growing visibly nervous. "I've been sent here to help you," he said. "There was a technical malfunction, and you ended up here. They sent me to try to bring you back."

A likely story.

"Where is *here?*" Quynn asked.

Saul looked around as if seeing things for the first time. "This is a planet called Eryn. One of the seven. One of the three."

Why did that ring a bell? Quynn was pretty sure he'd never heard the name Eryn before, but something about it seemed familiar.

"You're lying," Quynn said. "I know Talon sent me here on purpose. Why?"

Saul cocked his head, as if listening to something. Then he bowed submissively.

"You are correct," he said. "We did send you to Eryn on purpose."

Quynn felt himself growing angrier. "Why?"

"The people I'm working for—they don't want me to tell you just yet. There is a reason, though. A good one. When the time is right, you will know."

In a flash, Quynn darted forward and grabbed Saul, twisting him around and putting him in a headlock. "Give me one reason why I shouldn't kill you now," he said.

Saul was trembling. "I'm your only hope of survival here,"

he said, his voice coming out strained. "I can help you find food and safe water. And I can get you back to Valaralda."

"Maybe I'll just find some natives and shack up with them. I can breathe the air here, so things can't be *too* different. Maybe I don't need you."

"The indigenous intelligent life on this planet is long dead," Saul said. "And you would *not* have wanted to meet them."

"Fine," Quynn said, releasing Saul. "You get to live—for now. But you are going to tell me everything. Starting with why all intelligent life on Eryn is dead."

"Simple," Saul said. "It was the Sundering."

THIRTY-THREE

ELANIL ENCOUNTERED three more Trees before she made it to the end of the strange gauntlet. The purple sky was starting to get to her; she felt a headache beginning to form behind her eyes. She'd answered the last three Trees distractedly, her mind focused on her mother, trapped in the Tree. As with the others, Elanil had placed her hand on the Tree, feeling the soul within. Each time, the soul spoke to her, giving her the answer she needed.

It was like communing with the dead.

The fourteenth Tree drew aside, leaves and branches shuddering as it curled upwards, away from the path. She had made it—she was through. But somehow she knew that the real adventure was just getting started in this strange place.

She took a hesitant step forward. The road curved upwards, leading up a steep, green hill. The two shining Trees were at the top of the hill: one black, one gold. They both glowed, even the black one, giving off a kind of negative light around it. The Trees were enormous, bigger than anything she'd ever seen before. Bigger by far than a regular Prime

Tree. As she approached, she felt dwarfed by them, a tiny bug in the sand.

YOU ARE STRONG.

The voice was in her head, but somehow Elanil knew it had come from the black Tree, the one on the left. She stopped walking, craning her neck to look upwards at the massive Trees.

"Who are you?" she asked, her voice sounding small.

THE FLOOD OF SOULS HAS SLOWED TO A TRICKLE. WHY IS THIS?

Elanil didn't understand the question. "What souls?" she asked.

YOU ARE A SOUL.

"Am I dead?"

YOUR BODY IS DEAD. YOUR SOUL IS HERE.

"Where is here? What is this place?"

So many questions, little one.

It was a second voice, the one she'd heard before. It was emanating into her mind from the golden Tree, the one on the right. Its thoughts unfurled slowly, languidly, like a cat basking in the sun.

"I'll answer what questions I can, if you answer mine," Elanil said. She didn't have anything else to bargain with.

She felt laughter coming from the Trees.

QUID PRO QUO, the black Tree said. **VERY WELL.**

From which world do you come?

The first question. "Earth," she said. Interesting that they didn't know that already. Whatever magic was occurring here, the Trees weren't omniscient. She could use that to her advantage.

"How many worlds are there?" she asked, but regretted the question immediately. She didn't know how many she was going to get—she shouldn't waste them.

Our reach is far, little one. Seven planets are strongest, but three are stronger still. Valar, Mar, and Eryn.

"Who are you?"

OUR TURN, the black Tree thundered.

"Sorry."

HOW MANY SOULS REMAIN ON MAR?

"I don't know what you mean. What is Mar?"

YOU CALL IT EARTH.

"How many souls remain on Earth? I have no idea. A few million? More if you count the floating cities. Who are you?" It was her turn. Time to get to the bottom of this.

Surely you have guessed who we are, little one.

She had, but she wanted to hear them say it. "Tell me anyway."

YOU NAME US TWINS, BUT THAT IS NOT OUR NAME. I AM NELENOR. THE OTHER ONE IS VELION.

"Are you gods?"

OUR TURN.

Elanil sighed. "Sorry."

What was your Talent?

"Leafrunning."

The Trees were silent for a moment, as if thinking.

THE FIFTH ASPECT. BLUE.

Elanil wasn't sure if she was supposed to answer that. She didn't know what an Aspect was, or why it was blue. Was it her turn? She decided to venture a question. "What is this place?" she asked. It seemed the next logical thing she needed to know.

This is Ambarhal, the gold Tree said in her mind. *Guruthos made it, and we reside in it, gathering souls until our return. What is your name?*

Elanil felt flattered that they cared to know her name. But why should she? These beings, whoever they were, were obviously powerful. But that didn't mean she should worship them, cower before them.

"I'm Elanil," she said. "From Sylrantheas." She felt like she needed to add that last part. "How did I get here?"

You took the path of violence.

She was shot, they meant. By Lorelei, the madwoman in red leather. But their answer was interesting: could there be other paths? Other ways to get to Ambarhal? Would one *want* to get here on purpose?

WHAT YEAR IS IT?

"2312," she said, "on Earth." Did the Trees not experience the passage of time here?

The year draws near, the golden Tree said. It sounded excited, almost giddy. That probably wasn't a good thing.

"Are you gods?"

Our influence in Ambarhal is great, but it is limited in the corporeal world. Our power comes from the weapon. With it, we are like gods to you. You have none who can face us and live. On Starmist Prime, perhaps...but they will not be coming to your aid. They are long, long gone, scattered to the celestial winds.

She sensed laughter rumbling through them.

WHAT DO YOU FEAR?

That was an odd question. "I don't know," Elanil said. "Death, I guess? But I'm already dead. So nothing, I guess." She was lying. She feared this place, whatever it was, very much. But that was not something these strange Trees needed to know.

Nothing is the wisest fear of all, the gold Tree said.

She realized in that moment that the Tree was right.

"You said earlier that you will return," she asked. "How?"

EVEN NOW, THE DOORS TO OUR PRISON CRACK. THE KEY DRAWS NEAR. GURUTHOS SHALL USHER

IN OUR RETURN. THE HUNDRED THOUSAND YEARS HAVE ALMOST ENDED.

Well, that whole answer had been useless. Elanil had no idea what the black Tree was talking about. She wished Arra were here—her sister would surely be able to help her. She missed her sister, missed her father and friends and the whole village. She felt a sudden urge to dance, to run away. A tear came to her eye as she asked her next question:

"How can I get out of here?"

You have passed through the Fourteen and Chosen your allegiance. You are free to leave whenever you wish.

"But how do I leave? What allegiance did I Choose?"

NO MORE QUESTIONS.

"But—"

Your allegiance was chosen the moment your body died. You will make an excellent subject.

"I'm no one's subject."

The gold Tree laughed. *The choice is not your own. When the time is right, I will call. Now be gone from this hill. Others approach.*

Elanil looked around, but she didn't see anybody else coming. "How do I escape this place?" she asked again, hearing the desperation in her voice. "Help me!"

But the Twins were silent. She was once again alone in this violet world. She turned and trudged down the hill, tears rolling down her face.

THIRTY-FOUR

ORYM'S EXPEDITION was set to start the next day. It might be dangerous, and it might be long. There was a good chance he might even die at some point during it. So he decided to take the time for one last pleasure, in case things went to shit.

It was nighttime in Ilyrion, and he was in the richest part of the city: the Ecological District. One might think that a district named after *ecology* would be all farmland or forest, green and full of natural life. And it *was* a forest, or at least there was a forest floor and trees. But buildings crept up around those trees, clustering and circling in metal and glass, made to fit in perfect harmony with nature. It was a fitting dichotomy; a symphony of nature and technology that only Ilyrion could produce.

The Ecological Department received the very highest dole from the government, after all, and their budgets were never threatened. The members of that department were paid well for their efforts, and they in turn spent their money on material pleasures, not on nature.

The irony was apparently lost on them.

The Ecological District was eight city blocks that

surrounded the largest Prime Tree in the city, a Prime Oak. A series of skyscrapers took up most of the space surrounding the Tree, but they weren't like skyscrapers on Earth—going straight up, flat rectangles pointed at the sky. No, these were unconventional buildings, with structures that angled and curved outward, impossible feats of engineering that only worked because of the gravitonic engines that kept them up. The result was a series of beautiful bridges and balustrades, parapets and glass roads that curved around and around the Tree, integrating with it in a way that traditional construction techniques never could. It was a fantastic waste of resources.

Orym loved it.

He arrived at his destination, a tall building that was mostly residential, but with a restaurant in the first floor, basement, and top floor. The restaurant was *Turuvoite*, one of the finest establishments in Ilyrion—so of course Orym had immediately gravitated to it. In such a short time it had already become his home away from home.

A thick door marked the entrance to the underground bar, the part of the restaurant that Orym preferred. He noticed a poster pasted to the wall next to the door: it was advertising some kind of magic show, being put on by someone calling themselves Erodar the Prime. It was a bit of an arrogant title, Orym thought, but he supposed magicians were supposed to be arrogant. The poster called it the greatest series of illusions ever attempted on stage.

Orym very much doubted that was true.

He pushed open the thick wooden door and stepped through into darkness, taking in a deep breath. Candles lit the dim room, making it just possible to see where he was going. His nose picked up the scents of good strong ale and pipe smoke. Quiet conversation filled the room, and under that he could hear *lindalë* playing: elven music, its faint jazz-like tones lending a cozy ambiance to the place.

He stepped up to the bar and placed his order: bourbon, new stuff from Louisberg. He'd sold the barrels of bourbon to this bar as part of his move to Valaralda, but that didn't mean he'd stopped drinking it—it just meant he had to pay four times the price he'd gotten for the stuff.

But he didn't mind, and neither did the bar.

Louisberg was populated by a special kind of Remnant. They called the city Lusvunub, and they were almost civilized —*very* civilized, really, if you took their distilleries into consideration. They were also whizzes with mechanical things—their tanks and tricked-out trucks were a wonder to behold. And although they'd *probably* shoot you if you arrived in the city unexpectedly, they would at least maybe ask you if you had anything interesting to trade. So he and Quynn had brokered an uneasy peace with the Louisberg Remnant a long time ago, trading as much tech as they could get their hands on for the only thing the dirty humans had to offer: bourbon.

He took the glass of bourbon—neat, of course, barrel strength—and headed toward his favorite spot: a deep leather couch in front of the roaring fire at one end of the room. A few of the customers nodded at him as he passed—those were the ones who had picked up a taste for bourbon, knew he was the supplier. If nothing else worked out, he realized, he could make a healthy living brokering liquor trade between Earth and Valaralda. Might make for a nice retirement plan. Those Louisberg humans wouldn't talk to anyone else, after all.

The couch was warm, and the bourbon was warmer. The first sip burned pleasantly, and he set the glass down to let the finish linger. If anything, bourbon out of Louisberg was better than before the Sundering. Fantastic stuff. Maybe it was the cleaner air, the better water the Earth had now. Or maybe the extra three centuries had allowed the humans to perfect their technique even further than they already had.

Tiala would have liked it here, with the bourbon and the wood. Twins—he hadn't thought of her in a very long time. Regrets began forming as they always did, and he took another sip of bourbon to quiet the thoughts. He should have married that woman when he had the chance. Then Dillon would have grown up with his mother.

It wouldn't have lasted, though. Relationships never did. True, Tiala was special—but she wasn't the problem.

Orym always was.

He pulled out the handheld Arkiem had given him. Short of optical implants, this device was as good as it got on Valar-alda. It was paper-thin, rectangular with rounded edges. The machine could respond to voice, touch, or optical stimulus, and its output could be routed to headphones or beamed directly to the user's eyes. It wasn't quite the same thing as the implants worn by most people, but it was close. It allowed the user a high degree of privacy, since no one else could see anything on the screen.

Orym popped in an ear bud and activated the handheld, opting for a local news feed on the video program. The broadcast was in 3D, beamed to his eyes stereoscopically. He took another drink, feeling the bourbon and the fire spread their warmth pleasingly through his body. There was a cute news reporter on the program, and he settled in to listen.

"The United Sky Cities of Mar have elected their first President," the reporter was saying. "Alexander Greyson, formerly on the Board of Supervisors for New San Francisco, is the President-elect."

The image switched to a shot of Greyson, and Orym raised his glass in a silent cheers. At last, all that work had paid off. Greyson would make a great President. Orym would have to remember to congratulate him, if he was ever in the cities again.

"Meanwhile, underneath the Sky Cities, young people continue to flock to the charismatic leadership of President Greyson's son, Shane Greyson. Reports indicate that Shane—who goes by the codename 'Shot'—has successfully integrated over four hundred disparate groups of kids from all over the Sky Cities. The President has pledged funding to enhance areas beneath the city streets, giving the kids a safe —and legal—place to stay, while ensuring the continued operation of city infrastructure."

Orym smiled. Leadership ran in the Greyson family, apparently. He hoped Dillon was doing well. Last Orym had heard, his son had been heading to Nekhrumet, in the Thesserin Desert. He hadn't heard from the boy in some time.

"Now we move to the ground," the reporter continued, and the video changed to a sweeping overhead shot of a forest. "So far, most Remnant factions have been unwilling to speak with representatives from either Mar or Valaralda. Some altercations have broken out as negotiations have been attempted, and there have been a few casualties. The Mar High Council voted yesterday to take a unilateral "hands-off" approach to the Remnant, allowing them to remain in their communities for the time being."

The shot changed to another overhead view, this one of a line of humans trudging through the forest. They were carrying tiny yellow flags, shaped like triangles. The humans looked tired, but also happy. Orym didn't have time to wonder who they were before the reporter continued.

"It appears the Remnant are not content to remain isolated, however," she said. "Observers have seen many bands of humans like this, migrating to a central point in the Muir Woods. They are converging on a town, the newly-rebuilt settlement called Pano Sylrantheas. Formerly the home of Senator Alleria Starglow and her consort, noted historian Tarathiel Riverbow, this village was completely destroyed during the altercation with the rogue Eldrim element just one month ago."

The camera changed to a shot of Pano Sylrantheas. Orym could see dozens of buildings already completed, with many more in various stages of construction. Elves and humans were milling about in organized fashion, carrying wood, consulting blueprints, even drinking ale. Orym felt a little pang of loneliness—he missed the village.

"As you can see," the reporter said, "Pano Sylrantheas is well on its way to being rebuilt. Interim Council Leader Bellas has claimed that they target completion of the initial construction by the end of the year. Yet more and more humans still continue to migrate to this city in the woods. It appears that the citizens of Pano Sylrantheas will have their work cut out for them in the coming months."

Orym took another sip of bourbon. Things were going well on Earth. A little *too* well, if Orym was any judge of these things. The other shoe would drop soon—*must* drop. What would be the spark to ignite the powder keg? Would the kids in the Under overthrow the Sky City leadership? That seemed unlikely, with father and son effectively running things above and below. Would it be the Remnant? Nobody had been able to talk to the humans. What did they think of all the new elves and technology that were invading the planet? Maybe they were biding their time, planning to strike.

Orym sipped again. None of these things were problems he could solve. And maybe nothing would happen. Maybe Earth had actually entered into a time of peace.

Maybe.

"Now we return to Valaralda," the reporter was saying, "where we are delighted to have with us Donar Cresius the Twenty-Fifth, Research Director for the Department of Magical Research."

The video changed to a shot of an older gentleman, dressed in a long purple robe with a thick gold chain around his neck. Attached to the chain was an elaborate icon depicting the Twins: two Trees crossed together. It was meant to symbolize the source of magic, but Orym couldn't help but see religious significance to it as well. He wondered how devout the Department of Magical Research was.

He'd heard the Believers could be a real problem.

"Thanks for being here, Director Cresius," the reporter said, bowing.

Cresius bowed back. "My pleasure."

"What can you tell us about the phenomenon the Space Agency is observing?"

"We know very little about the object from a magical perspective," Cresius said. "From the images the Space Agency has shared, it appears to be a physical object, traveling at a significant fraction of light speed. The object appears to resemble a near-parabolic comet with a highly eccentric orbital period of somewhere in the range of 100,000 years."

"Would you mind explaining to our viewers what that means, in simpler terms?"

"Certainly. Comets that orbit the sun have what are called *orbital periods*, which is how long it takes for the comet to make one full traversal of its orbital path around the sun. The term 'near-parabolic' indicates that with just a little more velocity, the comet would be able to escape the solar system, effectively ending its orbit entirely."

"Interesting," the reporter said. "But is it a comet?"

"We don't know," Cresius said. "The Space Agency is sharing all its data with the Department of Magical Research, and we are doing the best we can to understand the object. From a magical standpoint, nothing appears to have changed. Yet."

"Do you expect anything to change?"

"We don't know. If this comet-like object is in fact related in some way to our magic, we may see some effects as it nears Valaralda."

"What do you think it is?"

"There are references littered throughout our histories to Guruthos, the ancient specter of death. In these texts, Guruthos is usually tied in some way to magic, power, or the Twins. So if the ancients can be believed, then this object very well could be linked in some way to magic."

"The scholar Tarathiel claimed the object had been here before."

"That is correct," Cresius said. "And now that we can observe the object's velocity and angle, we can calculate its probable perihelion—that is, the point at which it is closest to the sun. With the orbital period we're seeing, it does seem very likely that the object was visible to Valaraldans about 100,000 years ago."

Orym couldn't decide whether to frown or smile. On the one hand, Trey had been right about the Fall. Now that the Department of Magical Research was publicly validating his claim, perhaps people would listen to him more. Maybe he'd be able to reclaim his research, continue his fight against the Fall.

But on the other hand, it also meant the Fall was probably *real*. And if Trey was right about what it could do—what it was for—everyone was in a hell of a lot of trouble.

Orym sipped his bourbon, contemplating death.

THIRTY-FIVE

THE NEXT DAY found Orym at the Space Agency, prepping the expedition. He was standing in a large hangar that held a silver submersible, cylindrical and shining underneath the bright white lights hanging from the ceiling. The submersible was mounted on a massive trailer, which Orym had learned would be used to move it into the spaceship. The spaceship, then, would fly everything to Earth.

A submarine inside a spaceship. Not exactly what Orym had pictured himself doing.

He smiled. It seemed that even after twenty thousand years, there was still plenty of fun to be had.

"What do you think?" Director Arkiem asked as he entered the hangar. "It isn't much, but hopefully it will do."

"I'm not sure I want to know what would qualify as 'much' to you, Director," Orym said.

Arkiem smiled. "This *is* the Space Agency, after all."

"Point taken."

"Ready to meet your team?"

"Sure. But Director?"

"Yes?"

"Are you sure I'm the right one for this job?"

"I'm sure, Orym," Arkiem said. "I read through your dossier. You have quite an accomplished career."

"Very well," Orym said. "Let's do it."

Arkiem's eyes flicked to the left and his jaw muscles moved, sending subvocal commands to his implant. Orym watched a pair of workers loading a series of hard plastic crates into the submersible. Supplies, no doubt. Orym was glad he hadn't had to actually coordinate any of this.

There was a loud screeching sound, and a metal door in one wall slid ponderously open. Orym watched as people filed in, feeling his body growing tense, his shoulders drawing together in anticipation.

"Greetings," Arkiem said as the people assembled. There were four of them—three women and a man. "Team, may I present Orym Duskmere, formerly the Scientist General for the Cothellon on Mar."

The team bowed appropriately—all very respectful. Orym wondered if it had been difficult to convince them to come. He was a complete unknown to them, after all.

"Orym," Arkiem said, "let me introduce the team. First up is Shara, the submersible pilot."

The first woman nodded at Orym. She was short, with blonde hair and a pixie nose. She looked rather young.

Orym nodded back to her.

"Next is Mistale, our archaeologist and cave expert. She has braved some of the most remote regions on Valaralda, and is excited to see something new."

"Greetings," Mistale said, inclining her head. She was muscular and petite, with short, dark hair and flinty blue eyes. She didn't smile.

"Greetings," Orym returned.

"To her left," Arkiem continued, "is Elasha, our head diver."

Elasha was wearing a navy-blue jumpsuit which reminded Orym distinctly of the maintenance uniforms they'd used to wear in the Under. He'd worn one of them once, when he'd first met Trey. When he'd been pretending to be Marcus.

"Thanks for coming," Orym said.

"My pleasure," Elasha said. She was rather cute, with long, curly, dark hair and equally long and dark lashes.

"And finally," Arkiem said, "this is Tarron. He will be operations support for this expedition. Anything you need—provisions, armory, medical—he's your man."

"Hello," Orym said.

"Greetings," the man said. He was tall and well-proportioned—probably a hit with the ladies. The three ladies in *this* particular group, though, paid him no attention whatsoever. Orym could already tell that this would make for an interesting dynamic.

"Orym," Arkiem said, "why don't you tell everyone a little bit about yourself?"

Orym shifted his weight to a different foot. "Well," he said, "as the Director already mentioned, I was the Scientist General for the Cothellon. On Earth, I was responsible for discovering darkprime magic."

There were a few grimaces at that—darkprime magic was illegal on Valaralda, after all. Maybe he shouldn't have led with that.

"I've been involved with many scientific disciplines over the years," he continued. "Optics, space travel, communications, weapons research. My team created Fennas Elenathon, the device that brought Earth to this solar system."

"We heard you discovered a Prime Mage," Elasha said, and Orym heard a few snickers.

"Just so," Orym said. "I was partially responsible for unlocking Tarathiel's latent powers."

Everyone was looking at him sort of sideways. Did they not believe him? He hadn't expected that.

"And Prime Trees," Mistale—the archaeologist—said. "You *made* some?"

Orym nodded. It was a memory he'd rather not revisit.

The whole group burst out laughing.

"Everyone knows," Mistale said after she'd recovered, "that Prime Trees can't be *made*. They originated during the Great Awakening."

"Well," Orym started.

"And Prime Mages," the woman continued, "are just legends from the storybooks."

Great. So *that's* how this was going to go. Orym took a step forward. Arkiem was watching him, waiting to see how he'd respond.

He could kill them with kindness.

Or—

"Do you know who the first President of the United States was?" he asked, looking at Mistale.

"I don't see how that's relevant. I'd never even *heard* of the United States until a few weeks ago."

"He was a man by the name of George Washington. A visionary. A great leader. He knew that the country's independence only mattered if the right systems were put in place. And he knew there was no *point* to independence if he remained in charge forever. So he created the model of peaceful transition of power, a model that was followed with but one exception until the Sundering. He was a good man.

"And he was my close personal friend."

"I fail to see how this has anything to do with—"

"George Washington was a man of many words," Orym continued. "But one thing he said will always stick with me. He said, 'Associate with men of good quality if you esteem your own reputation; for it is better to be alone than in bad company.'

"Now I ask you, Mistale: are you a woman of good quality?"

She frowned. "Of course I am. Otherwise I wouldn't even be here." The others were nodding.

"So you accept Director Arkiem's selections for this team as valid and appropriate."

"Well—yes."

"As do I," Orym said. "Washington also said something else: 'Be courteous to all, but intimate with few, and let those few be well tried before you give them your confidence.' I don't mind you questioning me, Mistale. I'm a scientist—I only accept what I can observe with my own eyes."

He took a step forward, closing the gap between them.

"But I do mind you questioning Director Arkiem. He has proven himself to you—you yourself have just admitted as such. And he chose *me*."

He let his voice grow quieter in the vast room.

"You haven't seen what I've seen," he said. "Vast machines of metal, powered by thousands of human slaves. Billions of people killed in a flash. Children with the power of gods. Entire Forests in the sky. Mages who could kill hundreds of people with a thought."

Mistale swallowed, her eyes a mix of confusion and fear. "Who *are* you?" she asked.

Orym spun abruptly, returning to his place beside Arkiem. "Ladies and gentlemen," he said, "I thank you for coming. If circumstances allow in the future, I would be happy to arrange for a demonstration from one of my Prime Mage friends. But they are presently engrossed in important work, attempting to save this planet and all its people. You should be grateful to them—I know I am. But I am sure they wouldn't mind showing you a few *tricks*."

Everyone was silent, watching him.

"The expedition we are embarking on is one of similar importance. You may not understand it, but you don't need to —you just need to trust Director Arkiem. Which means you also need to trust me. I can tell you're all equal to that challenge. Am I right?"

Everyone nodded, somewhat hesitantly.

"Good. I expected no less from men and women of your stature and experience. We are scheduled to depart in six hours. Please stow your gear and meet me in the briefing room in fifteen minutes. Dismissed."

Everyone gave a sharp salute, then left to do as ordered. Nobody raised any further questions.

Orym finally allowed his shoulders to relax.

"See," Arkiem said, smiling at him, "you'll do just fine."

"ORYM?" a voice said.

What now? Orym turned to see a familiar man tottering through the main door to the submarine hangar. He had a smile on his face.

"Luthar!" Orym said. "So good to see you. Or should I call you Smoke?"

"Either works," Luthar said.

He was elderly-looking, especially for an elf. He walked with a definite hunch, and he had a shock of gray, curly hair about his face. But his eyes still sparkled, still held the intelligence Orym knew was lurking in his mind.

He and Luthar had worked together for hundreds of years. Luthar had been the research assistant that helped discover darkprime magic. And when the Cothellon army had attacked the Eldrim in the Prime Forest, Luthar has been there to lend a hand—and a few guns.

He was a good man.

"What are you doing here?" Orym asked.

"Got wind of a trip you're taking," Luthar said. "Want some extra help? I could do with one last adventure." He stepped closer. "And besides—this Valaraldan air doesn't agree with me. I need to be back home."

Orym clapped him on the back. "I think we're full," he said.

"Actually," Arkiem said, "there's room for one more crew member, if you think he'll be useful. I can have the ship loaded with extra provisions."

"This seems to be a pretty cutthroat group," Orym said to Luthar. "You sure you want to come?"

Luthar barked a laugh. "After everything we've been through together, you ask me *that*?"

Orym smiled. "Good point, old friend. Get your things—the bus leaves in six hours. Briefing in ten."

Luthar stood straighter, his hand coming up in a sharp salute. "Yes, sir!" Then he left.

Orym wondered if it was a coincidence that the two people who had discovered darkprime magic on Earth were the very ones going to investigate it now.

THIRTY-SIX

CARIEL WAS A CAT. She could see herself, her body, her mangled face. Her elven self was still there, and she could still feel it, feel her head and feelings and brain. But she could also feel the wildcat, the great beautiful beast who hadn't killed her and was now entwined with her somehow, breathing shallowly, mouth slightly parted, whiskers twitching.

She *stretched*...and the cat's back arched up, sinuous legs stretching forward, claws extending. The cat—*her* cat—yawned, a low growl escaping its throat. The languidness, the elegance of this cat almost took her breath away. It was effortlessly dangerous, like a taut bowstring waiting for release.

And it was gorgeous.

What was happening, exactly? Cariel quested about with her mind. Through the cat's eyes, she saw her own elven hands moving, waving about in the air. She continued reaching through her mind, feeling the connection point. There—there it was, a bright spark in the darkness of her brain. There was a thread connected to it, spinning outward through the air, tracing a bright arc toward the sky. She followed it, felt its shape and motion, running along it until she found the wildcat's mind. And there the line stopped, with a corresponding bright spark of connection.

It was almost as if the two of them were bound together, two souls twinned. She could perceive through the cat, breathe through it, *control* it.

This would prove useful.

Was it magic? Cariel didn't know. Was this what Hloldr had been talking about, the day before during the cavek hunt?

Had Cariel been able to do this all along?

Or was it something else? Something to do with her eyes?

She shuddered, suddenly, aware again of the pain in her face, the pain in her body. Blood was still seeping from her leg wound. Through the cat's vision, she could clearly see that the lower half of her left leg had been shorn off somehow. She turned / the cat turned, and she used its eyes to look up at the ravine she'd fallen from. It was high—easily fifty feet up, maybe more. Shit. No wonder she was crippled now, broken and bleeding on the jungle floor. She was blind. She hadn't seen where she was going. The jungle in this area was *full* of ravines like this, irregular drop-offs and river canyons. The Wilds were treacherous—everyone knew that. Yet Cariel had just tromped off, crawled off, moving through mud and leaves, unaware of where she'd been going.

She'd been mad. Mad with pain. Mad with fever.

And she'd been blind.

But now that she had the cat, she was blind no more.

She still had the fever, though. She could feel it burning on her face. She watched, detached, as Cariel's body spasmed, twitched. Her skin was growing pale. She was bleeding out. She was dying. She may only have moments left to live.

What could she do? Now she was a cat—*she was a cat*—but what good did that do? She knew it was just a link, just a thread of awareness passed between two souls. If Cariel died —if her body died—the link would end. And then there would be nothing left. Nothing but the beyond, whatever *that* was. Her soul would travel on.

But Cariel didn't want to die just yet.

Then she remembered something. It probably wasn't true, but in rylak lore the wildcats—they called them *kabul*, an ugly word—could heal you with their saliva. Rylak sometimes hunted these big cats when they were injured. Some of them even made it back alive.

She had control of this cat now, so she might as well try.

But what could a cat possibly do to heal someone? She bent the cat's head forward, feeling its mind dimly within her own. It was resisting her, just a little, but she clamped it down, asserting her control. The cat bent down, sniffing at her injured leg. The wound there was vast, raw and red and terrible. But she felt a little spark inside the cat's brain—an instinct, maybe, the thing it would have done if she hadn't been there to take charge.

It wanted to lick her wound.

So she let it. What harm could it do? She would die in any case—might as well let this cat get a meal if it could.

She almost shrieked when she felt its tongue. It was huge and rough and far stronger than she'd expected. She could feel her flesh pulling as it licked. She could feel excruciating pain as its saliva mixed with her blood and nerves and splintered bone. She almost screamed, almost lost consciousness— but then she noticed something else.

The bleeding was slowing.

The cat kept licking. She gave it almost free reign, letting it control its actions. The cat didn't know precisely *why* it was licking her, but it wanted to nonetheless. It enjoyed the metallic taste of elven blood, the warmth of it. It enjoyed the feeling of raw, uncooked flesh.

And it was *healing* her.

It was definitely helping. Her bleeding was slowing, somehow, as the great cat licked. There must be a coagulant in the cat's saliva. Had the rylak known this? How did Cariel know what *coagulant* meant? She was positive the rylak wouldn't have a word in their language of growls that would be anything similar. But no. It didn't matter. Her leg wasn't bleeding anymore, which was incredible. She might actually have a shot at surviving this.

She allowed the cat to keep licking her, prodding it mentally when needed, sealing up all her wounds. It was amazing, almost like magic.

Magic.

She couldn't help but feel that this...this *thing* she was doing, this binding of souls, had to be powered by magic. Something in her told her that magic did exist, that it was a real thing. Magic had brought her to this planet. Magic—somehow—was to blame for her whole terrible existence.

And now magic was helping her survive.

So. Perhaps she could *use* this magic. If she could discover this...this *soulbinding*, what else could she find out?

What else could she do?

She grinned / Cariel grinned, her teeth black with blood and dirt. The fever still shone out in her mind, but for the first time she realized she might actually have a chance at surviving.

She might actually have *power*.

THIRTY-SEVEN

"I NEED TO TALK TO TREY," Lorelei repeated. She was standing freely now, without Allain's assistance. Her eyes were clear, focused.

She looked angry.

"Didn't you try to have Trey killed?" Allain2 asked.

"That was before," Lorelei said. "I didn't have all my memories back then."

"And now you do?"

"Most of them, yes."

Talon stepped forward suddenly. "Do you remember your parents?" he asked, his tone strangely cold.

Lorelei cocked her head. "No," she said. "Memories of my family are still dark. That's strange."

Talon smiled. "Memory therapy is never usually one hundred percent effective," he said. "We can try again, if you'd like, although you might end up losing memories rather than gaining them."

"No," Lorelei said.

Allain caught Talon trying to hide a smile.

"Let's go," Lorelei said.

"Go where?" Allain asked.

"To find Trey."

"But we have no idea where he *is*."

"Oh. I guess we don't." She frowned.

"I do know someone who might be able to help," Talon said. "She's a bit eccentric, but a lot of people pass her way. She might have seen him, or know somebody who has."

"Alright," Allain said. "Who is she? Where do we find her?"

"She's outside the city," Talon said. "I can send you to her, though. I even have someone who can drive you there."

"Can't we just call her?"

Talon grinned. "She doesn't believe in that sort of thing."

Allain looked at Lorelei. She was obviously flustered, impatient, but her memory had returned. Shouldn't she be back to the way she'd been before, as leader of the Cothellon? Shouldn't she be ordering him around, maybe smacking him around or—worse—*killing* him? That's what she'd done before, after all. She was cold and heartless. She'd shot Elanil. Surely now that she'd regained her faculties, she'd be a force to be reckoned with.

But she was just standing there, looking at him, waiting on him to make the decision. She was beautiful, standing there, and she didn't look intimidating at all. Allain felt suddenly important, having her look at him like that.

It was a feeling he was not used to.

"Alright," Allain said. "We'll go see your friend."

Talon's lips split into a grin that he didn't try to hide.

THIRTY-EIGHT

TREY AND ARRA decided to take some time to stroll through Errenmel before leaving for the city. The end of the world was coming, but Trey figured maybe it could wait for a few more hours. Errenmel was beautiful. They couldn't let it go to waste.

They walked down the cobblestone street, not quite hand in hand, gazing at the quaint thatched-roof houses and the gardens and the little horse-drawn carriages that went from place to place. It felt to Trey like an old European town, a village disconnected from time. As if Errenmel wasn't part of the same universe, the same problems.

He liked it.

But he knew it was a veneer. Underneath all the low-tech appearance was a suite of high-tech things: nanorobotics to clean the surfaces, impact-proof polymer weaves to form the walls and roofs, three dimensional display technology to create the illusion of paradise. Oh, it *was* paradise, to be sure. But not entirely all of it was real.

Lashel was walking with them, explaining these things. "I've been doing a little digging," he said, "ever since Mar entered the solar system. The dichotomy between humans and elves interests me—biologically, we are very similar species. Elves' eyes are different—we almost always have less pigmentation in our eyes, and we can see a tiny band of ultra-violet light that humans can't. Plus we benefit from a slower aging process, and a *much* longer modern history. Our whole genome is tailored to long, slow life with minimal reproduc-tion. It's an interesting outcome, given that the ecological situation on Valaralda isn't substantially different from that of Mar. But other than those changes, and our ear tip shape, we're pretty similar to humans. It's remarkable."

"Have you met Orym?" Trey asked. "He'd like you."

"Not yet," Lashel said. "I'd very much like to."

"I'll arrange it."

"Anyway, I was thinking about why elves tend to be more peaceful, less confrontational. That's not actually true, of course—elves aren't *that* peaceful, we just tend to express our conflicts on other levels—political, emotional, sometimes economic."

"Not with magic?"

"There was certainly a time when magic was used to fight, especially during the mythical age of the Prime Mages. But as those mages declined, and as elvenkind evolved, we gradually became used to magic, integrating it into society in a more constructive way."

"You mean you restricted it to death."

Lashel barked a laugh. "That's part of it."

"What's the other part?"

"Religion." He pointed up ahead. They were approaching the Church of the Twins, and Trey could see a line of people out front, carrying signs. "The Devout," Lashel said.

"I thought they were called Believers?"

"Either name works. But I think the term 'Believer' is too

mild. Yes, they believe in the Twins, but so do most elves, even if just in passing. These people—these Devout—are something more. They devote their *lives* to the faith, often to the exclusion of everything else."

"Are they a problem?" Trey asked.

"Not usually. In fact, the Devout are one of the reasons our culture—at least Esaran culture—is as stable as it is. The Devout are extremely pacifist, claiming that the Twins decry violence in any form. They are disciplined. Some would say they are slavish in their loyalty to the Twins. And there are enough of them that it has a cooling effect on society."

"Interesting."

As they approached the church, Trey was able to read some of the signs:

END MAGIC LICENSING
FREEDOM OF ALIGNMENT
SEVENTH ASPECT REIGNS

"What's the seventh Aspect?" Arra asked. "What are they protesting?"

They continued approaching the church, the stained glass windows looming brightly in front of them. The protestors—for that was what they appeared to be—had taken notice of the trio. They started turning toward Trey, shouting stuff at him he couldn't hear.

"The soul has seven Aspects," Lashel said. "The elves on Mar practice the Ways, correct?"

"Yes," Arra said. "But there are only six Ways."

"Right. The seventh Aspect is the primal one, the one that powers soulsundering and gatesending."

"But why are they protesting?"

"They want gatesending made legal."

"Why?"

Lashel shrugged. "Who knows? The Devout have grown more restless of late. That they would dare to stage an open protest like this is indicative of that fact. And it won't help—the Department of Magical Research won't budge on any of their policies."

It was an interesting situation, and not really that different from those found on Earth. Trey was surprised protests like this hadn't occurred earlier and more frequently in the past. What was different now?

"Lashel," Arra said, "do the Devout have a uniform? Do some of them wear gray robes, with belts made of colored string?"

Lashel frowned. "I think I've seen a few that meet that description. Why?"

Arra described the mage that had attacked them the other night. The mage had turned into six copies of himself, all fighting expertly. And in the end, he had stolen the Book of Amplification. And Trey still didn't know *why*. Or *how*, for that matter.

"Interesting," Lashel said when she was finished. The shouting from the protesters was getting louder. "It certainly *sounds* like that was one of the Devout. Maybe a leader, or a highly ranked member. Obviously a mage."

"Do you know how he split himself like that?" Trey asked.

"No idea. That's not any magic that I've ever heard of. Except…"

"What?"

Lashel stopped walking. Trey and Arra stopped beside him, ignoring the angry protesters. "After the Great Awakening," Lashel said, "there were stories of incredible magical feats. One of the more prominent accounts was of mages breaking up into parts, able to turn themselves into miniature armies. They could split and recombine at will. But the magic was supposedly unstable, dangerous. Many of those mages did not survive."

"But those are just legends, right?" Trey asked.

"Indeed. Legends. Like Prime Mages themselves."

Trey ran a hand through his hair. Prime Mages were real. And mages who could split like that were also real—he'd seen one with his own eyes. What other legends from the past might be true? Was there some connection between these powers and the Devout? He'd have to investigate, once he got back to Ilyrion.

Suddenly something big and wet hit him in the face. He flinched, wiping a red smear away with his hand. A tomato fell to the ground.

Then another one hit him, and Trey saw that the protesters had escalated beyond simple words and signs. Now they were throwing vegetables.

Great.

"Let's go!" Lashel shouted.

"Why are they so angry?" Arra asked.

"I don't know," Lashel said. "I don't know."

"I thought you said they were extreme pacifists?"

"They are. They were. Come on."

They turned and fled, dripping tomato juice on the cobblestone street. And Trey couldn't help but wonder what the world would be like if the Devout decided to drop their tomatoes and pick up swords.

THIRTY-NINE

"DID LARA TAKE THE BAIT?"

"Yes," Talon said, the sound of the word grating in his ears. He flexed his fingers. "She remembers about twenty thousand years now, give or take a few millennia."

"Good," the voice on the other end of the line said. "That will propel her, at least for now."

"You're stirring the pot," Talon said.

"She will tear them apart. I know her." The person on the phone almost sounded like they were smiling. "She is strong."

"Will that be a problem?"

The person laughed. "Of course not. Her companion might be, though. What was his name?"

"Allain. He is soulsplintered."

"His knowledge must remain limited. If these mages learn too much about soulmagic, it could be our undoing."

"He's not a risk," Talon said. "He has no idea what he's doing."

"Good. How fares the Device?"

"Done," Talon said. "The last Book was installed today. Now we're just waiting on your command."

"Excellent. Let me spin a bit more web, and then I'll be ready. It's close now, Talon. I can feel it. After all this time, it's almost here."

"I can feel it, too."

"They will be very pleased with me."

"With *us*," Talon said.

"Of course."

"I want her," he said. "When this is done."

"Lara?"

"Yes." He licked his lips.

The other person sighed audibly. "My old friend, you'd think that after a hundred thousand years you would have changed at least a *little*."

"I can't help my nature."

"No, I suppose you cannot. But *I* have changed." The person's tone grew lower, more dangerous. "Cross me, and you'll be worse than sundered. Worse than dead. You won't know pain, or torture, or rape.

"I'll soulburn you myself."

Talon felt a chill run through him. "Of course not," he said. "I would never dream of it."

That got a laugh. "You're a terrible liar, my old friend. Always have been."

There was silence for a time.

"Very well," the other person said eventually. "When this is done, if you do your part, I'll let you fuck my sister. Twins know she deserves it."

Talon's lips split into a grin.

FORTY

WHEN TREY GOT HOME to his apartment in Ilyrion, he was immediately conscious of how terrible it was. It was too small, too modern, too shabby by far. It lacked character. It wasn't *home*. But it was all he had—for now. Maybe some day Arra and he would reconcile. Maybe at some point she would feel something—love—for him. But that day hadn't arrived yet. She seemed distant from him now. Reserved.

And he didn't know why.

There was a console on his desk, a little thing Orym had given him, courtesy of the university. It beamed video right into your eyes, which was creepy. Orym had said it was like an advanced computer, but Trey had never *used* a computer. He'd heard of them, from ancient books and a few videos Quynn had smuggled into New San Francisco, but he'd never held one in his hands.

As far as Trey could tell, he hadn't actually been *alive* during that period on Earth. There were just no memories there. None at all. Only blackness, and sometimes a violet sky.

Strange.

He tapped what he hoped was the icon for *messages*, just in case somebody had tried to contact him. Sure enough, three messages were waiting. He fished around on screen with his finger, clumsily trying to open the first one. Eventually, he made it work. The message popped onto his retinas, startlingly clear.

To: Tarathiel Riverbow
From: Donar Cresius XXV
Subject: We need to talk

Tarathiel,

I would like to speak with you at your earliest convenience. It is a matter of urgent importance. Please contact the DMR and my secretary will clear my schedule.

Respectfully yours,
Donar Cresius XXV, MrD
Director of Research,
Ilyrion Department of Magical Research

THAT WAS INTERESTING. Was Trey finally getting some *respect* from someone? Who was this Donar Cresius, and what was he the twenty-fifth of? Trey had heard of the Department of Magical Research many times since he had arrived on Valaralda, but he'd never actually met anyone from it. All he knew was they were responsible for the licensing and restriction of magic. Those people in Errenmel—they'd been protesting the Department.

What could this person possibly want?

He tapped the next message.

To: "Trey"
From: A person who knows
Subject: Careful

You're treading on dangerous ground. Don't go poking into places you aren't wanted—you never know what you might find. Akhenaten was wrong.

T

WHAT WAS THIS—SOME kind of threat? Who the hell had sent this, signing it only with a single letter? How did he know Trey? And what, precisely, was he worried about Trey finding?

Things were getting curiouser and curiouser. This "T" person had mentioned Akhenaten, the Moon God of the ancient denizens of Nekhrumet and surrounding areas. He'd been a real person, Trey knew, not actually a god. Akhenaten had featured strongly in his research.

There'd been an Akhenaten on Earth, too, Trey suddenly realized. He felt a chill run through him—that was *way* too much of a coincidence. He remembered reading about Akhenaten the pharaoh. He'd lived on Earth during the Eighteenth dynasty of Egypt, in the 1300s BC. He wasn't featured as a god himself on Earth, like he was on Valaralda, but he did encourage worship of Aten, the sun god.

Trey paused. How the hell was his memory this good for *that* particular fact, when he couldn't remember half his life? He had no idea of his childhood. He couldn't remember actually marrying Arra. He only had dim memories of the Sending, of the time before. But this—this obscure piece of Earth history—*this* he knew perfectly.

He sighed, pulling back from the computer. Two messages, both confusing. He should probably contact Donar Cresius, find out what he wanted. Maybe tell him about this T and his strange message.

But the name Cresius rang a bell. It was familiar to Trey. Why?

He mused for a minute, thinking on it. His stomach rumbled. How long had it been since he'd eaten? He stood, about to go make some food, when suddenly it hit him.

Cresius. Yes. The name *was* familiar.

It was the man he'd punched, way back twenty thousand years ago, in the Senate hearing. As Tarathiel. Cresius was a vocal opponent of the Sending, but he'd ended up going along with it, in the end. This Donar Cresius must be a distant descendant. This man was in charge of the Department of Magical Research? If he had half the temperament of his ancestor, Donar Cresius XXV would be one hell of a handful.

Maybe that explained why the Department had such a bad reputation.

Something was flashing on the screen, still connected to his eyeballs. Trey flinched, looking to see what it was. Oh. Yes. He had *three* messages, and he'd forgotten to look at the last one. He pulled it up, his hunger momentarily forgotten.

To: Trey

From: A friend
Subject:

You don't know me, but I've been watching you. There are things you need to know—dangerous things. You're her son in law, and I believe you'll need our help. I'll find you when the moment is right.

Be careful in the tombs. Shadows gather.

THERE WAS NO SIGNATURE, no name at all on the message other than "a friend." The message said that Trey was "her" son in law, which meant...Arra's mother? Who was Arra's mother? He thought back, memories returning as he tried to remember.

ALLERIA WAS COOKING in the kitchen. Tarathiel stepped as quietly as he could, barefoot, hoping the hardwood boards in the kitchen floor wouldn't squeak and betray his presence. It smelled amazing in here—she was stirring something in a pot, oil crackling and popping, a hint of garlic and scallions and something else—cayenne?—swirling in the air, tickling his nose.

He sneezed.

Alleria glanced at him, not turning. "Hey," she said. Her face was slightly red from the heat coming off the stove. She was radiant, as always.

Tarathiel took the remaining three steps and put his arms around her waist from behind. "Smells good."

"It's not nearly done yet. Have you set the table?"

"Yup. Tell me again why we're having her over?"

Alleria put the wooden spoon down and turned, giving him a little kiss. "Politics."

"I thought you *hated* Selenia."

"Selenia is a kind woman—I don't hate her. I hate Leriaar, the damn Speaker. I hate the way she looks at you."

"She doesn't mean any harm."

"Trust me," Alleria said, "she means a great deal of harm."

"But you and Selenia never usually speak. Why invite her over now?"

Selenia was blonde, always with braided hair, with that strange way of walking up and down the aisle. He remembered the last time he'd visited the Senate, the way she'd tapped each desk in turn as she walked. She had an odd way of moving, but she seemed nice enough. If anybody in the Senate could be considered *nice*.

"Selenia is well-connected," Alleria said, turning back and resuming her stirring. She reached over and grabbed a glass bowl filled with diced zucchini, tossing it into the pot. The crackling sound intensified. "She can help us pass the motion, if we play this right."

"Okay." Tarathiel was still holding his wife, feeling the tantalizing curve of her waist and stomach. "I'll play my part." He continued running his hands along her body.

"Stop it," she said, laughing. "I have to finish this."

"Let me help."

She snorted. "The day you cook is the day I write a dissertation on the history of the Prophet of Nekhrumet."

"Hey," Tarathiel said, "you're a great writer!"

"And you're a terrible cook."

"Fine." He withdrew his hands. "I think you'd make a really good mother, though, for the record."

Alleria dropped the spoon. "That was out of the blue, even for you." She turned, her eyes veiled. "What made you bring *that* up?"

Tarathiel shrugged. "Just something I've been thinking about. Where we came from. Where we're going. My parents are great—I only wish you knew yours."

Alleria's face was motionless. "I wish that too," she said. "I wish I'd known my mother."

"I'm sorry," Tarathiel said. "I just don't understand. How can you not remember her?"

"I'm an orphan, Tarathiel. Orphans don't *have* mothers."

"Everyone has a mother."

"Maybe so, but mine left. Mine abandoned me. So the next time you're in a *family* mood, leave me out of it."

She turned and picked up the spoon. He could tell from the tenseness of her body that she was angry, that the conversation was over. It was always like this with her, always anger and hatred whenever kids or parents were brought up. He'd known that. It was always like this. Why had he been so stupid to talk about it again?

"I'm sorry," he said, and he saw her shoulders twitch. Then she turned, and there were tears in her eyes.

"Your mother is so great to me," she said.

He stepped forward, taking her in his arms. Dinner was forgotten, for the moment. "She loves you. So do I."

"I know. I just wish I'd known her. My mother. My father. Anyone. I try not to think about it, you know. And I do want kids…I do. It's just…"

"Not the right time."

She nodded, sniffling. "Sorry. I'm a mess. Can you keep stirring this while I go clean up?"

She looked up at him, blue eyes glistening with tears, and he felt love dripping through him, running through his veins like the water on her face. He leaned in, kissing her, using his fingers to wipe away her tears.

"You'll be such a good mother," he said.

"Thank you."

She left. Tarathiel stirred the pot, thinking about daughters and sadness while the steam and oil rose.

TREY GASPED, coming awake from the memories. He'd been right—Arra had no mother, at least not that she'd ever known. He remembered it now. She'd been left as a baby on the doorstep of a Church of the Twins. The deacon there had taken her in, raising her as one of his own. But she'd never known her *true* parents. She'd never had a real family.

But Trey—Tarathiel—had.

Not Quynn, of course. Quynn wasn't his real father. No, Trey had actual parents, way back then. Adamar, his father. Delana, his mother. He actually *remembered* them now, their faces, their voices. They were real. They were his.

And they were dead.

They'd been there, he remembered, on the Sending platform, saying goodbye to him and Alleria. There had been tears in their eyes, as well there should have been. It would be the last time he would ever see them, his flesh and blood.

He felt tears welling up. His life was a whirlwind of mystery, a maelstrom of fragmented time. It was coming back to him in bits in pieces, like segments of a puzzle beginning to form. Not all of it made sense to him, yet. He didn't have all the information in place. He hoped that if he just kept going, somehow everything would finally make some sense.

He wondered what Arra was doing right now. He should go to her, comfort her if she needed it. Find out what she was thinking, feeling. Find out what he could do to help. Maybe she was cooking, like she had been in that memory. Maybe she was standing at the stove, a wooden spoon in her hand and tears in her eyes.

Maybe she needed him.

But no.

Arra was her own woman now. She was an archer, a warrior, a mage far better than Trey was. She was strong.

She didn't need the likes of him.

So he made himself some food, all the while thinking about what he should do. There had been three messages, all of them mysterious. Cresius, T, and "a friend." They all wanted to speak with him, or to warn him of something. But of what?

He had a sudden vision of a tomb, of a dark doorway, runes inscribed into sandstone, of a pit and a trap and a hallway filled with cobwebs and stone. He remembered a room and a casket—no, a sarcophagus. He remembered death. No, that wasn't right. It wasn't *his* death—it was someone else's. Someone on his team. Was it—

Cresius.

Wait. Hadn't Cresius been with him for the Sending?

No. No now he remembered it. Cresius had died. He'd died there in the Tomb of Akhenaten, died a long way from his friends and family, away from everything he'd held dear to him in the world. He'd died trying to *prove* something, trying to show that Tarathiel was wrong, that there was nothing to be afraid of, that there was no evil, no Fall, no ghastly menace heading towards them at a million miles a minute.

But Cresius had been wrong.

And then Trey realized something else. Cresius had triggered a trap, way back then. The door to the chamber they were in had been closing, he remembered. He would be trapped—they all would be. He'd had to leave, had to escape the tomb and all its mechanized strangeness. He'd had to run with what he'd had, take it to the Senate, try to convince them of what he'd found.

But it hadn't been enough.

Because there had been *another* door, just beyond that chamber, waiting a few feet past where Cresius had died. There was another door, which meant there were more secrets still to find underneath that pyramid, way down deep where Akhenaten was buried.

Trey needed to go back. He needed to revisit that tomb, delve into the secrets that lay beyond, waiting to be discovered. He needed to travel to the desert and learn anything he could. For he knew—*knew*—that there was a secret there. Something big, something that would prove once and for all that the Fall was coming. That death was on its way.

But that wasn't all. That wasn't why he actually wanted to go. Because he *remembered* now. He remembered what his research said was buried in that tomb.

It was a Key.

The Key to end the Fall.

The Key that would awaken the Defense Mechanism. The ancients had built it, and it was just waiting for release, waiting to destroy Guruthos and the evil that it brought.

He could find the Key. He knew where it was. The fix for everything was there, just waiting underneath the ground.

All he had to do was look.

THE
END

TO BE CONTINUED...

THE STORY CONTINUES

*Excerpt from **THE CRYSTAL CURSE**, book seven of The Metalwood Saga:*

Cariel wasn't bleeding anymore. And she could see, if only through the wildcat's eyes. She could also move, but only as the cat. Which left just one problem.

She was *starving*.

By her count, it had been at least a full day—maybe two—since she'd eaten. She'd been so preoccupied with being blind, with falling off the fifty foot ravine, with losing her damn leg, that she hadn't paid attention to her stomach. But now she needed to. It was time. She desperately needed to eat.

So. Could the cat do the work for her?

She flexed her mind, Willing the cat to move, and it did. It flexed a paw, claws unsheathing, teeth bared. She could feel it resisting through the bond, but only a little bit. It was manageable, as long as she kept a strong Will.

So. Food.

She sent the great cat out into the jungle. Its vision was incredible—so different from her own, or at least how her vision had *used* to be. The cat could see a great deal: movement where she might not have noticed, peripheral information she might not have been able to see, detail in the dark. She'd never been able to see in the dark before. It felt like magic.

The wildcat prowled the nighttime forest, and it didn't

take very long to find something: just a vole, a little mouse-rat, a small rodent. But it would be meat, even if she couldn't cook it. It took barely any effort for the cat to capture the vole and bring it back to her, blood dripping from its jaws.

The cat deposited the rodent next to her, and Cariel grasped out for it, struggling to find where it was on the ground. Her movements were opposite of what she expected, like looking in a mirror. She was watching her mangled body through the cat's eyes—the cat that was hovering over her, eyeing her every move.

Eventually she got it. Her hand closed around the furry, bloody vole. She brought it up to her mouth, and for a moment the smell was overpowering. For a moment she almost threw up, but her hunger was stronger. She needed protein. Never mind that it was raw, bloody, and smelled like wet rat. Never mind that she'd have to crunch through little mouse bones and brains and teeth and claws.

Never mind that the vole was still alive, wriggling in her hand.

She watched herself through the wildcat's eyes. She almost thought she detected faint amusement in its mind as her body—her destroyed, elven body—ate the raw, wriggling rodent.

It tasted like death.

It took several kills before Cariel's strength was somewhat restored. By the time it was finished, daylight had returned. She was exhausted. She needed sleep.

But first she needed water, and this was something her own body had to do. So she turned over onto her stomach, crawling with her one leg and two arms, inching through the muddy jungle ground toward the stream. She knew there was one nearby—she could hear it / the cat could see it.

It took nearly all her strength to get there. Every move was agony, pain shooting through her. She felt wounds reopen—the one on her leg stump was the worst. Without actual medicine of some kind, she'd probably grow infected and die. She probably already *was* infected.

But she had to continue on.

She finally got to the water. It was just a little stream, but the water looked fresh. She dipped her fingers in / the cat watched the ripples of the water as she dipped her fingers in / feeling the coldness as a shock to her skin. Then she crawled an inch further and lowered her face to the water and drank.

It was the best thing she had ever tasted.

The water rushed over her face, soothing her eye wounds, cleaning some of the blood and dirt away. She lifted her head to take a breath, already missing the coolness of the jungle stream, the way the water felt running down her throat.

But there was something wrong.

She / the cat noticed something reflecting on the water. It cocked its head, then abruptly looked upwards at the sky. And there, flying right toward them, was a sakul. One single sakul, the murderous white bird floating alone in the sky, wings outspread. It had only been a few days since she'd last seen one, during the cavek Hunt.

Cariel knew that one peck from that bird would kill her instantly. And the cat seemed to know it too—it tensed, ready for action, every muscle poised and ready.

What could she do? The sakul was still moving toward them at an incredible rate, feathers fluttering as it winged around tree branches, intent on them.

And she was stuck. She couldn't move—not quickly, at least, and certainly not well. She could control the cat, but she didn't want to risk it dying to the bird. And she couldn't send the cat away—she didn't know how far it could go, if there was a range on this soulbinding thing.

She didn't want to lose her only friend in the forest.

But then an idea started forming in her mind.

She / the cat paused, staying completely motionless. Cariel's hand was still trailing in the water, but she kept it still, allowing the stream to ebb and flow around her fingers, looking for all the world as if she were dead.

The cat stood motionless as well, tracking the bird's movement with just its eyes. The cat's muscles were taut, ready to spring into action in a flash. Cariel hadn't needed to force the cat to do any of this—it was acting out of instinct. It had seen sakul before. It knew what to do.

But this time, Cariel was going to alter its approach.

Just as the sakul reached them, Cariel encouraged the wildcat to jump. And it did, but not *exactly* where it had originally intended. It had wanted to catch the neck of the bird, but Cariel had other ideas. So the cat sailed upward toward the tail of the sakul instead, where a few stabilizing feathers connected to the bird's body. And just as it jumped, Cariel's hand flicked the water, flicking it upwards as hard as she could. And as she did so, she reached out through the wildcat's mind.

Hard.

Everything happened at once, as if in slow motion. Stream water flashed into the air, the droplets catching glints from the sun. Some of the water hit the bird. She watched it through the cat's eyes, saw as the great wildcat sprang upwards, launching itself into the air with hind legs primed for action. It sailed towards the bird, jaw open, paws outstretched.

She / the cat saw the bird veer slightly, just an inch to the right, in response to the sudden shower of water from below. She watched her mouth / the cat's mouth plunged into the bird's rear feathers, wrenching downward and carrying the bird with it. Bird and cat were in the air, all motion halted for the briefest of instants.

In Cariel's kabul's eyes, everything seemed to stop. The drops of water hung there in mid-air, gleaming. The sakul bird twisted and paused, its beak turning to inject its venom into the cat. The kabul's muscles rippled slowly, perfectly, its black fur reflecting the sun as it leapt to grasp the bird. And Cariel's fingers, her hand, her arm, were reaching outward toward the pair of deadly animals.

Time resumed.

The cat brought the bird crashing down, beak and claws and whiskers and tail thrashing, the bird screaming, the cat growling. Cariel couldn't tell where sakul ended and kabul began, but she reached out for it anyway. She reached out for the bird. Her hand met it, found its beak, risking instant death.

And in that moment when she held its deadly instrument, she saw a soul there. A third soul. A bird soul.

And Cariel *took* it.

She captured it, this time violently, this time on purpose. She knew what she was after, and the soulmagic obliged. And as the cat and the bird finally hit the jungle floor, she subverted that bird's mind, claimed it, enslaved it.

Bound it.

And then she / the cat released its jaws.

And she / the bird alighted softly on the ground, preening its tail feathers, annoyed at the small amount of pain that the cat had inflicted. Cariel / sakul / kabul stood there in the mud, aware of each other's presence, conflicted and reserved and afraid. Only the sound of the stream and the three beings' breath pervaded the air. Only the beating of three hearts. She was the bird now. She was the cat. She was herself. She was three.

And now Cariel could *fly*.

To be continued in THE CRYSTAL CURSE...

To purchase, head to **jtf.link/metal7** or scan the QR code below.

ENJOY THE BOOK? HELP SPREAD THE WORD

Reviews are the most powerful tools in my arsenal when it comes to getting attention for my books. Much as I'd like to, I don't have the financial muscle of a New York publisher. I can't take out full page ads in the newspaper or put posters on the subway.

But I do have something much more powerful and effective than that, and it's something that those publishers would kill to get their hands on.

A committed and loyal bunch of readers.

Honest reviews of my books help bring them to the attention of other readers. If you've enjoyed this book, **I'd love it if you could leave a quick review.**

Head to **jtf.link/metalreview6** or scan the QR code.

ABOUT THE AUTHOR

Jeremy is a fantasy and science fiction author, living and writing in the San Francisco Bay Area. Fantasy is his first love —there's something about magic and mayhem that has interested him since he first cracked opened Lord Foul's Bane in the seventh grade. Also archery.

There always seems to be a lot of archery involved.

When not writing, Jeremy is a graphic designer, software developer, game designer, and music composer. He makes a really great Old Fashioned.

Check out his other work and sign up for his newsletter at **www.jeremythomasfuller.com**.

facebook.com/JeremyThomasFuller
instagram.com/jeremythomasfuller
amazon.com/author/jeremythomasfuller
bsky.app/profile/jeremythomasfuller.com

www.ingramcontent.com/pod-product-compliance
Lightning Source LLC
Chambersburg PA
CBHW030646020726
47493CB00006B/1888